EXPIRATION DATE

EXPIRATION DATE

MARDINE PERRINS

KAT BIGGIE PRESS
Columbia, SC

First Paperback edition 2021
ISBN: 978-1-948604-93-2 (paperback)
ISBN: 978-1-948604-94-9 (ebook)
Library of Congress Control Number: 2021900828

Cover design: Michelle Fairbanks, Fresh Design
Prepared for publication by Write|Publish|Sell

*Thank you, for the endless enthusiasm and support
I received from my children, family and friends.*

To all those who I've borrowed your names for my characters.

*To my young son, Hunter, who was a frequent reminder
that I should have been done with this book three years ago.*

*And finally, thank you to my husband, for making
sure none of us starved while I was working.*

For all of you, I am truly grateful!

-|-

Melissa Morrison put her feet up on a chair in the break room, resting her head on the table. The door opened slightly and June, a student nurse, poked her head in.

"She's ready, ten centimeters dilated."

Melissa lifted her head slowly and dropped her feet to the floor. The dark circles under her eyes told of the last eighteen-hour, three-day shift she'd been working.

Melissa entered the room as the laboring mother—Shauna, she reminded herself—screamed with her next contraction. She watched the woman's husband, David, get swatted away each time he tried to dab her head with a cool cloth, and wondered how much longer she would tolerate the attention.

One wall was painted with a mural of lilies, lupine, peonies, primrose and asters—an English garden to soothe the trauma of labor—while the other featured lambs and geese frolicking together in the countryside, washed over with a melancholy overtone contrary to its playful characters.

Melissa was happy to see the friendly face of the woman's cousin, Elisa, who was standing by the birthing bed.

David was pacing. "Is the doctor coming soon? I think she's ready!"

"He's on his way," Melissa said.

"I'm going to be a dad in like five seconds and I don't exactly know what to do here."

Melissa glanced at Shauna, panting and gripping the sides of the bed—she let out a grunt.

"Okay well, I'm pretty sure there's not much for you to do here. I believe Shauna will do most of the work," Elisa assured him. "Your job is to be supportive."

Dr. Reed Frederick entered the room. "Elisa, I didn't expect you to be here."

"Hi Reed. I'm here for moral support." She side-eyed David with a smirk.

"Great, the more the merrier."

The room was set up for expectant moms to deliver on one side of the room with a half wall separating the newborn baby area. The baby's nook was filled with baby supplies and brightly lit with white walls.

Melissa observed as June pulled the sterile drape off a covered table and began to prepare for baby's arrival.

"Melissa," Dr. Frederick glanced at the nurse, "informs me that you are completely dilated and ready to go."

"I'm ready," Shauna panted.

Elisa scrunched her face as Shauna contorted hers with a contraction. She let out a little scream and immediately resumed her breathing exercises.

Everyone assumed their positions, with David holding Shauna's hand repeating, "Breathe, breathe."

Elisa stood at her head as silent support, though occasionally giving words of encouragement. The only wall not adorned with animals or flowers was the one facing the birthing bed—it was a plain lavender.

Melissa smirked, glimpsing Elisa mouthing the screams with Shauna as she pushed with each contraction.

Twenty minutes later the shaky cries of a five-pound baby girl filled the room—Jessica, they decided. The anxious mother grappled for her daughter, rapidly searching for the birthmark, as the baby was whisked away to be inspected.

"I'll have her right back to you in a moment," June promised.

David turned back to his wife, while she lay back to rest, wiping the stray hairs away from her eyes and sweaty cheeks. He looked down at her, meeting her unsettled gaze.

Elisa backed away, not wanting to intrude.

In the baby's nook, Melissa instructed June on how to examine the newborn infant using the Apgar score system—the practice of quickly assessing a baby's health moments after birth.

She noticed June's hands trembling, so she placed a reassuring hand on her shoulder. June closed her eyes for just a moment and took a deep breath in to block out any distractions before performing a second test, checking the baby for signs of anything less than healthy.

"Heart rate's good—110 beats per minute," she blurted out, talking herself through it. "Reflex response." She gently let Jessica's head drop into her hand. "Spontaneous movement, sluggish. Next check," she flipped the baby slowly from side to side, "baby's… color… is… good." She looked again and lowered her voice. "Hands and feet, slightly discolored. Respirations… slow and irregular." Melissa watched over June's shoulder as she finally wiped Jessica down, while apprehensively searching her tiny body for the same string of numbers Shauna had so desperately tried to catch a glimpse of earlier. Finding them, the date was clear. The birthmark read, 7152168. She looked up at Melissa and grimaced.

June loosely wrapped Jessica in a blanket and carried her to Dr. Frederick, who stood at the end of the birthing bed. She gently slipped the blanket away, positioning the foot so he could see the numbers. His weary eyes looked up, then from father to mother. "I'm so sorry," he said quietly, glanced at Elisa, and mournfully left the room. There's nothing more he would do here.

Shauna cried out. "Nooo, not her!"

Wails echoed throughout the ward from room 701.

David let out a bloodcurdling howl.

Cupping her mouth, Elisa stood silently waiting in the shadows now, allowing the distressed parents space to absorb their child's fate. A fate that is always possibly looming with each birth, but never easy to accept. She wiped the tears from her cheeks.

His eyes red and swollen, David reached toward Shauna, trying to console her. She flailed her arms, rejecting his efforts.

"Please God, no, no, no!" she cried desperately. Elisa moved forward and placed her hand on her cousin's shoulder only to get pushed away— she crossed her arms and again receded to her haven against the wall.

David continued to attempt to console his wife, though he didn't really have the will to completely contain her. Her arms still pushing him away, she inadvertently hit him in the mouth, causing a trickle of blood to form on his bottom lip. He noticed, but didn't care, though he stopped trying to hold her. Distraught, he wasn't sure how to calm his wife or even sure if he wanted to.

June swaddled Jessica and carried her to her parents. The new mom's gaze followed her as she got closer, as though her baby would disappear if she turned away. She took her in her arms and kissed her forehead; her dad bent down to do the same, nuzzling his cheek against his daughter's as if to take a little bit of her with him when he retreated.

"Check again," he whispered to her. "Check again, maybe they're wrong, maybe it wasn't clear. Check again."

Shauna opened her eyes wide. *Another chance.* A small wrinkled foot popped out as she meticulously unwrapped the pale pink blanket Jessica was swaddled in. Inching closer, Elisa fruitlessly tried to steal a glimpse from across the room. Everyone waited in anticipation knowing the result, but maybe…just maybe there could have been a mistake?

They both looked so quickly—perhaps they didn't see well! She unwrapped the last layer and looked away briefly, then turned back. She raised Jessica's foot, searching as if trying to focus on the words on the page of a book. Her face scrunched up and distorted into what was an unmistakable answer; she sobbed. Unable to hold his stance, David collapsed onto the side of the bed, and this time she allowed him to throw his arms around her and they wept together as a family.

Silently, Elisa made her way over to join Melissa and June.

"What's the date?" she asked in a whisper.

Melissa somberly looked into Elisa's eyes. "July fifteenth, twenty-one, sixty-eight."

Elisa gasped and softly said, "That's three days from now!"

Suddenly, David pulled away from his family, turned and hit the wall, crushing his hand. He winced, but picked up the chair he'd been sitting in moments before and hurled it across the room, nearly hitting June. Melissa raced to push a button on the wall, while Elisa rushed toward mom and baby to act as a shield of protection.

The hospital loudspeaker urgently announced, "Code orange maternity, 7th floor, Code orange maternity, 7th floor."

On Elisa's hip she heard her pager, "Beep, beep, beep…"

- 2 -

IN ANOTHER WING of the hospital, Dr. Jack Derrin was called in to check on a patient whose life monitor had been alarming. As he entered the patient's room, a sudden overhead announcement—"Code orange maternity seventh floor"—flooded the halls.

"Hello, Mr. Czekowski," Jack said, looking at the reading from his life monitor. "Looks like you have bought yourself a midnight rendezvous with the on call cardiac catheterization team."

Mr. Czekowski was sitting up in his hospital bed patting his right upper chest where his device was implanted. "My life monitor said I have a problem." He waved his hands over his body. "Somewhere."

"Yes, it's indicating that the problem is your heart. Are you having pain, Mr. Czekowski?"

"I'd never seen a day in the hospital till yesterday, but I can't breathe, my chest hurts and I'm dizzy! It's this place I'm telling you!"

"Yes, well are you having any pain anywhere now?"

"This can't wait till morning, doc? I've had this pain coming and going for weeks!"

"As much as it is my pleasure to be woken up out of my sleep at midnight and rush into the hospital, it looks like, according to your life monitor and our heart monitors, you *are* having a heart attack. So, you have two options." Jack raised his voice only slightly.

"One, we can take you to the cardiac catheterization lab and see what's going on with your heart and maybe fix it… or two, you can potentially die a stubborn man."

"Well I'm just telling you, I didn't have any problems till I got here. My monitor said I'm fine!"

"Your monitor says you're not fine." Jack tried to patiently explain. "Well why do I need a monitor to tell me I'm fine anyway?"

Jack closed his eyes briefly; the dark circles underneath contrasted his lily-white skin. He sighed and sat in the chair next to the bed. "Everyone has a life monitor, Mr. Czekowski. You've had it forever. It's there to detect if there are any abnormalities in the body's system so we can escalate treatments. Like for you—today, we can fix your heart if we need to, okay?"

"Whatever."

"Elisa and Grace!" Jack exclaimed, looking toward the entrance to the room. "Great, the crew is here!"

"Okay, Mr. Czekowski." Jack placed his hand on his shoulder. "I'll see you upstairs in a few minutes." He raised his eyebrows to Elisa and she detected a smile underneath his nicely trimmed beard, while he rushed out the door.

Being summoned for an emergency procedure was the last thing Elisa needed right now. She wanted to stay by her cousin's side while her husband went on his rampage. Shauna needed support, but instead, when the pager went off, Elisa washed her face, sucked in her emotions and went to work.

"Hi, Mr. Czekowski," Grace confirmed, looking at the name band on his wrist. "I'm Grace, I'm going to be your nurse for this procedure."

"I'm Elisa, a cardiovascular specialist, I'll be assisting as well, we're going to bring you up to the cath lab, okay?" She forced a smile.

"Yes," he muttered, as they quickly move him out of the room.

"Code orange, maternity, seventh floor," continued to be repeated and Jack was forced against the elevators while the responders rushed by.

"What are you waitin' for, the train, man?" the familiar voice called from behind.

"Hey," Jack replied, as he turned and recognized the voice belonging to his long-time buddy.

"Reed. I was actually on my way to the cath lab to do a case when I ran into the crowd on their way to the code. Do you know what's going on?" he asked, motioning to the crew that had just passed.

"Yeah, unfortunately another short date," he said, shifting his eyes to the floor. "Elisa's cousin's baby, by the way."

Jack frowned. "Ah, geez."

"I delivered twelve this week—others delivered more. It's not getting easier."

"Twelve, wow! I suppose it wouldn't, but that's about the fifth code I've heard overhead," Jack said.

"Tensions are high with parents. Apparently, we're not immune to the effects of this random phenomenon that's been going on all over the world."

"Phenomenon?"

"Seriously?" Reed pulled his head back. Jack shook his head.

"You need to get out more; keep in tune with the happenings around you! There has been a record number of short expirations – short as three days. Personally, I think they've blown this thing up. I'm sure it's one of those things that just… happened, and we won't hear any more about it in a couple of months."

"Really! Don't *you* find that a little strange?" Jack asked.

"Nothing more than a coincidence," Reed said, shrugging his shoulders.

"Maybe you're becoming too desensitized to it," Jack suggested. "I have to run."

-**3**-

In a small office at Exylon Pharmaceuticals, Mike waited in the dark with the exception of one small lamp shining on the virtual cybernetics computer in front of him. An illuminated green leafy plant twirled mid-air as he spun it with his finger. The phone rang, jarring him from the monotony. He slid his hand across the small silver disk on the desk just below, and as if sucked down into it, the hologram of the plant disappeared. He hesitated a moment, having expected this call long ago, but answered on the first ring.

"John, you must have been busy, my friend," he said.

"To say the least. This really has been the first chance I've had to call."

Though the situation required an aggressive repercussion, Mike was not surprised by the low-key tone in John's voice. John always carried himself in a congenial manner, but his inflection was always felt.

"Need I tell you that this hasn't gone over well with Mr. P? He is demanding answers. As is the president, from what I gathered from the response I received from him earlier. I'm flying out now to meet him, so I need some answers myself. What happened?"

As semi-retired professor at Harvard University, head of the Division of Population Control and Statistics, and one of the top biochemists in his field with a long list of credentials, John Vanburen was known for his unyielding will to have things done in accordance with the way he needed them done.

"I have traced the source of the situation and I am in the process of rectifying it," Mike nervously stated. He had a great respect for his mentor; his nerves stemmed from not wanting to disappoint, rather than fear. He could feel the smile on the other end of the line, though it was not one of delight.

"So, what do we have?"

"Well," Mike began, "apparently, a shipment of the Restore nutriment injection vials went out to several different hospitals and clinics to which only the regular nutriment injection vials should have gone. As is evident with the aftermath and news reports. So our Restore nutriment was given to women who were not on our selected list of regions, which means these injections were not distributed by our own providers, who are very careful *not* to inject so many fetuses in dense areas at once. It took a little bit to figure out how that happened, since this all took place five months ago, but I finally traced it back here to Exylon." He paused, waiting for the verbal punch that didn't come. "I haven't addressed him yet, but it appears that Claude sent out the injections."

"I see. Do you know why Claude may have done that? And how he had access to those Restore injection vials?"

"An accident, of course, but I've yet to figure out what actually occurred. Those vials are locked up in a room off the lab—only I have the key. Yet, his signature was on the shipment. I'll address him carefully tomorrow; I don't want him to suspect what he's actually done."

"Perhaps if you'd brought Claude in on what we were trying to accomplish, as I suggested, this wouldn't have happened," John calmly, but firmly, pointed out.

He's not one of us, he wanted to say sharply.

"Maybe. But I still don't think he's mature enough to understand our beliefs. I think he would be trouble."

"I don't understand your animosity toward Claude, he's a smart boy and a damn hard worker." John shrugged it off as old business. "Whatever you think, but I trusted you with this division, so don't make me regret that." *Actually, this may work out better than planned,* John considered.

~

John disconnected with Mike to find one of the young pharmacists that worked at the nutriment plant in the doorway.

"Oh, Derrick, you startled me, didn't hear you come in. What are you still doing here?"

"Finishing up on some work."

"Oh, okay then. Go home boy, it's late." Derrick stood, contemplating. Grinning. John looked up again from his desk. "What?"

"There's a lot of buzz going around about the short dates," he said smugly.

"Yes, there is."

"This is a step forward for Restituere."

"These short deaths are not happening in our targeted regions," John pointed out.

"Not the regions the very few Restituere members decided on, like yourself and Mr. P, but this is what we wanted nonetheless."

John focused on Derrick. "What are you getting at?"

Derrick stepped forward. "Look what I did! What everyone else was too afraid to do! Expand our targeted regions; move faster. Your blueprint—Restore—will have us die out before we've reached all the areas of focus that we'd projected reaching! I have expedited the same plan we put in place. Yes, Restore was a good start, but we're moving too slowly. We've had meetings with the same ol' chatter… time for action!"

John stood up abruptly, gripping an object from his desk and moving around to face Derrick. "You sent those Restore shipments out?! You jeopardized our brotherhood! Went off on your own! Now everybody around the world is looking for answers! Looking for us!"

"Good, they should be! We shouldn't be hiding! We should start our revolution now!"

John had already made the decision—he knew what he needed to do. He approached Derrick, who barely had time to feel the sharp puncture in his arm before John threw all his weight against him, knocking him into the bookcase, scattering books across the floor.

"John, what… !"

The blood rushed from Derrick's face when he suddenly realized that John had injected him with nanobytes.

I just need to keep him down until they take effect, John thought. More than twice John's age, he struggled to hold him, now that Derrick was no longer caught off guard.

Three hundred seconds left now until the nanobytes reached their objective. John's full body weight was elevated as Derrick used the floor as leverage to lift himself, tossing John onto the floor.

"What did you do?" he asked rhetorically.

Panting, John scrambled to his feet. "I'm sorry, Derrick. You're a liability to our cause."

One hundred and twenty seconds—the tiny programmed bytes raced through the bloodstream, rapidly targeting each cell in its host.

"I am what Restituere is all about!" Derrick said, lunging at him, his knee catching John's side.

John doubled over, but mustered all his strength to match his young fellow Restituere brother's. He grabbed the tail of Derrick's shirt, pulling him down before he could reach the door, again throwing all his weight on him.

Thirty seconds—cell death had reached most of the organs. Derrick's eyes bulged and his breaths became raspy; his strength was fading fast.

John eased up on his hold. "I'm sorry," he said again.

Complete cell death. Derrick's body went limp. John stood and straightened his shirt and pants, now feeling the complete impact of Derrick's side jab.

"This will not be an easy call," he sighed.

"Sorry to wake you, Louise. Can you get me the family of Derrick Monahan. Yes. Immediately, please. I'm afraid our young friend reached his expiration date."

- 4 -

Jack found the cath team already in the lab as they wheeled Mr. Czekowski into the room on his stretcher.

"Good morning, Paul!" Grace screeched, interrupting the recap of her day she was giving to Elisa.

Paul, also a cardiovascular specialist and the first assist tonight, shuffled in behind them with disheveled pieces of brown and blond hair peeking out from his baseball cap. Approaching Elisa, he shot Grace an annoyed look.

"Whaaaat the hell, it's almost one a.m., pleeease make her stop," he groaned, before exiting to the control room just outside the lab. Elisa gave him an understanding glance, too tired herself and upset over Jessica's impending fate to want to listen to Grace's shrilly blabber.

Paul stepped into a glass chamber that reached from the floor to ceiling.

"State your name," the mechanical voice commanded.

"Paul Rivera," he called out clearly. A ray of light appeared, scanning his body from head to toe and up again, with the second scan leaving a form-gripping barrier impenetrable to radiation from his thighs to his chin.

He exited the chamber and donned his surgical hat and mask while Jack entered behind him. The Cardiac Catherization lab was a large room containing a huge camera, which glided full circle around the table the patient was lying on. Next to the table, there were three monitors suspended from the ceiling, with two main monitors allowing the doctor and team to see while working on the patient's heart, and the other reflecting the patient's vital signs. Equipment was laced around the room; a code cart and other essentials needed to perform procedures throughout the day and for emergencies sat in one corner. As they worked, the lights were low. The crew moved like a well-oiled machine, getting Mr. Czekowski on the table and set up quickly.

"Elisa Quinn, monitor verification; ready to record," Elisa called out, activating a full disclosure virtual monitor to record a three-hundred-and-sixty-degree view around the room. She verified its detection of Mr. Czekowski on the cath table, scanning his heart rate, blood pressure, and saturation and adjusting to detect any variations in his vital signs. She wiped the nearly dried tears from her face and yawned, physically and emotionally exhausted. Using two fingers to grip the images floating in the space in front of her, she pushed away the images irrelevant to their current procedure on the holographic display, bringing forth and calculating their present situation.

"You okay?" Jack asked Elisa, approaching from behind. "I ran into Reed on the way over. I'm sorry to hear about your cousin's baby."

She nodded, stifling her tears.

"Sure you're up for this?"

"I'm good," she said, watching Mr. Czekowski's vitals. "Two milligrams of versed," Grace shrieked aloud.

Scrunching her face, Elisa responded, "Got it," verifying that the medication and dose populated in their designated location.

The staff checked the schedule to make sure they were not on call the same nights Grace was on. Everyone at some point got stuck with her, though. A veteran of twenty-six years at the hospital, she was an excellent nurse, but there was no compensating for the high-pitched tone that reverberated out of her mouth when you had already been jolted out of your bed in the middle of the night. Though lately, she'd shown signs of fatigue and occasionally disorientation. Her normal three-course lunch had turned into an apple and cheese. Pretty soon, she'd likely begin to slip in her job duties. As was government mandated, two months before her expiration day, she wouldn't be able to come to work. Not that she'd feel up to it. With this in mind, for most of the staff in the lab her screechy voice had become considerably more tolerable.

"I was actually still up when the pager went off, watching the news because it was the first chance I got to watch it today. Fifty micrograms of fentanyl!" Grace called out. "Jerry had to work late, so I had to run some errands for him…"

Paul glanced out at Elisa, who watched him as he banged his head against the air as if it were a wall. She gave him a short smile.

"Hey doctor, have you found something?" Mr. Czekowski asked, poking his head up to see, and banging it on the camera.

"Keep your head down, Mr. Czekowski," Jack instructed, "or we're going to require neurology to look at you next for the bump on your head. Rule is, I get the best seat in the house."

"Yeah, okay," he muttered, returning his head to the pillow.

"One milligram of versed," Grace called out, injecting more medication in his IV line to put him to sleep.

"Okay," Elisa returned.

After the third injection of contrast into the patient's coronary, Jack said, "Looks like a pretty tight blockage, let's fix it."

Grace began to open and hand off the equipment normally used for an intervention to Paul.

"So, Benita, ya know from News Eleven, did a story on the expiration dates here in the Albany and Troy areas. She said that these dates are abbreviated! That's the word she used, *abbreviated*. We've seen short expiration dates—but there's so many at once! Said they'd been reported over the last month, but the public is just learning about it." Grace adjusted the patient's oxygen level and continued.

"Then my sister called…" she went on.

Paul turned toward Elisa and inscribed the word HELP in the air with his finger.

"… in Minnesota. Don't you guys find all these coincidences strange?" she asked, taking in a deep, necessary breath.

Jack placed a catheter at the edge of the blockage, injected Serous

Stent, a medication that dissolved the plaque completely from the vessel, followed by an anticoagulant sealer that gripped and adhered to the vessel, preventing regrowth. Mr. Czekowski squirmed slightly with discomfort. Jack took another x-ray picture and retrieved the equipment from his patient's heart before turning to address Grace.

"Haven't really heard anything about it, Grace. Sounds like they're already investigating though," he said, finishing up with his patient. He pulled off his sterile gown, tossed it in the garbage and continued. "Maybe it's not as unusual as we think; maybe this kind of thing has happened before somewhere else, in another state or country perhaps. I'm sure they don't always report on that sort of thing worldwide."

"Where have you been, Jack, in a hole?" she said. "The last forty-eight hours, the whole country's been buzzing about it! This apparently had happening over the last month, but the magnitude is just being realized."

"You heard about this, Paul?" Jack asked. "Yup!"

"Actually," Elisa interjected, "I've been watching too, Jack, and they have been reporting this peculiarity in other countries but said they don't know what to make of it. The infant death rate, within three to seven days, shot up fifty percent in the last month in a number of areas. Of course, Orbis has yet to make a statement. This is all coming from local news sources."

"Our global government." Paul rolled his eyes. "Why don't they just disband and allow each country to run itself!"

"Paul, that has nothing to do with anything," Grace said.

"Sure, it does. Perhaps if each county ran itself instead of 'Living together as one,'" he mocked Orbis's motto, "they would have a handle on this thing by now. It's more like, 'One control, everyone thinks alike, each country believes they have a say, but it's still the stronger country's representatives that have all the clout,' motto."

"Wow, bitter much? Still has nothing to do with this situation, this is not a political issue," Elisa said.

He sighed. "Orbis hasn't made a statement because they probably have no idea why this is happening. They're in on it or they don't care!"

"Well, I'll buy the 'they don't know what's happening' part. I do however think they care."

"You're entitled to stay in the dark."

Elisa shook her head.

They delivered the patient back to his room, as Grace prolonged her report to the receiving intensive care nurse. She fiddled with the IV bag unnecessarily and offered to help get Mr. Czekowski settled. This would be one of the last times she'd get to go through this routine. Elisa gave Grace an unseen melancholy smile, wished her goodnight, and shuffled down the hall toward the parking garage.

"Hey, Elisa, going my way?" Jack asked in his proper English voice when he saw her at the door.

"Is that the heck out of here?" she responded in the same voice.

"Why yes!" he replied. He held the door and waved his arm, allowing her to go first. Elisa flashed a smile.

He frowned. "Hey, I know you and your cousin are tight, if there's anything I can do…"

"Everyone knows short dates can happen. They *do* happen. But it's different when it hits home, ya know," she said.

"I know."

"And, *could* she have been part of this phenomenon? Her date is in three days!" She wiped her sleepy eyes. "Aren't you at all curious about the stories Grace was talking about? Like I said, I've been kinda following the news reports too, and it seems as though something is definitely wrong."

"Apparently I'm out of the loop. I've been so busy I haven't really had time to catch up on current events. That said, Reed's on the front line and he doesn't seem concerned, though there have been many more deaths here at our hospital too, apparently."

"Well, do ya think it could be some sort of exposure to chemicals or radiation or something?" she asked, grasping for answers.

"Don't know. Again, Reed thinks it's something that is going to pass soon enough.

"I'm sure there'll be more information to come. See you in the morning," Jack said, continuing to his car after leaving Elisa at hers.

-5-

In contrast to its more formal, dignified surroundings, the library in the White House had a quaint, non-threatening presence. John was pleased with the president's choice of location to meet for what he assumed would be an uncomfortable discussion. He tugged his earlobe in an effort to scratch the itchy security tag in his ear. He admired the infamous lighthouse clock while he waited, exhibiting his appreciation for the arts, and vintage collectibles in particular. The rare lighthouse clock had been a fixture in the White House since the year 1824, a commemorative of the visit of the Marquis de Lafayette. His pause for admiration was cut short as the president entered the room. Over the years he had learned that the president, Harrison West, was keen on punctuality, a trait John also possessed.

"John." The president greeted him when he entered the room. John stood and responded, "Mr. President."

"Please." President West motioned for John to have a seat. He walked intently over to the heavy cherrywood desk and leaned against the edge with his arms crossed, towering over John. President West's presence usually commanded attention. At seventy-nine, he was the oldest president to have held this position in a long time, but at six foot two, with a rigid exercise regimen and perhaps his ethnic African-American genes, he looked twenty years younger. John attempted to straighten up slightly, feeling as though he was about to be reprimanded by his teacher. Being a professor, a pillar, a leader himself, he did not like this feeling at all.

"Talk to me, John," the president said firmly. "I don't have to tell you how detrimental this situation is and how much worse it can get, so I need to know two things: What is happening, and is it under control?"

"Sir, it appears that one of our newer employees to the division, Claude Monark, made a grave error." After only leaving Derrick a couple of hours ago, John thought it best keep the focus on Claude, rather than mention Derrick. "Five months ago, he shipped the nutriment supplement injections to clinics to be distributed to women in their fourth month of pregnancy, as usual. However, the nanobytes in these supplements happened to all have similar dates, which are within three to seven days instead of the mandatory variation of dates. Those injections were unknowingly given to thousands! It's created the dilemma we have now, mass infant deaths within days after birth, ultimately causing the alarm we are currently seeing all over the globe."

"Who is Claude Monark? What do we know about him? We cannot afford for this program to be exposed! People are rightfully upset. Families are terrified that they are going to lose their children to an untimely death. I don't have to tell you what happens to parents when they are defending their young. John, this could get very ugly!"

"It was a rookie mistake: he's a brilliant scientist. Young, but hard working, energetic, committed. Not someone I would like to lose, sir," he appealed. *Careful, John,* he said to himself, *you need to make sure Claude keeps his position in the bureau.*

"You will vouch for him?"

"Yes sir. I understand your concern, Mr. President, but we, like our predecessors, have dealt with similar situations in the past," John pointed out. "Questions, inquiries, probing from the likes of many. We handled it then, we will handle it now."

"Okay, how?" West asked, tightening his posture and raising an eyebrow.

"Our best defense, I think sir, is to play ignorant on this one."

"What? That's absurd! People want answers, not ignorance!"

John could see the vein bulging from the side of the president's neck.

"I understand sir. We are going to give them ignorance with a strong stance!"

The president leaned in slightly, focused on John's next statement.

"Expiration dates are already a mystery—have been for the last hundred years. There has been speculation about their origin, ranging from radiation to aliens being responsible; religious conviction increased by eighty percent! But, of course, expiration dates ultimately have just settled in as a part of life, right?"

President West nodded, still unsure where John was going with this.

"We hold a press conference. Orbis… holds a press conference telling the people that we have exhausted every possible avenue that could have caused such a travesty." John maintained eye contact with the president while pacing the room. "You address the concerns that are floating around. You assure the public that testing has been done to ensure that nutriment injections were not contaminated and that these regions do not have chemicals seeping into the water or food supply. Every precaution has been taken to make sure that there has been no foul play in our communities. And then we present it as a fluke—a hiccup in our genetic material. Give them a history lesson in some of the ways we have mutated, if you will, that cannot be explained. Such as conjoined twins, pituitary hyperplasia, you know," he grappled, pointing to the president, "the condition that causes a man to grow to over eight feet. Being born with additional limbs. The list goes on."

The president walked to the window, peering out into the darkness, considering this. He turned to John.

"I would ask you to come work as my adviser, but you are too valuable to me at the bureau." His expression was stony. "I'm not completely comfortable with this, but I think it may be the only solution."

Acknowledging both the compliment and President West's concern, John continued.

"Mr. President, we must maintain the trust of the people or the questions are not going to go away. And there will be those who will not stop until they get some answers."

He gave the president a minute, then locked eyes with him.

"We know there is only one answer. That answer cannot be revealed. So, we must create another."

-6-

NO NATURAL LIGHT SHONE in the voluminously large chamber, though Mr. P preferred it bright. The fluorescent lighting he'd installed illuminated every corner of the room. To some, in spite of its size, his workspace might feel like a tomb, but it served his needs. He enjoyed the realistic, life-sized vision of ocean waves crashing on a rocky beach, pictured against a far wall, and bopped his head slightly to the faint sound of music coming from the speakers installed alongside the lighting. He stopped only long enough to carefully fill the quarter-inch cartridges, attaching the needles of equal size. Gathering the cylinders, he filled a drone designed to hold ten, gently placing each cylinder snugly into its own holder. In the notebook next to him he crossed off, "Palace Square-St. Petersburg, Russia."

Carefully lifting the drone, he carried it to a metal cart already loaded with fourteen cartridge-filled others and proceeded to exit through a large metal door opening into a tunnel. While making his way through, the clanging of the cart mixed with the vaguely audible sounds of water movement surrounding the tunnel. He exited through the door on the other end and was met by a smaller room than the last. This room was a little quainter, with a brick fireplace to the left, wood floors, and soft lighting extending from the ceiling. The drones were wheeled to join others just outside a small two-person elevator to continue their journey.

Almost there! Concentrating on a large black sphere, he strode to the other side of the room. Stroking both rounded sides of the orb simultaneously, four doors on the flattened top slid opened from the center out.

Identification, the orb demanded.

He bent slightly over the opening and spread his eyelids wide. Another door slid to the side.

Password, the orb demanded.

After typing in his password, he added some numbers on the keypad presented.

Mr. P dropped his head at the interruption of a call.

He swiped the black band on his wrist; immediately an illuminated panel, containing a myriad of functions, wrapped around his wrist. He brought forward telecommunications.

"Yes, make it quick," he snapped.

"Hello to you, too," John quipped. Silence.

John continued, "Though unfortunately an unforeseen necessity, I'd say the unscheduled test of the newly programmed nanobytes was quite effective. The false medical report that Derrick's life monitor was defective and had not revealed a detrimental heart defect was everything."

Mr. P continued to punch numbers into the keypad of the sphere.

"There is sure to be an uprising about the legitimacy of that report," he informed John. "There haven't been any malfunctions with the life monitors in almost a hundred years—since the early days of their initiation. Once the push to examine the device reveals it indeed was not the issue, in addition to him clearly not reaching his expiration date, since what'd his birthmark say, fifty years from now, further investigations will certainly ensue. However, at that point we will have already accomplished our goal and that will be the least of their concerns."

He slid his hands along the sides of the orb, causing the doors to slide shut, and sat in the chair beside it.

"And your meeting with President West?"

"Successful as well. I explained that this was strictly a nutriment injection programming delivery faux pas, leaving him no reason to believe there was anything actually wrong with the injections themselves."

"Good news. And John, I understand that Derrick went off on his own, but you need to keep a tighter rein on your people."

"Will do." John heard a disconnect on the other end.

His first meeting with Mr. P was unexpected. Restituere was very new, with only a handful of members, and really all they had to talk about was their disgust for the current condition of the world and their hopes for a new one. The meeting was held in London that night, and John remembered Mr. P fading into the shadows in the small auditorium, remaining silent throughout the meeting. He approached John afterward, extending his hand and introduced himself.

"Interesting perspective you have on the state of the world."

"Yes brother, that's why we're all here, to share our views."

"It seems to me that you could use a little help and a little more organization."

"Anything you have to bring to the table, you're welcome to."

"Let's meet again," Mr. P suggested. "I have your number; I'll be in touch."

John still didn't know how Mr. P got his number, but he was very impressed with his poise that night.

-7-

Her eyes burning from staring at the ceiling, Elisa turned to the clock next to her bed. "Ughhh." *Four more hours to sleep.*

She couldn't shake the distraught cries of Shauna and David in the maternity ward. It had been a very long and disheartening journey for them. When they married four years ago, they had planned for lots of children. As a child, Shauna was always the kid playing the mom. The one who took care of the neighborhood kid who fell and got scraped or the one who was getting teased. She was *the* babysitter in the neighborhood, often taking care of Elisa's younger sister, Ashlei, as if she were her own sister.

When it was time for them to start a family, she'd had trouble getting pregnant, followed by several miscarriages, and though they had suffered such losses, they never lost hope and stayed encouraged. After two years, they finally were able to share the news that they were expecting. Elisa couldn't have anticipated that she could be so happy for another human being. This wasn't just news of another baby in the family, it was cause for celebration after their discouraging journey. The whole community celebrated—Shauna's trials had been felt by everyone she had touched. *Was this Jessica's natural expiration date or was she part of this... new occurrence?*

She reviewed the discussion with the others in the lab and with Jack about the expiration deaths. Was she thinking too much into it? *You don't need to concern yourself with everything!* she scolded herself, remembering the last time she felt the need to investigate suspicious activity and write about it—ending up being reprimanded by the authorities, her notes disposed of, and having to apologize to the "perpetrators." She glanced over at her desk. *And there it sits among all the others, shut away in a drawer, along with my confidence. Let this one go! Go to sleep!*

She drifted into thoughts of her mother's voice. "You can't fool your heart. Trust it, it will always lead you in the right direction."

And with that advice, she did just the opposite and went into the medical field.

Still, she thought, the deaths of so many in such a short time seemed to be a bigger story to be investigated, and maybe told.

Expiration dates were not a discussion in her home—they were still a taboo subject. She and her sister were not allowed to know their expiration dates. Her parents preferred they, "live every day like it's your last." She heard this mantra many times growing up, and secretly challenged that rule on her eighteenth birthday. As she stood in front of the mirror, excitedly stirring up the nerve to finally search for the answer she'd longed to know since early childhood, the words played over and over in her head. *Live every day like it's your last.* And at that moment she decided that in her parent's "old" wisdom, she wouldn't have the ability to live each day as it came, if she anticipated when *her* last day would be. She and Ashlei were two of the only people on the planet, she felt, who didn't know their expiration date. Nothing to look forward to; no pre-expiration date parties, no last-minute whims, no scrambling to make everything right before they go or even choosing a more adventurous way to go. No making *any* decisions, because they didn't know when their last day would be.

Elisa's mother and inspiration, Rachelle Quinn, instilled in her daughters the importance of the written word. She recited more than once, "Without the written word, history would be lost, experiences not shared, imagination would be untapped." As a writer and the owner of one of the last standing privately-owned bookstores, Rachelle wrote and often read one of Elisa's favorite children's stories—"Seventy-nine Lovely Dreams." *I loved that story,* she fondly recalled. The tales of a young girl's many different opportunities and explorations. *Another way Mom tried to foster the idea of following my heart.* She turned on her side, trying to get comfortable. *At the rate of these mass deaths, there won't be any children left to enjoy these stories.*

Elisa still took pleasure in helping her mother with the promotional "Corner of the Month," which showcased different parts of the states and countries. This section housed books, music, and art from parts of that particular area featured for the month. As teens, Elisa and Ashlei were given the assignments of setting up these corners so they could learn about other cultures. They would each get a month and the rule was no technology, so their competitions were fierce, she recalled fondly, as to who could be the most creative with their corner. They put together word searches and scavenger hunts to find artifacts from these places, among other activities. Elisa would act out scenes from books, improvising a great deal of the time. She especially loved setting up the corners when they featured Haiti and Ireland, her mother's and father's heritage, getting lost in the history of the two countries. As her mother instilled the love of literature, her father, a police officer, made sure that she and Ashlei learned the art of self-defense from a very young age. Finally beginning to doze off, she smiled warmly, remembering what great memories her childhood held.

$$- 8 -$$

THE FIRST EXPIRATION DATe was documented at St. Lukes Hospital in
Troy, NY on September 1, 2068. This baby was known as Little Owen.
It was the nurse in the room who first noticed the date. Owen Cross
was born to parents George and Sabrina Cross. He was whisked away
by Sabrina's nurse, Anna, as soon as he took his first breath. She cleaned
him, the Apgar test was done, and he was found to be completely healthy.
Just as Anna was swaddling baby Owen, she noticed a faint dark mark on
the crown of his head. Concerned that he was injured during birth, she
brought him closer to the light, slightly separating the soft dark hairs to
get a clearer view. *A birthmark?* she pondered. She stood, mouth gaped
open, not quite sure what to say. *It's so absurd!* Dr. Green was the physician on call who delivered Owen; he caught a glimpse of the perplexed
look on her face.

"Anna, you alright?" he asked, carefully choosing his words wisely so
not to upset the new parents.

"I... umm... hmmm, baby's fine." She made sure to get that out,
realizing she was blabbering and not exactly answering the doctor's question. "Doctor, could you just take a look at this marking?" Her eyes
remained on the mark. "It's a little unusual."

Sabrina looked at her husband, gripping his arm. "Is everything
alright?" the new father asked.

Doctor Green didn't acknowledge George's question, but tilted Owen's head, while cocking his own like a dog questioning his owner's command.

"What the… hmm." Owen, who had patiently tolerated the attention, began to wail as Dr. Green shifted his head again from side to side searching to get a better angle.

"Do you have a flashlight?" he asked the nurse without looking up, while she was already extending it to him. This time it was Sabrina who spoke up.

"Is someone going to tell us what you're 'ummming and hmming' over there about? You're scaring me!" Jarred from his focus, Dr. Green looked toward the concerned couple and apologized for the delay in responding.

"I don't really know what I'm responding to. Your son has a mark on the crown of his head. Do either of you have any birthmarks or anyone in the family have any that you're aware of?"

The couple looked at each other, confirming, and simultaneously said, "No."

Sabrina took it a step further and finished, "Not that we know of."

George asked, "Is it that big a deal… really?" Dr. Green let out a puff of air unintentionally and drew his arm up, scratching the back of his head.

While Anna handed mom her swaddled baby, Dr. Green looked up at them and said, "Well, it's the darnedest thing, the mark on Owen's head is a seven-digit number."

Owen Cross, George and Sabrina Cross, Dr. Alvin Green, Anna Carrington, RN, and a few others who managed to involve themselves in this marvel, went down in history as the first to see such an unbelievable sight.

At this time, it was a local story of interest. This number on baby Owen's head was a curious thing and had hospital staff talking among their coworkers and family members, but it eventually made the *Times Union* newspaper and *Troy Gazette* as a human-interest story. It wasn't until a few weeks later that it had captured the interest of more than just the local community.

Owen Cross was the first documented case of what is now called the expiration date. Little Owen's date read 7102135. Sixty-seven years after his birth, just like the others before him who had reached their dates, Owen began to go into multi-system failure a month prior to his expiration date. He lost interest in eating, had difficulty following conversations and was short of breath most of the time. On July 10, 2135, as the date had predicted and as expected, Owen Cross just slumped over, dead in his easy chair.

The second documented case was thirty-six days after Owen's birth, at Trinity Hospital in Moldova, a small country in Eastern Europe. Alexander Roman was born to Mihail and Lilia Roman on October seventh at 6:51a.m. At the moment he was born, he was blue. He was rushed into another room and upon evaluation, his respirations were shallow and weak. His cries were labored and whiny, and his heart rate was slowed.

Shortly after Alexander's birth, Dr. Dorian Luca felt for the infant's pulse; it was absent. Alexander was lifeless.

As the grieving couple held their son for the first and last time, Mihail tried to wipe a spot from his newborn's foot to no avail. He squinted, his eyes moved in closer and he pulled back in horror when he realized that the spot was a group of numbers that read 1072068—indicating that very day.

Alexander Roman, Mihail and Lilia Roman, and Dr. Dorian Luca also went into the history books as the first to discover what the numbers on these babies actually meant.

Owen's funeral was a huge event that droves of people gathered for and tuned in. News media from all over the world were in attendance. East Greenbush, New York, Owen's neighboring town, was busting at the seams as people streamed in and out of the funeral home in a steady flow, some only staying for a moment to give their respects or maybe just to be a part of this rare occurrence—a part of history. For some, it may have been just to confirm what had been confirmed so many times before—that the expiration date did indeed mean just that.

Owen was not the first person to live up to his expiration date, however, he was the first to be born with one, as far as anyone knew. Following his delivery, birthmarks identified each newborn's expiration day. Like everyone else affected by the post-war fallout, Owen struggled, but lived a good, long life. He went to a local college and became an engineer, marrying and living with his college sweetheart, in the small hamlet of Wynantskill, where he grew up in a house with a white picket fence. He and his wife had three kids, two grandkids, one dog, two cats, and a hamster.

Owen was interviewed several times over the years. He'd been asked questions like, "What does it feel like to be the first person born with an expiration date?" "Do you feel like you've led a happy life?" and "Do you think that since you were the first that maybe your parents were receptive to aliens?" For the most part he enjoyed the attention. It was like being a celebrity.

The day Owen was born was referred to as "E" day.

$$-9-$$

July fifteenth. Elisa quietly entered the bedroom after David left sobbing. He and Shauna had just shared their last moments together with their daughter, Jessica. Elisa eased down at the end of the bed, not sure if Shauna had even noticed her enter the room. Shauna's puffy red eyes were glassed over, her vacant stare contorted and doleful while gazing down at her daughter, who had passed on. Elisa stayed silent, watching her cousin—her best friend—mourn the loss of not just a child, but a dream, a life, a future.

Shauna was still wearing the same t-shirt and sweatpants she had two days ago. *She seems so small and frail,* Elisa thought. Shauna caressed Jessica's head with a shaky hand, tears falling from her cheeks onto the pink blanket which swaddled her daughter. Elisa startled when Shauna began to speak to Jessica in a whisper.

"You were right to wait. The anticipation was almost as magical as you being here in my arms. Your arrival compares to no greater feeling. You are everything we expected. You are amazingly beautiful. You fill us with hope, joy, love, acceptance—all the things we wished for you, you have given to us in this short moment."

She pulled Jessica into her embrace, resting her head in her baby's chest, and sobbed.

- 10 -

JOHN WAITED AT THE CARGO doors of the plane for the attendants to retrieve the large silver cases that made the trip with him. He cringed, observing the end of one of the crates slip from the shorter of the two attendant's hands.

"Seien Sie bitte vorsichtig, sie handhaben eine sehr wertvolle kiste!" John called out.

"Jawohl," the other attendant said, bowing his head, complying with the request to be careful.

"Folge mir," John commanded and the attendants followed.

It was his second trip to Germany in six months, and he'd decided he would rather not have to make a third trip.

"Welcome to Berlin. The truck you requested, sir," the gentleman said, holding the door open and nudging his head, instructing the two attendants to place the cargo in the back. With the wheels tucked up in their wheel-wells, the truck hovered four feet from the ground ready to transport.

Looking toward the back, John pursed his lips. *If those idiots drop these cases, this will surely be a wasted trip. If anyone knew what is in those cases...*

"Sir." The gentleman motioned for John to get into the car. "I will make sure your packages arrive safely in the vehicle."

John nodded his head and got into the driver's seat. *"Danke schön."*

Once everything was loaded, he handed the gentleman a handful of euros through the window and motioned for him to share it with the others.

"Thank you, sir," he said, quickly backing away from the truck as John sped off, kicking up dust in his wake.

"Arschloch! Berechtigte Amerikaner! Entitled Americans!"

John softened the further he distanced himself from the minor irritations at the airport. As he refocused on his agenda, he felt a strong sense of patriotism. His mission—to save the world from itself! If it weren't for him and Mr. P, there might be no hope. He fondly recalled Mr. P's speech as their organization began to strengthen.

~

"Restituere is an idea. A movement. A brotherhood. I understand we are few now, but there are so many other civilized intellectuals out there that believe as we do. They too will want to be a part of rebuilding our home, in order to see progress in regaining the dignity and hope that this planet used to depend. To see our world flourish again we will need to bring the minds of the brilliant and accomplished together and make a plan. We will need to take action!"

Restituere rose from discussions of disappointment in the current state of the world and how it was imperative that something changed before it fell into disarray again. They spoke of making it better for those who earned their place in it. Ideas began to develop here and there as the group grew through word of mouth across the globe. They still weren't very big then, but they felt as though they could make a difference. That difference came in the form of "Restore."

~

Several hours later, John pulled off into a field which housed a barn, careful to hover just behind it, out of sight. Shivering, he reached back in the truck to get the jacket he kept in the front seat. *I never know what kind of weather to expect here in the summer,* he thought, rolling his eyes and recalling his previous visits, when rain poured the entire time, yet it was extremely hot. He opened the back of the truck and pulled one of the cases close to him, placing his right index finger and left thumb on a pad hidden by a golden plate with the name Samsonite embedded on it. The case clicked, and he opened the top and pulled out a drone.

The sound of crickets permeated the early evening air with no other sounds to drown them out. In the hours of dusk, he was comfortable enough that he shouldn't stand out. John circled around the perimeter of the farmhouse barn carrying the large drone; he looked around before entering and stepped through the partially opened old barn door.

"Where will the best place be for this guy to reside for now… ?" he said, looking around the barn, suddenly jerking his head upward. The hay that was dripping over the edge of the wood beams above him shifted. *There's someone in the rafters!* John didn't take his eyes off the loft as he moved further into the barn. His heart was racing now. He looked around for a weapon, prepared to fight, although he was the one trespassing. *Too late now, I'm here.* He gently put the drone down and picked up a shovel he found resting against a wooden post. "Show yourself!"

He dove to the ground as two glowing eyes arrowed straight for him, just missing his head. Following its courageous attack, the owl flew out of the barn and into the night.

Jumping up, he took a deep breath, not sure if the screeching came from the owl or from him. He shook his head and chuckled, put down the shovel and proceeded to wipe the dirt off his jeans—fully aware that his slightly plump physique may not have been a match had his assailant been a young strapping country boy. He peeked out the door to make sure the commotion hadn't attracted the local residents, though the closest house was a quarter mile from the barn.

He ascended the ladder to the rafters, and after searching for a place it most certainly wouldn't be seen, he carefully placed the drone in a nook that was safely hidden yet allowed it to extract itself when commanded. As the late day turned to night, with the moon lighting his way, he traveled the countryside, placing hundreds of drones in a similar manner. He located barns, trees, abandoned buildings, alleyways, anywhere that the drones could stay hidden until they were summoned to complete their task.

- 11 -

ELISA'S ONE-BEDROOM APARTMENT filled with the smell of sautéing asparagus and fresh garlic, complementing the aromas of grilled chicken and rice.

Her head swirled with thoughts of Jessica, dead babies and the devastating repercussions of the string of deaths all over the world. *A multitude of parents grieving just like Shauna—the thought is just unimaginable.* She struggled to pry her thoughts away and focused on her sister's recounting of how she had gotten the "in" at one of the most innovative companies in the world.

"So, Professor Aster said, 'Uncle Bob, you may not want to overlook this young lady as I may have to overlook your Christmas gift this year.'"

"So, she wasn't asking any favors?!" Elisa said sarcastically and smiled.

"Well, I *was* her best student. And look at that, hard work does pay off!"

Ashlei leaned in on the counter, her voice softened. "It's nice to see a smile on your face again."

Elisa returned her sister's smile. "Shauna getting any better?"

"Not really. It's only been a couple of weeks. How long does it take to get over the death of a child—weeks, months, years, never?" she replied and took in a deep breath. "Anyway, I'm very proud of you, Ash, you definitely earned your spot at Exylon!"

"Thanks E," Ashlei said, pleased.

"So, since you've already bypassed the other new hires and are already involved in some of their more important projects, are you working with a bunch of stuffed shirt geeks or what?" Elisa snickered.

"Ha, you mean like me? Yes!" she laughed. "And, I love it! I've learned so much in such a short period of time. And they are not, actually, all stuffed shirts. Most are really cool, down to earth."

Ashlei set the table in the dining room, which extended off the kitchen, while Elisa finished putting the meal together.

She continued, "However, there are a couple weird guys there. They don't speak to me or anyone else much."

"Weird like how?" Elisa asked, serving dinner.

"Well, they don't speak to me or anyone else much." She laughed.

"Ha-ha, I mean other than that!" Elisa rolled her eyes.

"I don't know, like, just creepy. Like Mike, 'the eyebrow' Khoury for instance."

Elisa snickered.

"He's got these dark bushy eyebrows that almost form into one. It makes you think he's up to something sinister. It doesn't help that his body language always appears as though he thinks you're going to steal the wallet from his pocket or something."

"Well maybe that happened, ha-ha," Elisa joked.

This time Ashlei rolled her eyes. "Yeah well, most likely! He's a dork, but all jokes aside, I definitely didn't imagine him to be so... awkward. He is actually a brilliant genealogist that has done groundbreaking work in the field of DNA mutation, among a long list of other accomplishments. I've been following him throughout my studies—a bonus to working there, as he also only started working out of Exylon not too long ago, transferred from Manhattan, I think. And the other guy I mentioned, Claude, he's a bit of a mystery, verdict's still out there. But, he hangs around Mike, so I'd say he's weird by association."

Elisa laughed. "Oh, is that how that works!" Ashlei laughed too. "Yeah!"

"News flash, if Mr. Kourey's going to lead you to your chosen path, you're going to have to talk to him. So, what happens when you tap into his brilliance and start hanging with him too? Will that make you creepy?"

"Probably. I'll have to get past it if I'm hoping to work more in my field of study because, yes, that would most likely lead me to him. I've been given a couple other projects right away, though, that are more structured around fundamental research—boring! Not that I'm complaining, I'm grateful to have the opportunity to work there."

"Maybe they're testing you to see what you can handle, get your feet wet."

"I hadn't thought about it like that." Ashlei bit into her asparagus.

"My goal is still to research expiration dates, especially after Jessica and what's going on all over the world right now. Investigations are not active any longer in our scientific community, so someone has to take on that albatross and revisit its origins." Ashlei dove into her chicken.

Elisa pulled her head back. "Do you eat at home?"

"No. I'm still living like a starving student!"

"So other than taking on that mountain, what *else* do you want to do, specifically?"

"Well." She finished chewing. "Have you ever thought about how our senses work and relate to everything we do, every second of the day?"

"Not really," Elisa said.

"I had been doing a lot of research over the last year based on a study that I came across while I was doing my dissertation in school. I had to dust off some pretty old books I'd found in the archives to continue reading up on it. I'm guessing, like so many other break-throughs and studies, that after the Transitional War it was put on hold and eventually got lost to scientists. It all ties into human DNA and my interest in mutation."

"Researching the senses. So, can I move objects with my mind?" Elisa asked in jest.

Ashlei's posture straightened with her excitement. "Some say that we harbor the ability to do that! It's just a matter of unlocking that part of our brain. Problem is, we haven't figured *that* part out yet."

"Or maybe we have and it's just locked up in the archives," she tapped her head, "with the rest of those old dusty books."

- 12 -

MIKE'S CONVERSATION WITH JOHN was brief—his instructions clear. "Find out if Claude was an accomplice or if Derrick went rogue on his own." Mike hadn't been happy when John assigned Claude to work with him at Exylon nine months ago. Mike's temporary reassignment had taken him away from his current project, VM9, requiring Claude to continue Mike's work so that his project could stay on course. John favored Claude, calling him, "an up-and-coming star," but Mike had his own ideas about Claude based on his stereotypes.

"He's green and I'm not comfortable with him fooling around with my life's work."

"He's young, yes, but mature, ambitious, and he comes with skills that surpass any of my other students. That part of him reminds me of you. I've been working with him for a couple years now, Mike, he has some great ideas!"

"I'm not debating his intelligence, but where he excels in academics, I think he will lack in critical thinking and logic. Do you know how he showed up to the lab? A t-shirt, jeans, and sneakers. Hair disheveled; he could use a haircut!"

John chuckled. "So, he has a personality. Change of pace from your current surroundings, you can use some of that. Work with it!"

My life's work, in the hands of... a fool!

Though not happy about the change, Mike would never turn down an instruction from his mentor. It was John's research, specifically on vegetation mutation, that Mike had built his theories on and how he had been able to make further discoveries. Noting his natural academic skills and social awkwardness, John had taken Mike under his wing when he was a student at Harvard University and helped him to grow and tap into his potential.

Mike was well-known in his field, writing papers on his innovative research on DNA and genetic mutation, and altering life spans. He graduated from Harvard at a very young age with degrees in Biomedical Science, Genomics, a PhD in Bioinformatics, as well as many other accolades. His research was talked about, debated, and taught around the globe.

Mike's opportunity to begin and run the sister division of Population Control and Statistics in Albany, New York, facilitated by John, was an honor for him. A more controlled environment was needed for their intended plans and Exylon Pharmaceuticals, a government-run company, was an ideal location for him to work undisturbed. And now here he was, as predicted, cleaning up a mess that had something to do with Claude. He would need to question him carefully.

- 13 -

THERE WAS NOTHING extraordinary about the exterior of the Exylon Pharmaceutical Technology Company. It was a generic building that stood alone on several acres of land, separated from the city surrounding it. Security was prominent around the perimeter and within, however, the company prided itself on fostering the idea that a comfortable, welcoming workplace would produce a more productive outcome for the thousands of expert scientists, researchers, and engineers employed there.

The interior was, to some degree, like a small city, and though there was much activity throughout the building, it engendered a tranquil, peaceful state outside of the labs and work areas. Soft sounds and scents permeated the building, encouraging a pleasant demeanor. At its hub, beneath a skylight, the flowing water fountain created a central meeting place for employees to gather for a quick conversation or just a brief neutral getaway from a heavy workload. Exylon played a key role in revitalizing the industry at the beginning of the transition era, from the Virtual Cybernetic Computer with a design by Robert Frederick to creating organ cloning for transplant.

Exylon was usually silent after everyone had gone home, so the reverberations coming from the research lab fell on deaf ears other than its recipient.

Frequently one of the only staff members here working late, Claude found himself the object of Mike's disgruntled rant, which seemed to have come out of nowhere.

"Why did you send injections out without my authority?"

"I didn't think I needed your authority to send out nutriment injections, we send out shipments all the time."

Mike ignored his response.

"It's not your job to change anything or go off on your own! Your job is to do exactly as you are told!" he scolded. "A job, by the way, that you are getting paid very well for and could have been given to someone who follows orders!"

"I didn't change anything! I sent out the shipments as I always do."

"Idiot!" Mike yelled at Claude, while pacing back and forth past his desk. "Very careless!"

Mike had worked himself up into a sweat, repeating the last twenty minutes of Claude's inquisition.

"So, five months ago there was a shipment that went out of here. You signed off on it and sent it out."

"Mike, how am I supposed to remember exactly what went on here five months ago? There was nothing unusual going on."

"In the business you're in, you'd better damn well remember what goes on around here!"

Claude couldn't recall Mike ever using the word damn. He was definitely riled up for some reason.

"I'm just trying to figure out where those injections came from. They weren't shipped in from the nutriment plant, but they weren't the injections for my research that I already had here to send out."

Claude was tiring of Mike's relentless repeated questions. He rolled his eyes. "There was nothing unusual about the way I sent out any injection shipments!"

"Idiot!" he said again, shaking his head.

"What is the problem here, Mike?" Claude was rapidly trying to think back to the day Mike was questioning, to recall if there was anything off or different that he could have done wrong. They sent shipments out all the time, what was so special about this one?

"Does this have anything to do with the news reports about the mass surge of deaths?"

Again ignoring Claude, Mike asked, "Exactly where and how much went out?"

Claude untucked the back of his shirt to let air climb in through the bottom. "Umm," he stammered, placing his hand over the silver metal virtual cybernetic computer (VCC) disk on his desk. A blue ray of light shot up from the disk. He typed his passcode into the free-floating keyboard and an owl head greeted him. "Hello Claude."

Mike rolled his eyes.

Claude cleared his throat and continued to type. "Not quite sure why this is such a big deal. It's just a mat—"

"No, I guess you wouldn't," Mike mumbled, cutting Claude off.

Pulling up all the files from five months ago, Claude found the shipment Mike was going on about and could see why he didn't have those injections in his records.

Derrick had called Claude, that night—frantic, afraid of losing his job. He was already on his way from Washington D.C. It was Derrick's job to send the nutriment injections vials from the nutriment plant, scheduled for the Albany site, to Mike; but he screwed up and they didn't go. Since he was unauthorized to send them himself, he covertly transported them, hoping that Claude, who had authorization, would send them out and that Derrick could avoid having to deal with Mike at all. Claude didn't think this one little favor would come back to bite him, but Mike was proving why Derrick was so nervous to tell him he screwed up in the first place. Claude documented the shipment in his own log and sent it out. Since Derrick had only worked at the bureau for six months, Mike would have crucified him for a mistake like that. If he were alive, Claude would try to find a way around explaining the truth, but it wouldn't hurt now to let Mike know.

Claude attempted to speak, but Mike clamped his fingers together in his direction. "Irrelevant!"

Claude's nostrils flared.

Mike continued, "You do realize that you have brought an insurmountable amount of attention to what we're trying to do here, and go figure, people are going to start inquiring!"

Claude stared at Mike, raising his eyebrow.

Mike stood back, his tone calmed. "Everything has an order here. We need to document … document everything, that's all."

Claude stood with arms crossed and face tight, pointing to the list projected before them.

"Here's the list of exactly who those batches went out to and their destinations."

"Okay," Mike said, beginning to recite the list quietly to himself—skimming through most.

England: Olivia Addington, PhD, MD—Biomedical Scientist—Bristol Medical Center. 3 Old Gloucester Street, London WC1N 3AX ph: 020 7956 2000

England: Damian Farley, PhD, Biomedical Science—

Temple Clinic. 190 Oxford Place, Leeds LS13AX ph: 0113 292 6666

China: Mae Ling, PhD, MD—Lead geneticist, Fudan Woman's Clinic. 107 Box, 233 Meilong Rd, Shanghai, China ph: +27 11 202 4450

Russia: Petrov Alexander Ivan, MD, Bioinformatics Research Scientist—United Clinic. ul. Lesnaya k. 9 g. St. Petersburg 564890 Russian Federation, ph: +7 319 877 92 29

Russia: Tarasov Adam Igorevoich, MD—Moscow City Medical Clinic. ul Mokhovaya k. 3 g. Moscow 678396 Russian Federation ph: 8 904 947 25 94

Canada: Liam Tremblay, PhD, MD—Lead geneticist—Ontario Health Clinic. 15 Rue Nepeau, Ottawa, ON K1P ph: 413-867-7896

America: Monica Darby, PhD, MD—West Park Center. 135 Canyons Ct, San Diego, CA 22434 ph: 619 679 9809

America: George Terrance, MD, Bioinformatics Research Scientist—Los Angelos Family Clinic. 302 Adams Blvd. Los Angeles, CA 90007 ph: 213 678 9302

America: Lorie Angle, PhD, MD—Lead geneticist—Mid City Health Center. 24 Blackwell St., Anchorage, Alaska 99737 ph: 907-3236918

America: Michael Portsmith, PhD, MD—Bioinformatics Research Science—Athol Technology Center. 1 Terry Rd., Hartford, CT 06105 ph: 203 457 6809

America: Theodore Rheinhold, PhD, MD—Biomedical Research Scientist—Citizens Health Clinic, 1345 Victoria Ct., Portland, ME 04953, Ph:207-368-7312

Moldova: Cristian Popa, MD—Moldovia Medical Center N 77, AL, Genovia str. MD-0098 Chisinau, ph: +(373 22) 77 99 0972

America: Rafael Delgado, MD, Lead geneticist/Bioinformatics Research Science—Albany Medical Center. 2218 Ontario St., Albany, NY, ph: 518-367-8980

A sharp throbbing began at the base of Mike's skull and he took a deep breath in.

"Moldova!" he said in a whisper.

One of the first countries to witness an expiration date?! A country whose very name signifies the 'birth' of expiration dates for some! No one's going to notice that! he thought sarcastically.

"All of our injections, as you know, are accounted for, for obvious reasons."

Mike finally gave Claude the opportunity to speak and he explained that he sent them out for Derrick as a favor.

Claude was the vessel Derrick used to send those injections to unauthorized sites. Although irritated that Claude did it behind his back, it was innocent enough. Mike was confident Claude had no idea that the shipments carried Restore nutriment injections with nanobytes that would guarantee a very short expiration date.

And just like that, the rant was over and Mike rushed from the lab, leaving Claude baffled and more curious about his abrupt mollification than the rant itself.

-14-

The two men entered the "Transitional Era" museum exhibit, the lights gradually coming on as the monotone automated recording sprang to life.

"As the global struggle for dominance erupted into the conflict that became known as the 'Transitional War,' whole countries were destroyed, and the planet was left in disarray. Between the destruction, germ warfare, bankruptcy, barren land, and no hope for rebuilding, East Africa, Western Asia, most of Eastern Europe and many other parts of the world were abandoned—the damage irreversible. Standing territories embraced the surviving displaced population. Miraculously, something positive emerged from this war: a greater understanding of the human race."

As they walked through silently, the pictures completely filled the wall, gradually changing from the devastation seen around the world to a calm flowing brook.

"The hundred and sixty-four remaining countries were able to come to many universal agreements. A union was formed with representatives of all countries to decide and enforce new international rules for humanity. This global committee is known as Orbis."

The pictures now moved to a council of men gathered in a conference room, followed by the spinning Orbis insignia.

"For the first time ever in the history of the world, all countries came together

as one for the greater good of all people. From that time on, every decision made was for the benefit of the planet."

Just as they exited the exhibit, a gaggle of school children entered, ignoring their teacher's plea for silence and order as they ran around giggling. John turned and smiled.

Mr. P ignored the children, focusing on the reason for their meeting.

"I infused the last of the needles with the nanobytes and attached them to the drones—they're all completed now. We need to distribute the last of the drones by tomorrow so I can go over the trajectory again. We can't afford any mistakes here."

"I'm afraid you're on your own there, that technology is beyond my comprehension. You're positive they'll follow your instructions?" John asked.

"Since we know where the targets are located, the information we gathered within Restituere, setting the latitude and longitude coordinates are pretty simple really—the drones do all the work. We've done the hard part—the tedious task of delivering the drones to each region here and to the other countries, leaving them close enough to continue to their projected targets. The complicated part was making sure that they know what they are targeting so they proceed directly there. I've worked with infrared in the past, but not on such a large scale, nor from this distance. In any case, secondary detection is rhythmic pulsation. In other words, a human heartbeat. The drones were programmed to follow both within the one-mile radius." Mr. P smirked. "It's smart technology, there shouldn't be any change in their course. And currently, after following the flight pattern I programmed for the drones we couldn't person-ally deliver, they will have already found their resting spot, in the trees, barns, rooftops, all the places we designed them to sit, and they will just lie in wait."

Stopping in front of the true-to-life whale skeleton, Mr. P stood firm, hands behind his back. "And of course, as you said, there will be many targets who aren't reached by our nanobytes, and that's okay… we'll get the bulk and that will serve our purpose for now."

They continued to walk.

"How'd the drop go in Germany?" he asked John.

"About as smooth and as tedious as all the others. Though bringing the drones all around the globe was laborious, it has its perks. In Tokyo, I found a restaurant that makes the best nigiri sushi I've ever had." John grinned.

Mr. P smiled. "You'll definitely have time for travel when things have settled down."

He asked John to meet him at the New York State Museum—for him, it harbored a nostalgia—it had always been his sanctuary. The museum was partially destroyed when the Transitional War reached American soil. The rooms housed local antiques, as well as artifacts from the cities in the lower parts of the state, the Adirondacks and Finger Lakes regions, and beyond, telling stories of their way of life, the native wildlife, and local and global tragedies. Many years after its destruction, architects were careful to salvage the original sections that had survived, and a newly expanded addition included the transition era and the many ways the locals had adjusted and survived all the way to present day. For John, the addition represented a symbolism to Restituere's cause—a rebirth of their nation.

Mr. P couldn't resist stroking the fur of the preserved wolf in its display as they walked by the "DO NOT TOUCH EXHIBIT" sign.

"After the launch, we'll need to gather all the members of Restituere together and announce our next move. Once the shock of the situation has subsided, after the news reports and Orbis's speeches, we'll embark on our projected vision. We'll enlist volunteers to head up committees, we'll need organizers to delegate tasks such as educating communities about the opportunities that lie ahead," Mr. P said.

"Do you think, at that time, we should let the other members of Restituere know we were responsible for opening this pathway to continue our work?"

Mr. P shook his head. "I don't think that's necessary. To them, we will have been given a gift."

I don't agree, John thought. *Restituere are our brothers, they should be a part of our plan. I know they would all want to belong to this triumph!*

"Just playing devil's advocate here, but we may get questions as to why we needed to do anything at all. I mean, this to them will be a miracle, a gift like you said, and the suggestion may be to not look a gift horse in the mouth."

Mr. P raised his chin slightly. "And we will respond that you cannot simply expect a plant to grow. It needs water and sunlight, right? Plans also need to be nurtured. Great things don't just happen, they're reared."

They walked around the large moose, a surviving relic in the old section of the museum. The moose, standing in a stream of water surrounded by its native habitat, had always been a symbol of the New York State Museum. Children and adults alike gathered and wondered at its size, tossing a penny into the water, making a wish.

"We need to be ready for what comes next," Mr. P said, admiring the magnificence of such an animal, which had become extinct.

"I'm prepared!" John said, feeling energized. *This has been a long process; a lot of thought and work has been put into making this happen. Oh, I've planned for this and I'm ready for every obstacle!*

"I'm talking about your psyche." He looked at John and back at the moose. "Are you prepared to handle the aftermath and what is to come? I'm talking about your cognizance of the situation as it will be. Though this is what must be, it is a heavy responsibility to bear, and I need to know you are prepared for that."

"This has been my ambition, my very existence since its inception. No one can feel more passionate about what we are doing then me. My psyche is fine!"

Mr. P tossed a penny in the water, glancing over at John with a smirk. "Not that we'll need it."

- 15 -

Elisa heard laughter coming from Jack's office when she approached. She knocked on the door and entered.

"Hey, I have a question about a patient—some of us are working around here," she chided.

"Hi," Reed said, rising from his chair.

His captivating smile reached into her chest, igniting emotions she needed to keep at bay.

"I just stopped in to say hi. I won't keep this guy from doing any work," he continued.

She pulled her hair behind her ear. "It's not critical and I'm just teasing, you don't have to go."

"I wasn't staying long anyway," he said, staring in her eyes, making her blush. There was nothing really outstanding about Reed's face. She thought, actually, his face was quite plain. His hair combed neatly the way you would expect a legacy's heir to wear his hair. He stood tall, confident—good breeding. But there was something in his smile that glowed from the inside.

Jack's voice faded in, breaking her trance.

"Reed came to borrow some scrubs since his latest newbie showed him exactly what she thought of him." Jack laughed. "And her opinion covered his entire front!" He laughed again.

Elisa pulled her head back, questioning.

Reed quickly stated, "My off-color comment about her questionable skills may have hurt her feelings and she expressed her right to retaliate. I really meant no harm, I apologized."

"I suggested that maybe studies in women really aren't his thing and he should have stayed in the family business."

Elisa laughed too, putting that scene together in her head. She considered the affluential Frederick family legacy and felt compelled to ask.

"Actually, why did you choose such a different path than your family and pursue an interest in obstetrics?"

"A girl, ironically." He chuckled.

"Do tell," she said, easing down into the chair in front of Jack's desk. "My father *did* want me to go into the family business, especially at that

time. He was grooming me to jump into the VCC end of the business. At the time, it had been, what… about sixty years since our technology in Virtual Cybernetic Computers had had any real upgrades. It was my father who took that limited, cumbersome dinosaur of a computer and created the disk that gave us the ability to expand and utilize virtual cybernetics. So, he was looking to launch a new division introducing newer technology, with me at the helm."

"Got it, I'm well aware of your brilliant family history, get to the girl." Jack motioned to move along.

Elisa shook her head at Jack and looked to Reed to continue.

"Anyway," he cut Jack a look, "I was young and couldn't see myself locked into much of anything really, much less such a huge responsibility. Regardless, I went to school, did what I was supposed to; sort of." He grinned. "And there she was. Mary Windsor." Picturing her, he looked into the air. "Angelic really. She was standing outside of class talking to Professor Green, who taught Anatomy and Physiology. I approached her on several occasions, but she didn't give me the time of day, so with my connections, I had myself put in all her classes."

"That's extreme!" Jack said.

"Long story short, I ended up falling in love with medicine, obstetrics in particular. Not as much with Mary, though." He laughed. "Though, I do believe I was led to Mary by divine intervention—the medical field is my calling and where I hope to make my largest contribution."

~

After leaving Jack, Reed opened the door to his office to find Elisa waiting for him. He closed the door behind him; she heard the click. The smile on her face turned to a seductive pout as she reached out, pulling him in closer by his lab coat. "What took you so long?"

"It's been ten minutes since we left Jack's office."

"Exactly," she said, cutting off his grin by pressing her lips hard against his.

They kissed for what didn't seem nearly long enough for him. "I have to go back to work," she said, still wrapped in his arms.

"What are you doing tonight?" he asked.

"My place… drinks, dessert," she offered.

"How about I make you dinner?"

She hesitated. "Late cases, I'll be here most of the night."

"Okay," he said disappointed, "late night dessert it is."

Lately, he had reconsidered their stance on keeping their relationship, or whatever this thing was, a secret. When he was with her he felt invigorated; when he went home, he felt the pang of loneliness of an empty house. But he believed she liked the mystery and excitement of sneaking around. Which was great at first, but now he wanted more.

- 16 -

Ashlei approached the door to the lab labeled Room 211, her new assignment, with reservations. Still feeling as though she'd won the job lottery working at Exylon, she was among some of the greatest minds in the country. But now she would be working directly with a legend, Mike Khoury. Sort of. More like working indirectly. She took a deep breath in to keep from getting lightheaded as that reality set in. Exylon had the exclusive reputation of being the top biotechnological company in America; you had to either be a genius or know someone, such as her professor, who had an in to work here. *You earned your way into the company; you deserve this opportunity!* She grinned. *But it was nice having that in!*

Moving on from secondary school at only fifteen, she enjoyed full scholarships to Penn State and then Cornell University, graduating magna cum laude and one of the top in her class, earning degrees in neurobiology and genetics. Her young age and busy schedule didn't keep her from humanitarian projects, with memberships in the honor society, math, chess and debate clubs. She considered herself the quintessential nerd, despite her natural beauty. She found early on that the less noticeable her appearance, the greater respect she got for her work. She regularly pulled her hair off her face in a ponytail, avoided wearing anything too short or snug that showed off her curves, and rarely wore makeup. She even wore non-prescription glasses to hide her face. Still, with the same soft bronze complexion as her sister and emerald eyes, she radiated a natural glow and her beauty always showed through.

Ashlei patted her hair down and straightened her glasses before entering the lab where she would officially meet Claude, whom she would be working with for her next task. Her attention was drawn immediately to the layout of the room, divided into applied practice on one side and academic workspace on the other. At the lab workstation she observed an incubator, unopened sterile beakers, scales, and floating microscopes—named for their mobility. They extended from the lab counter and easily adjusted for any small workspace. Her eyes widened as she followed the windows from floor to ceiling, the entire room saturated in the sun's rays. After scanning the room quickly, her eyes rested on Claude.

Hearing the door, he turned. "Oh, hi Ashlei, come on in," he instructed, turning his attention back to what he was doing.

Ashlei was taken aback a little by the fact that he said her name as though he knew her well.

"Hi. Claude Monark?" she questioned, knowing exactly who he was. "I was assigned to—"

"Yeah, I know why you're here, Ashlei, I requested you," Claude interrupted, still focusing his attention on the vials and paperwork he was logging onto.

"Oh," she said, again taken aback, now by his abruptness.

He stopped what he was doing, swiveled around on his stool and gave her his full attention.

"Honestly, I work alone—for the most part. I prefer it that way, but I have deadlines too, like everyone else and I have a lot of research that, quite frankly, I don't have time for," he stated. "That's where you come in," he said, pointing to her with both pointer fingers.

"I need you to go through this file." He handed her a stack of bound papers.

This is heavy enough to be a door stop—for a very heavy door! she thought.

"Read it here, at home, I don't really care, but I need you to be updated by tomorrow, so I can go over the details with you then and we can get started. Okay?"

"Umm, so… you… want me to read this entire thing in one day?" She realized she sounded like an idiot when the words come out of her mouth.

"Umm, yeah," he said, staring her in the eyes. "Look, Ashlei, I chose you because your portfolio was ridiculously impressive. Also, the training you have is exactly what I need on this project. I've seen you run circles around those cretins out there. If I didn't think you could read that *book*," he joked, trying to lighten the mood, "in a day, you probably wouldn't have been the person for the job."

"Okay, no problem." She smiled slightly, lifting the file up in sort of a toast. "I'll get to work on it."

"Great," he said swiveling back to his station. He quickly swiveled back to face her again as she opened the door to retreat.

"Oh, I'll see you back here at seven a.m. tomorrow."

"Perfect," she said, rolling her eyes, careful not to let him see. *Cretins?*

- 17 -

CLAUDE STARED OUT THE WINDOW down at nothing, trying to bring his focus back to the Portulaca plant sitting in front of him. It was one of the thousands of plant life types that possessed properties key to his trials. This particular plant was able to thrive in barren conditions, with a promising ability to grow in the experimental soils he'd been working with.

He'd been replaying Mike's rant in his head. There were no red flags that indicated that those shipments shouldn't have been sent out or should have been sent elsewhere—*that I recall.* And why did Mike go from acting like a lunatic to temperate, like he got a good sniff of the lavender that's piped through this place?

Derrick Monahan had an uneasy relationship with Mike. After Claude sent off the shipment that day, they'd gone to lunch. Shoving down a burger while he spoke, Derrick asked, "What would you do if you thought someone was sabotaging the work you were doing? Wouldn't you try to get rid of them to protect that cause?" He thought those were odd, random questions till he asked, "How well do you know Mike? Do you think he's handling the program at this site properly?" He was young and immature and looking for an ally. Claude couldn't take him too seriously. He was hired to work at the nutriment plant only months prior to their conversation, challenging Mike's authority was pushing Derrick's boundaries and Claude shut him down before he got himself in trouble.

Since his death, though, Claude wondered if he'd squelched Derrick's concerns too quickly. What did he know? *Mike never did answer my question—whether the matter had anything to do with the recent mass deaths.*

Claude looked at the clock. Ashlei was right on time.

~

Fully prepared, Ashlei arrived in the lab promptly at seven a.m., as instructed. The shades were slightly drawn, leaving the room a bit darker than the day before. This time, Claude greeted her as she walked in the door.

"Good morning, Mr. Monark." Cringing inwardly, she lightly touched the lapel of her pants suit, while Claude sported jeans and a t-shirt.

"Good morning. I have a meeting to get to mid-morning, so I'm just gonna get started and throw you right in, okay?"

She nodded.

"First of all, it's Claude. And now that you have full clearance to work on this project, I want to reiterate that our work is confidential. Everything we are working on must not be discussed with anyone other than myself and Mike Khoury."

She nodded. "Understood."

"I trust you got through the manual alright?" he asked.

"Yes, I did," she said, patting her bag containing the data he gave her to read through.

"Good. So, you've got some history on our project and a whole lot of review of things you probably already know. Hence the fact that you graduated. Sorry, I couldn't deconstruct the manual, but I'm sure you noticed, it's all intertwined. So, here's what you don't know. We are in stage nine of project Vegetation Mutation or VM9. VM one through eight have been unsuccessful, but Mike—you'll meet him later if you haven't already—believes we are so close that this should be the one that succeeds. This project is Mike's baby, actually. His dream is creating vegetation that can change the way we look at growing plants. We're going down new roads with genetic mutation.

"In a nutshell, we're breeding plants with the best, most desirable traits. I'm talking about genetic engineering. Removing the DNA from one organism and transferring it to another. I know you've learned about that in your studies, but we've been working on the ability to not only mate vegetation, creating new breeds so that we're able to grow them in any kind of environment and atmosphere, but to grow them to immense size. Can you imagine what that would mean for the planet? For our communities to not have to struggle with tiny patches of land, not knowing if they will even produce anything?" he said, excited about the prospect.

"Can't wait to get to work," Ashlei said flatly.

Claude grinned at his own over-enthusiasm. "I know your studies are in human genetics and DNA and probably seem a little more interesting to you, but plants and people are closely related when it comes to genetics. But I know you know that. You never know what you'll get out of this research," he pointed out.

"Sorry, I actually *am* excited to be working on this project. I didn't want to steal your thunder by taking my enthusiasm a step beyond yours," she joked nervously.

"Ha," he replied, though not smiling.

Ashlei realized trying to joke was poor judgment.

While walking across the room to the lab station, he pointed back to the desk in the academic area and then to a lab jacket hanging on a hook.

"Throw your stuff on the desk over there and grab a coat."

She quickly did as he instructed, while he continued to explain what the project entailed.

"We're also looking into using different materials to grow vegetation. Rather than earth's soil, we have artificial soil created by a number of different substances. The ability to be able to grow vegetation with limited resources and limited light is our goal. We have already mastered cross-pollination, which means supplying different types of resources for essential nutrition. And we are pretty close to doing this in a fraction of the time that anyone could ever predict.

"Basic rundown. Plant breeders use what is known about genes of plants to select desirable traits—same with humans," he said.

"We breed plants with the best traits and use genetic modification to change the genetic composition by making crosses and selecting new superior genotype combinations. Genetic engineering removes the DNA from one organism and transfers the gene into another using gene cloning, designing it to work in another organism or plant."

"The new gene is inserted into some of the cells using various techniques, like the gene gun, and is delivered into the nucleus of a cell without killing it. The trans-genetic plants are grown to maturity and the offspring are repeatedly bred within this elite line.

"This traditionally takes six to fifteen years, but Mike is able to do this in less than a year. His ambition is to be able to do this with limited space, in a short time, in any kind of conditions, no sunlight, and no traditional soil. We're also working on amplifying the dimensions. In other words, to eradicate famine in ways that no one has done previously—maybe find ways to reuse the land that's sat barren since the war."

He stopped and turned to look at her. "Keeping up?" She was pretty sure he asked just to be a jerk.

"Yes, sir," she replied, following him around the lab. In the next hour Ashlei learned how to get into their virtual cybernetics files, where the equipment was stored that she would be using, and Exylon's rules about safety in the lab that Claude admitted to not always adhering to.

"Okay, if you don't have any current questions, I'll leave you to get started." He threw on a sports coat that was draped over a chair and left her alone in the lab.

"Great second impression I've made," she muttered.

- 18 -

JOHN HAD A CAR WAITING for him when the helicopter landed at the Bureau of Population Control and Statistics (BPCS) nutriment division facility. He sneered, as he always did, at the dry and dull landscape. Wind turbines, spinning consistently, stretched as far as the eye could see on either side of the plant. They were the only other structures within miles. The building itself was circular, built with the idea of conserving energy and also ensuring an even and constant ventilation.

As the driver got closer, John saw a couple of maintenance men cleaning up the carcass of what looked like a coyote. A couple of young vultures were testing their limits to fight for their share, getting zapped by the invisible perimeter fence when the men shooed them away. *Probably what took out the poor coyote*, he thought.

They came to a stop in front of a sign that read "Danger: Electric Fence" in several different languages. The driver opened his window, allowing in a silver ball about the size of a golf ball. It scanned his left retina, then the right, and retreated. A gate lighted up and an automated voice announced, *"Gate deactivated, it is safe to enter. You have three minutes to enter before electrification will re-activate."* This announcement repeated until the last thirty seconds of the countdown, by which time they were already on the inside of the gate.

Despite its barren landscape, the building's immediate surroundings were lush with a variety of green plants and shrubbery.

For his second round of clearance, John approached the military officers on either side of the entrance; one stepped forward and raised a thin gray box to John's ear and a green light flashed on—across the screen read "John Vanburen" accompanied by a head shot of John underneath.

The officer nodded, embarrassed, knowing that John was Head of BPCS, but not wanting to get caught slacking on his security responsibilities. John smirked and moved on.

Just inside the doors, he paused while fluoroscopy scanned for weapons.

The lobby seemed to be in constant motion as the walls on either side told the story of the facility's beginnings, from the process of producing nutriment serum to the benefits it brought to women and infants.

In the center were the administrative offices—desks, monitors, activity, all inside a large glass dome.

John waved to Monica on the other side of the glass, an administrative assistant who had been a staple at the facility.

The entrances to four hallways stood on the other side of the dome.

The far right led to the cafeteria and facility employee store, the next entryway led to the meeting rooms and conference center. He exchanged a quick greeting with Colonel James Stone, Chief of Security for BPCS, who was coming from the conference room hall.

John entered the one of two halls that housed the nutriment labs, research and development.

He toured once a month, inspecting the facility, nodding and smiling as he walked through. Most of the labs were semi-automated, so in each lab he found assistants, pharmacists, and scientists busily working, some covered from head to toe in white.

He stood outside Quality and Process Control, hands behind his back, observing through the wide glass window. The project team inspected units and equipment for defects and flaws; satisfied with the flow, he moved to the next glass window. Here he followed the machines moving in and out like oil pumps, auto-filling vials and ampules. Satisfied, he moved along.

"John!" The nutriment plant managing director extended his hand.

"Kyle." John stepped around him to observe the activity down below on the floor of the only open area in the building other than the lobby. Holograms of the facility's operations hovered in front of engineers while they inspected each one.

Kyle moved in next to John and began going over the monthly activity report.

"There's a break in a line behind us in the water treatment plant. It's created a bit of a mess and concern about system contamination."

"Have you taken the appropriate steps to fix the problem?"

"Yes. I have men back there right now."

"Okay, what else?" John asked.

Kyle hesitated. John turned to look at him.

"Well, there's been talk. Down in K. About … Derrick."

"What kind of talk?"

Kyle looked around and lowered his voice. "Well, that his expiration date wasn't up yet. That maybe he was… taken care of because he sent out those Restore injections to the high-profile sites. Finding out that he was the one who sent those out and the news of his death *did* come at the same time."

"Who's saying these things?"

"Well, it's in everyone's head."

"You too?"

Kyle stayed silent.

"I can tell you that it certainly was an expiration date that ended Derrick's life. I can also tell you that there is no room for rogue actions in a brotherhood."

He moved on to the next window, the lab which produced nutriment serum, spending only a moment before moving on. They bypassed an elevator with a sign next to it that read:

-Dispensing area Level B

-Drug product development packaging material warehouse Level C. They continued on to the elevator at the end of the hall labelled Restricted. Pulling out his passkey, John held it flush against the pad to the left of the elevator, and they stood inside waiting. Seconds later a small silver ball uprooted itself from a socket above the keypad and levitated toward his head. It glided around to John's ear and scanned the tag. "John Vanburen. Welcome." The elevator moved. The doors reopened four floors below on Level G.

They took a left and entered a control room, putting on the hanging white hooded jumpsuits.

"Hello, John… Kyle," Mohammad greeted them when they stepped into the lab.

John waved, Kyle said nothing.

They blended into the nearly all-white room in their suits. John walked to a large drum labelled "Nutriment infused Nanobytes."

"Any issues, Mohammad?" John asked, moving next to the connected glass case that enclosed five black mechanical arms. The arms moved quickly, extracting nanobytes from the drum; they received a number, filled a syringe and then were joined with a probe that moved simultaneously, just below the arms.

"No, sir. Everything has been running smoothly down here." Two more white suits came in from another door.

"Hello, Mr. Vanburen," they both said. He nodded.

Kyle hung in the background, ready to document any discrepancies or changes that needed to be made.

One of the workers sat down in front of the large screen on the wall, pushing buttons. The screen changed from the spinning Orbis insignia to a geographical map of America, then changed to sites to the midwest.

John concentrated on the small windows on the mechanical arms. The red numbers flashed so fast it was difficult for him to get a view of any one number. 1162209, 922261, 312172, 8132243. Random dates ranging from six months from this day to one hundred years from now.

"Any trouble with our expiration dates?"

"Uh, no," Mohammad said, continuing his work.

John followed the line to witness the last step prior to final packaging. They were labelled with batch number, serial code, product name, and sent off to be boxed and shipped.

"Jessie." She turned to John from the monitor. "We're careful not to clump any like dates together that may be distributed to the same regions?"

"Yes, Mr. Vanburen. All of our data has been checked and re-checked regularly since the increase in deaths occurred."

Their next visit was to Level K, which was classified, with entry requiring access to an elevator on the other side of the building. Kyle trailed behind. John pulled a different security key card from his jacket, the other nine in existence belonging to the only other people who knew this lab existed. They followed the same protocol for this lab, putting on white hooded suits before they entered. Miguel, a pharmacist, rushed to turn the music off and approached John.

"Hello, John. Uh, Mr. Vanburen. I didn't know we were expecting you today." He hurried to pick up a soda bottle sitting on a monitor and grabbed his sandwich wrapper from atop the tubing that transported the syringe and probe packaging to the distribution center in the next room.

John shook his head.

"Hello," Charlie said, and turned back to the large monitor in front of him.

John inspected the process, which was identical to the one on Level G, with the exception of the programming of the expiration dates.

"Miguel…"

"Yes, sir," he answered before John could finish his sentence.

"Have there been any issues? Is the programming running smoothly?"

"Yeah, I mean since, Derrick… that whole… ya know… since we have come off standby, this baby's been running great! Our Restore dates are back on track, seventy-two hours to a hundred and fifty give or take." He smacked the glass encasement the black mechanical arms were in.

"I see." John moved over to watch the arms vigorously working, just as they were on Level G. He took his hood off.

"I hear there's been some speculation over the circumstances of Derrick's death." Kyle put his head down. Miguel looked around and Charlie turned to look at John.

"Derrick was not thinking about Restituere, but only of his own personal agenda. I will say to you both what I said to Kyle. I verify that it was an expiration date that ended Derrick's life. And I will also point out that there is no room for rogue actions in Restituere."

On the way back down the dusty road to the awaiting helicopter, John closed the partition between the driver and himself. He swiped the band on his wrist, and immediately an illuminated panel wrapped around his wrist. He pulled forth a number, like plucking a petal from a flower. He swiped again; Mr. P. hovered above his wrist in a hologram.

"We're back on track with the Restore injections."

"Questions… death?" Mr. P asked, while his transmission was interrupted from the remote location.

"Yes, a few questions about his death, but I handled it." He paused. "We have another potential issue; Krish Persaud has gotten increasingly uncomfortable with his new partner's questions, I think he may be a threat to Restituere? He's been questioning Krish regarding his methods and treatments. Krish has a strong suspicion that his associate may reach out to someone about his concern."

"I see, I'll… handle it."

The image retracted, his wrist no longer illuminated. Gone before John could even say goodbye. He admired Mr. P's smooth demeanor. "I'll handle it." And John knew that he would. Enough said.

- 19 -

Lydia Kantell was going skydiving. It was something she had been planning since her tenth birthday, and today—thirteen years later—she'd showed up at the door of the only skydiving place in town. She'd been up since five in the morning anticipating this longtime dream, getting dressed and in the car before she realized she was standing at the front door of the school with her hand on the handle.

She hesitated for a moment and wondered if this adventure was such a good idea. She hadn't really been sure of any of her ideas lately. As she stared at her brown reflection in the glass that read, EXTREME SKY-DIVING. COME IN FOR THE RIDE OF YOUR LIFE, she said to herself, "Don't back out now, chicken!"

Smiling a little at her own insult, she pulled on the handle and entered a small brightly lit room with nothing more than a desk, a file cabinet, two chairs and some posters on the wall of accomplished skydivers. Dexter Morey was younger than Lydia had expected. Or so he looked. He wasn't much taller than her at five feet, six inches, and had the face of a twelve-year-old boy, but he had a smile that reached to the door. The tandem master got up from behind his desk and invited her all the way in with a hand gesture.

"Good morning!" He reached out and took her hand in a soft shake. His light grip didn't exactly give her confidence about "junior" taking her up in a plane, but lately she hadn't exactly been a pillar of strength.

"You're a bit early, but I can see you're anxious." He felt her hand was clammy. "It's normal to be uneasy your first time going up," he assured her. "We've had many people even throw up just before they got in the plane—not that that's what I'm recommending, but it's a little nerve-wracking jumping from twelve-thousand feet in the air."

"Not helping!" She shot him an irritated look.

"Sorry, I guess not but let me assure you, you are in good hands. And this will be an experience you will never forget."

Her lips tight, Lydia nodded her head in agreement as she followed him down a dark dingy corridor. A dusty chandelier hung above them, but with two of the four bulbs out, it didn't lend much light to brighten their walk. There were more posters on the walls in the corridor of happy people jumping out of planes with a tandem master attached to their backs. The anxiety rose in Lydia with each step. Her breathing was labored, and she could hear the crackles in her chest with each breath; it seemed as if they would never get to the door at the end.

Dexter was sole owner of this small, private operation. He had started it three years prior with the intention of bringing in big business from those who demanded a thrill before their expiration date. Businesses in other states had been doing very well with these thrill seekers, but there hadn't really been a place in Albany that offered skydiving. He thought he'd capitalize on the idea, but to his disappointment there really weren't too many people looking to jump out of planes in this area. Dexter was grateful for the business that came his way and tried to give each patron special attention and an experience they'd always remember. On the other side of the door was the hangar. A tall man in a green jumpsuit approached with a smile and handshake for Lydia.

"Hi there, I'm Sam. I'll be taking you up in this grand chariot today," he said, slapping the side of the plane. *A little over the top*, she thought, *but his greeting is genuine.*

"Nice to meet you," she said and just like that he walked toward the plane and climbed in.

Her chariot was a small plane that to Lydia looked like the model airplane her older brother, Philip, had put together when he was younger. *Philip,* she thought. *What will he think of my venture? What will any of them think!* Lydia had decided not to tell her parents, or anyone for that matter, that she was going skydiving. While Dexter explained how to put on the gear, as well as all the rules, regulations, and procedures, Lydia felt as though she were in a fog. She signed some forms relieving the company of liability should things not go as planned, nervously smiling as she sighed.

"The clips go on like this…" Dexter faded in and out.

Well here I am. I'm really doing it! she thought.

"You'll see the jump light turn green…" They go through a practice run and Dexter asked, "Ready?"

"About as ready as I'm ever gonna be!" she said, almost pushing herself forward with her words.

"Okay, let's go," Dexter said, clapping his hands together with enthusiasm.

Wearing her own green jumpsuit, which she was told was called a wing suit, she entered the plane with anticipation. They began to ascend, steadily rising to two thousand feet, then three thousand feet, ten thousand feet and finally twelve thousand feet. Lydia's breathing became rapid and shallow. The lump in her throat felt as though it would occlude her breathing at any moment. It was hard to hear in the plane as Dexter had told her it would be, so he gave her smiles and gestures. *He seems to be so nice,* she thought with a sigh. He opened the door, reached for her to connect their jumpers and just like that she pulled away and jumped. Dexter stood there staring, mouth open in disbelief.

"She jumped!" He gripped the opening of the plane on either side, looked down at her and again said, "She jumped!" and in that second, he jumped after her. *If I can pick up speed, I can make up that ten seconds I wasted. How stupid of me to wait. She jumped on purpose! Focus! Must reach her.* He drew his arms as close to his sides as possible and clasped his legs together. The ground was coming up fast, but he could see her coming up fast to him. Eight thousand feet, six thousand feet. *Not going fast enough,* he thought. *Must go faster! I'm not gonna make it!* He drew his limbs in closer and leaned his head down trying to will himself the speed he'd need with a little bit of experience thrown in. She came up a bit faster. Her arms were spread wide, brown strands of hair peeking from under her helmet were whipping all around. *Oh God, please let me get to her,* he pleaded. Approaching pull altitude quickly, he was running out of time. Twenty-five hundred feet above ground level. *I have to pull my chute,* he thought, struggling with the idea. *If I don't get to her, she dies. You're so close! You can do this!* he told himself, stretching out in a gesture grasping to reach her and pull her in, but she was at least five hundred feet from him. *I have to pull my chute.* He hesitated for a moment more. *Two thousand feet.*

Lydia's speed was at one hundred and fifteen miles per hour. Her fear had all but vanished as she flew… no, soared—through the sky like a bird. She felt a peace she didn't realize she would experience. She tried to smile, but the wind distorted her face to the point where she couldn't move her mouth voluntarily. *This is right. This was definitely the right decision,* she thought, trying to smile again in vain. *I'll never smile again.*

She continued to fall at an increasing speed and thought briefly about her failing health the last couple of months, her parents, her little brother, her longtime friend, Ash, and of course, poor Dexter and how sorry she was that she had to put him in this position. This was the clearest her head had felt in a while. *This was the way to go,* Lydia thought, that on her expiration day she would at least go out memorably. Dexter pulled the string on his chute and scrunched his face up in defeat and horror as Lydia rapidly pulled away from him and then hit the ground below.

- 20 -

FROM THE AIR, Exylon's insignia stood out on the helipad where the company's private helicopter sat dwarfed by Night Hawk, the government's own powerhouse chopper. Sleek and black with the Orbis logo on the side, these machines were known for their agility and firepower. Mike exited the building, fighting to keep the smile from his face. Don't walk too fast, he told himself, slowing his pace. He was wearing jeans and a short sleeve polo, fidgeting with the collar. He had to admit that he felt out of place in this attire—not prepared to make important decisions. He bit down on his lip—*just be cool, you're the man right now.* Approaching the helipad, he instinctively held the top of his head while the blades from the chopper blew his hair all around.

They must all be curiously watching through their windows by now. They'll see who this magnificent machine was sent for. Climbing the first step, he casually turned, smiled and waved to no one—the imaginary colleague who was seeing him off to his next important destination. Settling in, he was quick to suppress the giggle he had let out. For the remainder of his trip to Massachusetts, he beamed with pride. Mike enjoyed these rendezvous with John. There hadn't been many times in his life that he got to feel like the cool guy. He imagined that this would probably be one of the few chances he would ever get.

John's home in Boston would be, to most, considered a mini-mansion. He didn't really spend much time there, but his son stayed when visiting from Virginia occasionally. Paintings and sculptures were featured throughout the house, from what Mike thought looked like the nineteenth century. John was clearly an art lover. Mike was not, so he wasn't quite sure if the Da Vincis and Michelangelos were authentic, but he never really understood why that much mattered. To him, it all graced the walls and halls the same either way.

The largest room in the west wing was set up as a conference room otherwise known as the firebox room, as it carried the most fireboxes in the house—three. John had custom built a large round table that seated forty-eight members of Restituere. Representing the same circular interaction as the Orbis delegates shared at their conferences, he wanted each member to be able to look at the other and feel as though they all had a say, a chance to speak and be heard. He always said that he might organize and put together the meetings, but every member ran it.

The table was large enough to warrant each member wearing an earpiece, so they could communicate over such a large space and not have to yell or be asked to repeat themselves. As the group grew, John turned another room in his home into a conference hall that was set up more like a theater. Still, each member was equipped with an earpiece, but needed to stand when addressing the room. There's a large screen, podium and microphone placed on one end of the room facing all of the seats, so he could lead the meetings. There were just over a hundred members now. The conference room was large enough to fit just under a thousand people. John had ambitious expectations.

Mike was now standing in the firebox room, where they had had their first official Restituere meeting a year and a half ago. This was his favorite room. It was where he had discovered that he was part of something bigger than himself and that he wasn't alone in feeling the way he did. It was also where he met Mr. P for the first time. Well, heard him address the room via conference call. Mr. P was more of a private member. A very important and powerful private member. Mike had yet to meet him in person, and much to his disappointment, felt he never would. Mr. P met with John only, but to hear his voice and have him address the group was exhilarating.

Mike was proud to be part of an organization that had such an important role in forming a "better" world. He remembered the first meeting after being moved to the large hall.

~

It was six months after their inaugural meeting when John shared his epiphany on how to use the government-run expiration dates for their mission. Mr. P had instructed John to call a meeting of all the members who could make the trip on short notice, and to conference in the others, Mr. P included. John gave the floor to Mike to explain why expiration dates existed. He looked out on the faces of Restituere. Some from far away, some familiar—like Miguel and Derrick, pharmacists from the nutriment plant, and the only other two in the room who knew about the secret he was about to tell. He stuttered and paused a lot at first. He was sharing something that had been instilled in him to never reveal to anyone outside of the expiration date division of the Bureau. If someone was even thought to have disclosed this government secret, accidents would surround everyone involved—so he'd heard. But this was important. Vital to their future. It was a chance he was willing to take. He began with a global history and segued into the government's solution for population control. Not only were John and Mike the only government agents in Restituere, but they were in charge of a highly classified division of Population Control and Statistics—Expiration Dates. Essentially, he divulged the government's secret about their involvement with the expiration dates. There were a lot of gasps and chatter that went on for about five minutes. As instructed by John, Mike gave them the opportunity to absorb what was said before moving on to the reason they announced this classified information.

Mike then turned the floor over to John to share the idea about actually being able to realize what they were all there for.

He pointed out that, since expiration dates already existed, they could use this technology to their advantage, enabling their plan to make the world better by eliminating "undesirables."

He gave a glorious speech about how they had been fooled all these years, but that they could take advantage of Orbis's deception.

He cemented the brotherhood of Restituere and how, just as the government had established their classified secrets, so must Restituere. They would all be entrusted with the secrets of their brotherhood. Mike's pulse was racing—this was a new era for Restituere. They were about to embark on a new level of camaraderie—he'd never felt so alive!

"Just as the government has come up with a solution to our population problem, I think we can do one better." John addressed the wide-eyed crowd.

"We've talked about our planet dying at a rate that will not leave our children and children's children a viable place to grow and prosper." His voice rose, stoking the excitement.

"You know!" He pointed to a member in the third row. "George, we've discussed members of our society that have the minds to continue to conceive and produce technology that our world desperately needs. There will be no land, food, or future for them if the otheerrrs"—he dragged this word out, also dragging his hand across the room behind him, pointing at an invisible group of people which everyone seemed to be aware of—"are using all of the resources these great minds will need to create!"

He pointed again. This time at a tall, lanky member off to the left in the front row.

"Misha, your son just graduated summa cum laude! You expressed your concern that he had worked so hard to accomplish all that he had. And for what! What kind of a future does *he* have if resources are given to those who are not going to utilize them in a way that will be beneficial to all! Huh?!" There was a rustling in the room now. Shifting in seats. Some sitting on the edge, as if they wanted to jump up and sing "Hallelujah!"

He didn't let this momentum pass. He chose another in the group. "Lawrence Manning! Where are you, Larry?" he called and scanned the room. A dark-skinned man in his late forties stood up and lifted his hand.

"Right here," Larry called out.

"That's right Larry, stand right up there!" John brought his hand up as though he were magically lifting Larry himself. "You have great ideas on how to filter the filth and pollution from our air. Our very life-source!"

Larry nodded in agreement.

"How will that happen if you are halted by the very lack of oxygen you strive to save? You," he pointed at Larry, "are trying to do something great! You," he pointed again, "have a great mind that will bring good health and prosperity to all! And yet, there are those who are not contributing anything to our society, who will suck up every resource you need to thrive! It's not their fault! They're parasites and they don't even know it!"

The room was quietly still now, transfixed by the captivating man before them.

"The Transition Period!" Dramatically, he slowly paced the platform looking down at the floor and again up at the crowd, as if contemplating how to tell a big secret.

"You remember! The stories are all in our history books. The massive destruction from the war crippled everyday life, halting the ability to continue on as it had been. This era we call the Transition—when the planet went through its greatest change—from eradicating fatal diseases, growing advancements and technologies, to war and overpopulation, receding back to a primitive era. A *primitive* era! The destruction of electronics, communications, and medical advancements all brought life as it had been known to a standstill. It was as if the whole world went into their garages, attics, and warehouses, dusted off their old medical equipment, modes of communication, ancient computer technology, and continued to survive. Right! Globally, communication had to be rebuilt in order to maintain interaction." He punched his fist into the palm of his hand. "We're still here, folks! Still in this transitional phase where we are living as our primitive selves! We need advancements, not old technology! We need upgrades, not liabilities! We need a fresh start!"

He lowered his voice, looking around at everyone in the room. "What if, my friends, I told you, armed with the information you just learned from our brother Mike," he motioned towards him, "that there is a way we can all bring to fruition the ideas that we have only talked about—dreamed about! We have a vehicle to carry us to our destination!"

The members looked at each other with expressions of confusion. Some were still reeling over the admission that the government was behind the expiration dates.

Again, he gave them a minute to absorb all that had been said and then continued. "Without getting into the mechanics of the inner workings of the nanobytes, which are responsible for our expiration dates, I will give you a summation of what we have in mind."

He reiterated, "As you now know, expiration dates are programmed to cause us to… well, to expire at a particular time. What if we 'tweak' these dates to expedite the process already installed by our government? What if we programmed our own expedited short dates and distributed these 'special' nanobytes to a population of people who are a disease to our cause. They would be injected the same way they have been for more than a hundred years. We will be doing the work our government had begun, but better." He smiled and clapped his hands together. "Project Restore! Progress!"

He opened the floor to discussion. A member from New York City touched a button on her headset and now the entire room could hear her speak.

"Gentleman, we have something that I don't think we can even wrap our heads around. Clearly this 'miracle' of science exists, but we're now talking about our moral obligation to the people!"

Ebu Neigusse from Ethiopia spoke up. "We have an obligation to protect our people, even if it means from themselves!"

Arlo Fernandez, who had traveled from a small region in Cuba, shook his head with his hand behind his neck, still stunned from the announcement about the government controlling expiration dates. He stood. "This is so surreal. How can man change God's plan?! This has been going on for over a hundred years!" Looking up and around, realizing the vast range of religious, moral, and ethical beliefs in the room, he continued, "We all have our own beliefs about how and why we exist, and I'm sure none of them include man's 'divine' power to change humankind!"

Francisco Sosa fumbled with his headset and spoke so loudly into his microphone that the crowd pulled their headsets slightly away from their ears. "I will do anything to stop the murder and corruption that has been going on for centuries! The starvation and illness! We silently pray, and when a solution presents itself, we question it! Well, I will not question it! I will be a part of the solution!"

A voice overhead descended in an echo as if it were the voice of God. Mr. P began, "In my belief, my God allows man to grow and make his own choices, his own mistakes. We are what we are today because man developed penicillin to cure illness. Planes to fly across the world and share cultures. Machines to help us do our jobs faster, better, more efficiently. Who are we to say that we are not meant to prevent war, pain and suffering by creating a means to potentially stop it all?! I mean, isn't that why we are all here? In this room today! To find a solution to the depletion of resources, starvation, to help our fellow man thrive? To find a way to peace?" he emphasized. "Well, here it is my friends! The answer!"

This was followed by a roar of excitement.

~

Mike was startled out of his recollections when John entered the room and greeted him.

"Mike, you arrived quickly." He shook his hand and motioned for him to have a seat at the forty-eight-person round table. It seemed like such an unnecessary place to meet, but Mike felt comfortable in this room, in spite of its size.

"You can thank the Night Hawk for that," he said, relishing his ride. "I don't think they follow the speed limit."

John chuckled. "I imagine they don't at that."

"Thank you for meeting with me on such short notice. You know I hate those over the phone conversations; so impersonal. Anyway, can I get you a water, coffee… ?"

"No, I'm good, thanks," Mike declined.

"Well, then let's get right down to it, shall we. I don't think there's much we can do about the mass deaths at this point. I have assured the president that this was an isolated incident."

Mike gave a nod.

"Do I need to remind you, Mike, how important our work is here? We can't afford any screw-ups. This is bigger than us. We are advocating for the future of our people. If we don't come though, all will be lost to a dying planet, understand?"

"I understand."

"We should just continue on as planned and make sure nothing like this happens again. Here are the addresses that we need to be looking at."

Mike took the plain white envelope John had extended to him.

"How's your project coming along—Claude's been continuing your work, right?" John asked.

"Yes," he said, shifting his eyes downward. "He and one of our newer scientists, Ashlei Quinn, who has been assisting him."

John put his hand on Mike's shoulder and looked him in the eye. "Look, I know that your research is important to you. I promise, when all of this has been set in place and we're well on our way to accomplishing our goal, you will be able to return to it. Hell," he said, opening his arms wide, "we may not even need you to go through all that trouble when all is said and done! You may as well set your sights on some grander ideas, my friend, than that childhood goal."

This was supposed to make Mike feel better, but VM9 was more than just a childhood dream or an ongoing experiment. It might not even be the most significant thing he had accomplished in his lifetime, but to him, it was a promise to his mother and to himself that he could do this—he could make a difference. He loved the work he did. He was a scientist after all.

-21-

AFTER WORKING WITH CLAUDE over the past several weeks, Ashlei had gotten used to his contradictory way of working diligently, yet in the same moment saying or doing something absurdly entertaining. He had a very dry sense of humor, but she did not reciprocate his humor for fear of him questioning her commitment or her professionalism—she was all business when she was in the lab. Yet, noting that *he* wasn't exactly the epitome of professionalism, she admired his devotion to his research and work. So, she wasn't exactly sure how he'd take the interruption when her phone started vibrating in her bag from across the room at her desk. She continued working; she never kept her band on at work, she didn't like the interruptions. It vibrated again. Again, she ignored it. Lifting her head slightly to look at Claude to see if he'd noticed too. The third time it vibrated, Claude said, "Were you waiting for me to answer that? Because, I will. Sure you trust how that phone call will go?"

"Sorry," she said, jumping up from her station and rustling through her bag just as it began to ring again.

Ashlei swiped the band, it wrapped around her hand, illuminated, showing the name "Madre" with her favorite photo of her mom water skiing, hand thrown in the air; not the typical "book club" outing she was accustomed to her mother going on.

She swiped again, her mother hovered just above the band. "Madre, I'm at work," she answered and whispered, "I'll call you back later."

"Take a break, honey, and find a place you can talk," she said somberly.

Ashlei's heart began to beat fast. She pulled her glasses off and put them on the desk. "Madre, what's wrong?"

"Honey, I'm sorry, I don't want to tell you this on the phone, but I didn't know when I'd be able to see you with you working so much and I didn't want you to hear this from anyone else."

Ashlei gripped the band and her eyes began to swell with tears. "Tell me what, what happened?"

"Ash, Lydia died today. I'm so sorry, honey."

Ashlei fell down into the chair her bag had been on. Unable to get a sound out, she began to sob, suddenly recalling the date.

"Today was her day. Her expiration day. We always planned we'd handle it together. How could I forg…" she whispered and sobbed.

Claude kept his head down, trying to remain quiet and give her privacy.

"Do you want me to come get you, Ash? First Shauna's baby and now Lydia. I'm sure your boss will understand if you leave early."

"No, I'll take some time," she whimpered, wiping her tears with her sleeve.

"She went skydiving—she didn't wear a chute," her mom reported sadly.

"What?" She sobbed again.

"I have to go, Madre."

"Call me later, Ash, if you're up for it. Love you."

"Love you too."

Ashlei sat for a bit, trying to come to terms with the fact that she had just lost her friend. *I'd been so caught up with school and now work… we drifted apart over the last couple of years. I'm so sorry, Lydia.*

She was startled by the voice from across the room, forgetting where she was for a moment.

"You okay?"

"Not really," she replied, fruitlessly wiping her falling tears.

"Go ahead and go, come back when you're ready."
"Thanks." She grabbed her bag and left.

- 22 -

AT HOME, SLOUCHED ON THE SOFA, Jack mindlessly scanned the holo-vision channels, holograms flashing before him so quickly they looked like colored blurs of light racing across his front room. Sighing heavily, he grimaced at the soggy sandwich sitting next to him on the love seat, left over from the night before—and decided that he wasn't that hungry. Yet, he couldn't help but lift the bread, scowling at the now wilted lettuce and dried up cheese before pushing the plate further away.

It had been several weeks and the mass short expiration dates were all everyone was talking about. Jack had kept himself busy and hadn't had time to think about it himself—or, the stir hit a little too close to home and he'd intentionally avoided the conversations.

He scanned the living room looking for something—meaning? He was surrounded by a matching recliner to the loveseat, a coffee table and a floor lamp. The sparse pictures displayed on the wall depicted his few loves—holding a large rainbow trout he'd caught in Alaska, reaching the top of one of the high peaks in the Adirondacks, and one of him scoring the winning goal for his lacrosse team during his college days. On a side table next to the couch stood an antique wooden frame, with a photo in it of an attractive woman with brown hair that curled loosely around her neck. She was holding a baby that was six months of age. He sighed again.

Jack had grown up in Rockland County, in downstate New York. He attended Tufts Medical Center in Boston for his Interventional Cardiology fellowship following his Cardiology fellowship at Hellman Medical Center. As an avid hiker, he was drawn to the mountains of the Adirondacks further north and, falling in love with the area, he had decided to return to Albany to practice medicine.

He brought his attention back to the holo-vision when his favorite commercial came on. Anticipating the absurdity, he chuckled.

The man hovering in his living room began his spiel in front of a beautiful resort with palm trees swaying in the breeze.

"Hey, for you lovers out there, how would you like a two-night stay at a luxury hotel for two, all you can eat! Why not go out in style?"

The scene changed to a free-falling couple holding hands. "Choose what's right for you! Maybe it's skydiving to your death, chute not included, of course. For those of who enjoy the Old West, picture this scene," he said, spreading his fingers while throwing his hands out in front of him ready to wow his audience. "Husband and wife back to back. Ten paces, turn and shoot. How's that for—"

"Tacky?!" Jack inserted.

"Or maybe you'd like a nice double execution! Say to your honey, 'You're electrifying,'" he said, like a bad saying on a Valentine candy heart. "And for those who have the sea at heart, why not go down to the depths and enjoy the coral. Costs of retrieving your bodies are extra!"

Shaking his head, Jack muttered, "So ridiculous."

He'd read a pretty harsh article about the announcer in this commercial.

"Big Bob," the previous owner of "Die Happy Auto" has hung up his used car sales pitch and begun a new venture. Since bikes, trains, and buses were the more popular modes of transportation (or maybe it's because his cars were less than efficient), Big Bob has jumped on the bandwagon of some of the other successful companies capitalizing on human suffering and earning success with it.

Jack thought, *People must prefer that slimy pitch he spews in relation to their last hours rather than getting a crappy car.*

The article continued to talk about the beginning of expiration dates, how they changed the culture and way of thinking. Some people started fan clubs such as, "It's My Time Too," set up for a group of people with similar expiration dates who could chat about their "solidarity." Sectioned out into these categories, they shared what they'd done with their lives, what they wanted to do, what that date meant to them, and what they wanted to be doing on that day. Many people had made love connections through these type of organizations—one less loved one they'd leave behind. There had been jump-off sites pertaining to this that allowed couples with the same dates to choose the way they wanted to die together—like a vacation package.

The next commercial to air showed a middle-aged, balding man wearing a brightly-colored jacket, yelling at the camera in front of him.

"What are you going to do with the time you have left?!" He was pointing at Jack and the many consumers lured into watching his sales pitch. "Come on down to the Living Will Resort. Let us pamper you and give you the attention you deserve. Time is short! For some of us anyway." It ends with a close up of him winking.

This was followed by another commercial promoting expiration insurance.

He continued to stay tuned in as the EPAN news returned. "And we're back. Hi, I'm Ted Bertrum."

"And I'm Julie Schiffer," his co-host added, flipping her flaming red locks behind her shoulder, "and we're reporting the growing concern over the number of expiration dates in newborns all over the globe."

"Yes, Julie, we initially reported a week ago that these quick deaths were happening in our region and were spread all over America, but we have since learned that this devastating turn of events is actually happening all over the world!" he said, shaking his head. "Not only has there been an increase in these deaths, but they're being reported in Alaska, Maine, Los Angeles, London, Yemen, North Korea, even Moldova! The list goes on. There's lots of speculation as to why and how these occurrences are happening."

Julie chimed in, "So, these expiration dates are all short-term. Within seven days! And they are affecting so many!" She turned back to Ted. "Do we even have a count?"

"Not really, the numbers are still coming in daily, but it is said that as of right now, the deaths are an increase of about fifty percent compared to a month ago."

"Right now, we have Mark Goodman, reporting from London to get reactions from people in other regions.

"Hi, Mark. Are you there?" Julie asked rhetorically into her headset.

"Hi, Julie. Yeah, so here in London I've been chatting with some of the locals, and tensions are high," Mark stated, looking around and then back at the camera. "Most of the locals here have had the same concerns as we do in America and everywhere else, quite frankly. The fear of the unknown. Where is this coming from and will it end?"

She leaned in closer to the camera. "Yeah, everyone here is pretty scared."

Mark added, "I would imagine the questions being asked are pretty similar to the same questions that were asked a hundred years ago when expiration dates first began." Julie nodded in agreement as Mark continued.

"There was talk of conspiracy theories, genetic mutations, aliens, religious groups with their theories."

Julie chimed in, "Yes, we're starting to see the 'end of dayers' with their signs, 'Repent now, save your soul.'"

"Well, thanks Mark, we'll of course be continuing to search for answers here in the states," Ted said.

Mark signed off with a nod and, "Thanks."

"These questions still arise over the years because scientists, philosophers, physicians, *psychics*," he emphasized and grinned, "were never able to find an answer."

"Well, we'll be talking about this more and keeping you updated," Julie promised, looking into the camera. "For now, I'm Julie Schiffer." She turned to Ted.

"And I'm Ted Bertrum."

Julie continued, "We'll see you next time on EPAN, news channel seven." Simultaneously smiling they signed off, "Goodnight."

Jack turned off the holo-vision and pulled the silver VCC disk out of a drawer from the stand next to him to do his own investigating. Face-to-face with the photo in front of him, he picked it up, flipped it over and stared at the date written on the back. Recognizing the anniversary approaching, he slumped back into the couch. He turned it back over, gazed at the woman and child for a moment and replaced it on the stand.

"Beep, beep, beep, beep, beep…"

He grabbed his pager and headed out the door to the hospital.

- 23 -

The Medical Center had an unsettling silence after normal working hours, Elisa always thought. Whatever "normal working hours" were in a hospital. That said, she almost preferred to be here when everyone was gone, imagining the walls wanting to speak, if only they had a voice. Yearning to tell their story, a history of events that needed to be retold, the life that existed here at one point. The call tonight was a thirty-eight-year-old man with a strong family history of coronary artery disease. He was alarmed to discover that he had had a heart attack when, according to him, he took such good care of himself. She recalled his surprise.

"But I eat healthy, I exercise and practice keeping stress to a minimum. I don't understand!" he pleaded as if Jack could change the situation.

"Sorry, Lloyd, your life monitor doesn't lie. And it was right on time with this one. Sometimes, it's just all about the genes we carry. If you hadn't taken such good care of yourself, we might have seen you sooner."

"Uggh, wait!" Elisa yelped. Paul quickly stopped the elevator doors from shutting, just as they began to close. She hopped out. "I left my bag in the lab!"

Paul called after her, releasing the doors, "See you tomorrow."

"Gee, thanks for waiting," she mumbled.

Seeing Jack heading into his office, she stopped, holding the door open while he got his keys off his desk. "I thought you left long ago."

"Had to go up to see another potential patient for a cardiac cath, but she no longer has pain and doesn't meet criteria."

"Walk with me, I need to grab my bag."

It'd been over a month since the death of Jessica.

Jack took the opportunity to ask her how her cousin was doing and in turn, her.

Her tone softened. "She's getting through her days, but that's about it. I barely recognize her. I wish there was something I could do to ease her pain," she said sadly.

The light sensor in the lab came on when they entered. Jack looked empathetically at Elisa and revealed, "I lost a child."

Elisa fell still, not sure she'd heard him correctly. "What?"

"I was married about ten years ago. We were young and in love, of course. We wanted to get married right away to get our lives started and to spend as much time together as we could. She got pregnant immediately and nine months later, Peter was born." He beamed. "He was this amazing little thing." He brought his palms together as if holding him in his hands. "But," he took a deep breath in, "our joy was short lived, because his expiration date was one year to the day almost from his birth. I couldn't function normally for a while. Getting up every day was a struggle, but I learned to accept his fate as time went on. Miranda, my wife, was okay for the first six months. Well, as okay as someone can be expecting to lose a child. But then she began to act irrationally. Planning for his future. Looking at schools in the area, planning his birthday. She became despondent, just as your cousin has," he pointed out. "Not long after his death I came home one day to find her gone. She left. She just left."

Elisa felt a sting in her eyes as she sensed his pain.

"Wrote me a note explaining that she couldn't handle it all, couldn't go through it again. I was on track to becoming a pediatrician at that time. I knew after that experience, though, that I couldn't watch other parents go through what I had gone through, and so I switched my fellowship to cardiology. During that time, I'd seen parents go both ways. Some showered their children with love every moment of every day and some detached themselves in preparation for that devastating moment when they had to let go." Jack felt the heavy burden in his chest. "It changes you—changes everything, when you experience a loss firsthand." His voice cracked. Leaning in the doorway to the lab, he pushed his shoulder off to stand up straight. "Actually, Reed and I had done most of our pediatric rotations together." He sniffled. "It was probably a good thing I took another route, we were trouble together." He gave a short chuckle.

Elisa wondered if what was going on with the short expiration dates had fired up painful feelings Jack clearly had worked on concealing.

"I'm sorry to hear that, Jack; I didn't know."

"Yeah well, you wouldn't. That was a different life, I don't talk about it," he said. "I do, however, think of them every day."

Leaning against the lab table, Elisa crossed her arms, trying to stay warm in the cold air piping out of the vents.

"Jessica may not have been mine, but I'd been there for their journey from the beginning," she said, speaking of Shauna and David. "The excitement of the prospect of becoming parents and then going through all the miscarriages… I was so hopeful for them, ya know. And when Shauna was at the happiest I'd ever seen her, and they thought they were finally done with their struggles—Jessica's expiration date. I wasn't just an observer looking in from the outside. I wanted so much for them to have that baby, I almost feel like Jessica was a part of me too. David traveled for work, so I'd go to Shauna's appointments with her, for vaccinations, nutriment injection, even her birthing classes. Actually, I had fun in that class; interesting people!"

"However, I didn't enjoy the nutriment injection appointment. Believe it or not, needles freak me out. Outside of work, I avoid them like the plague!"

She stood up straight. "The plague! What about a virus? Could that be it? Vaccinations are susceptible to becoming contaminated with viruses."

Jack raised an eyebrow.

"Well, do you think that maybe there could be a problem with the vaccinations or nutriment injections? Some kind of micro-organism infiltration at a production level? It would make sense, right? Shauna received both injections. *Every* pregnant woman receives both of these injections. There's certainly a possibility that they could have been contaminated and bad batches went out!"

"I don't know, I'm not really familiar with them," Jack said. "My rotation in pediatrics was so long ago. I guess that's information I could get from Reed."

"Okay, do that. I'll do some of my own research and touch base with you tomorrow."

He yawned. "Go home and get some sleep, it's too late to think about this right now," he said, realizing it was one a.m.

-24-

ELISA HAD NO INTENTION OF sleeping when she got home. The apartment was almost completely dark aside from the night lights she kept on in the kitchen, bathroom, and hallway. She fired up the virtual computer and prompted her voice-activated search engine, Infinity.

"I should probably do a little background history first," she said to herself.

With a freshly brewed cup of coffee in hand, she stretched out on the sofa with her head resting back and feet on the coffee table.

"Infinity, find nutriment injections!" she called out.

Infinity's friendly female voice responded, "Found, 1,256 searches using the name 'nutriment injection.' Would you like me to read the selection from the beginning?"

Elisa quickly sat up, nearly spilling her coffee. "No Infinity, I will take a look." She touched the button in front of her and scanned the blue neon selections presented to her that were hovering above the monitor.

"Infinity, can we narrow the search to, 'What is the nutriment injection?'"

Infinity responded, "Found, 102 searches using the name 'What is the nutriment injection.'"

"Okay, much better." A tired Elisa exhaled. She scrolled through the selection, swiping away information she didn't need, until she found something that caught her eye. Pinching her fingers together she pulled forward and expanded the article. It read:

Nutriment Injections are defined as a supplement containing a variety of essential vitamins, minerals, and nutrients delivered to a fetus in order to guarantee proper absorption.

The nutriment injection is a minimally invasive procedure that delivers a nano-byte infused nutrient-based formula to the gestating fetus via a needle dispersing directly into the bloodstream, usually in the fourth or fifth month of pregnancy. This is followed by an ultrasound catheter verifying that the injection has infused properly.

This procedure is done in a specialist's office run by the government to ensure the injection is given and documented properly.

This much Elisa already knew. Every high school student was required to learn this in basic well-being class.

"Infinity, pull up, 'history of nutriment injections.'"

Infinity responded, "Found 136 searches using the name, 'history of nutriment injections.'"

Elisa scrolled down to the fifteenth option. "'Bring the past to light,' population well-being and women's continued responsibility to keep their offspring healthy for the future of mankind," she mumbled.

The blue lights of the VCC were taking their toll on her heavy eyes. She scrolled down to the twenty-first article, 'Reviewing the history of the nutriment injection' and opened it.

The first few paragraphs talked about the planet being saturated with people and lack of resources, then moved on to talk about why nutriment injections were important.

Babies being were born prematurely, deformed and sickly because mothers were malnourished and not able to provide adequate nourishment for themselves and their infants. Many care centers were put in place to help these mothers stay strong and healthy during pregnancy, but there was inconsistency and noncompliance among many. One of the first orders of business of the newly formed Orbis was to make sure that our planet would thrive under their order.

The nutriment injection was first created to supply infants in the womb the opportunity to grow strong and healthy. This was made mandatory to ensure that each mother would get the injection and create strong, healthy babies to be our future leaders. The first injections were given in 2067.

"Infinity, pull up, 'nutriment injection contamination.'"

Infinity replied, "Found, 31 searches using the name 'nutriment injection contamination.'"

She huffed, disappointed. They all described possible contamination having more to do with whether they were placed in cool, dry areas.

Elisa used her fingers to pull up a side article that piqued her interest. "Expiration date, begin."

Her sight began to blur, but she attempted to fight through it.

The article displayed a list of names and regions, starting with Owen in 2068.

"Hmm…" she slurred just before dozing off.

~

Elisa stirred when early morning rays of sun splashed her eyes. A little disoriented, with the VCC still illuminated from just five hours prior, she reached to swipe the disk, turning it off. She mentally replayed the dream of baby Jessica as a toddler running through a grassy field and felt a pang of pain. Rubbing her eyes and slowly becoming more lucid, *I made notes on Shauna's injection day!* she recalled. She often took notes about the people, places, and situations she encountered to put away to write about later. From the desk in her bedroom she pulled out notebook after notebook searching for the one she made notes in that day. "Napkin, random scrap pieces of paper, what is this…" She twisted her face and lifted a piece of material that was jammed in a notebook. "A green dried up leaf ?… Ah, notes from my hike in the park!" She shoved it back in the same notebook, causing it to crumble into pieces.

"Here we go." She pulled out the EKG strip she had made her notes on that day—all in broken language since she was usually writing quickly and on limited space so as not to lose her muse.

"Hmm," she said, turning it side to side. "'20cc syringe big needle/ interesting color—yellow tint/through IV, laparoscopic probe, verify baby position, probe/injection packaged together. Packaging—Exylon/Reed is looking good today/a little treat for me to gaze at.'

"Ha! Forgot about that little piece of information!" she giggled.

Glancing at the clock on the wall, she jumped up, "Crap, I'm late for work!" and dashed to get ready.

- 25 -

THOUGH IT HAD ONLY BEEN A DAY, Exylon was distant from Ashlei's mind—yet she couldn't just sit in the house, staring at the walls while her thoughts rehashed childhood promises made to her friend. The image of Lydia jumping to her death plagued her thoughts, denying her an escape from the guilt of allowing her friend to face her expiration date alone. Looking to the ceiling to catch the tears that had swelled in her eyes, Ashlei took a deep breath in and entered the lab. Claude swiveled around on his chair and she raised an eyebrow at his puzzled look.

"What are you doing here?" he asked.

"I work here," she responded.

"Yeah, I got that. I told you to take some time, to do what I assume was grieve."

"I'll grieve on my own time, thanks."

"Wow, that's hardcore, I don't think even I'm that tough." He waited for a response, but got no reply. "Well, if you need more time, take it, okay?"

"Yup, thanks," she said and situated herself on the academic side of the lab, in the corner she had personalized with photos of friends and family. She swiped yesterday's date to today from her inspirational calendar on the wall, revealing today's quote: "Accept what is, let go of what was, and have faith in what will be."

Claude glanced over at her, not sure if he should question her about the phone call yesterday.

"Ya know, if you wanted to throw a specimen at my head or something, today would be the day you'd get away with it."

Her furrowed brow required him to elaborate.

"I mean, you being upset and all, how could I get mad at you for throwing something at me—I'm pretty sure you have thought about it quite often."

Ashlei giggled, shifting her eyes to the side. "Yeah, there were a few times I wanted to trip you, anyway."

"I know, I have that effect on people." He smirked.

Ashlei slid her hands in her pockets and switched the subject to work.

"So, how long have you been involved in VM9, anyway? I mean," she clarified, "when did you take over for Mike? It seems as though you've already put a lot of your own work into it."

"Just a couple of months. I'm a workaholic, if you hadn't noticed." He smiled. "I can cover a lot of ground in a short period of time."

She nodded. "I am grateful for the opportunity you've given me. I understand this is a big deal," she said sincerely, tapping the files in front of her. "This is exactly where I was hoping to be when I graduated. What we're doing now—making a difference. Not everyone has the chance to do that. What they want, that is."

"I don't think you give yourself enough credit, Ash." She smiled at this, only her family and close friends called her Ash. "You are very bright and a hard worker. I've read some of your papers and your dissertation on this stuff. You have some great ideas! Stop chopping yourself off at the knees and own it. You deserve to be here."

"You read my papers?"

"Well, yeah. This is too important to me to leave to one of those pretentious jerks." He raised his hand, pointing to the door.

He spun the chair back to his lab station, flicked his military tag that hung off a knob a couple times, and then spun back again full circle to Ashlei.

"Is this your plan, or do you expect to do more?" Claude asked.

"Um, well, I was planning on getting a little work done and then maybe having lunch, but…"

"Ha-ha. I should have been clear. Do you want to work in a lab forever or do you aspire to other things?"

"Oh," she said, a little embarrassed. "No, I couldn't do this forever. Just this, that is. I really enjoy my time in the lab, but I want to get out into the field and actually get hands on putting my theories into play, and seeing real time results with real people. I understand some results will take years obviously, but lab rats and petri dishes can only motivate for so long."

"Don't underestimate those rats, they get to be your friends after a while."

She giggled. "I get that I need to pay my dues; you will find that I am the most patient, impatient person you may encounter."

Claude listened intently as she continued, "I'm actually all over the place. You read my dissertation on expiration dates?"

Claude nodded.

"I would like to submerge myself into researching why we evolved in that direction. I want to have my hands in so many other areas of the sciences, there's so much to explore and create, so much good that can be done. We haven't scratched the surface on all we can do, ya know."

She straightened up and shifted to the edge of her chair. "Like, are you aware that we are not tapping into all our potential as a species? Such as the ability to take our senses to an untapped level! The way our minds can adapt at will and be manipulated into exposing a deeper—" she paused, searching, "or heightened power, if you will." She noticed Claude was focused in on her, causing her to blush, and she flattened her tone.

"What I would really like to do, eventually, in the midst of all of this, is also be among people. Not doing my research studies behind closed doors in a lab. I like sunshine and air too."

"Getting out there is not out of the question. Your ideas, believe it or not, line up with a lot of mine. Maybe we can work on something together."

"Sounds great!" she said, realizing she had never really smiled around Claude too much, and now her cheeks hurt.

"By the way," he added, "in lieu of the fact that you may have actually taken me up on it, I switched the contents of that specimen container to just water."

Ashlei grinned. Moving over to her work station, she threw on her lab coat that hung on the hook and resumed her work from the previous day.

- 26 -

After working on VM9 into the evening, Ashlei's stomach was growling so loud that Claude took notice.

"I'm hungry too," he said. "Want to grab a bite to eat? There's a place not too far away that serves great food."

She grimaced at her body's betrayal. "Sure, I guess I didn't realize I hadn't eaten since yesterday morning."

She followed him away from Exylon, just over the bridge into the hub of Albany, driving past a cluster of dilapidated buildings—remnants of an old city. Ashlei passed by this way mindlessly almost every day. The abandoned province sat as a reminder of the darker days, when communities were crammed into what space there was to live. Each time she drove by, she felt a bit sad. *Do you continue to leave it as a reminder of a devastating era, or rebuild as a hope of a better future?*

The Domino Effect. She chuckled aloud. She always thought the play on words was a little juvenile for the government.

The Domino EFFECT was a program that was put together for just that reason—bringing attention to the path humankind had taken and the effects of that course, beginning with the eradication of diseases. This was followed by war, which ended with large regions becoming uninhabitable around the world. Then with an explosion of births and unequal number of deaths, came overcrowding and the depletion of resources, including the lack of grazable land for animals. Eventually this caused mass extinction for some species, which threw ecosystems into a spiraling anarchy with the food chain disrupted.

The focus of the group was to bring attention to the problem and begin to find ways to reverse the damage. It took several decades to see any changes, but once the changes began, they took off.

As things began to improve, land was made available and people were able to spread out. These tenement housing areas were filtered out until eventually they had been completely deserted, with the exception of small groups of vagrants. However, there were still similar pockets of rubble in almost every region.

Driving into the city at sunset, a wisp of breath escaped Ashlei's lips. The entire downtown area with its oddly shaped buildings lit up from the ground to display the breathtaking, artful architecture, was carefully showcased for just this moment, she felt. The Egg, which Ashlei thought was shaped more like a cereal bowl, was at the forefront of all the buildings. Housed in this building were many state offices, shops, and entertainment venues. She reminisced about the many plays and shows seen with her friends and family here over the years.

Claude led her to the Vintage House, a huge warehouse turned restaurant/bar, with quaint tables throughout the front. Ashlei hadn't gotten out much since she'd been home from school. This was one of the newer hot spots in the area. As they walked in, there was a calming waterfall simulation moving down the wall to the right. The building actually stretched back pretty far with a horseshoe bar in the center, high tables in the back and a stage to the left. The bartender smiled and waved in their direction and Ashlei realized that he was waving to Claude.

Busy for a workday, she thought. It was full of students and workers who had shed their responsibilities for the day, but most of the crowd was around her age and her generation didn't really care what day it was when going to hang out.

There was a steady buzz of conversations and laughter going on throughout the place, competing with the music piped through the speakers, which was just about conversation level.

"This okay for you?" Claude asked, choosing a high-top table in the back.

"Yeah, that's fine." She hoisted herself up in a chair. At five-foot-four, not all things were conducive to shorter women.

The bartender approached them and shook Claude's hand.

"Dude, haven't seen you in a while. What's goin' on?"

"Working man," he responded. "Dale, this is Ashlei… Ashlei, Dale."

"Hi, Ashlei." He shook her hand. "I can see why you haven't been around."

"Nice to meet you."

"What can I start you with?" he asked, looking at Ashlei.

"Umm, margarita on the rocks, no salt please."

Choosing the appropriate drink from a list that beamed up in front of him from his hand-held device, his eyes shifted to Claude.

"Lager, thanks."

"No prob." He pulled "lager" from the list and the beam was drawn back down into the device. "On the house!" He winked and walked off.

The illuminated menus, built into the table, were staring up at them, so Ashlei started swiping through the selections. Without looking up she said, "I guess you've been here before."

"Yeah, I probably stop in a few times a week to grab a quick bite. I'm not the best cook and the food's good."

"But not lately?" she asked.

"Working more lately," he said.

While picking at the edge of a napkin she resumed absently looking at the menu. Noting a silence, she looked up and saw him staring at her. "What?"

"Why do you always wear your hair up like that?"

She drew her head back, taken aback by his forward question. "Because I'm working and don't want to deal with it in my face."

"Gotcha," he accepted. She returned to the menu.

"You're not working now, let's see what you look like with it down."

She curled her lip. "I'd need to fix it, comb it out. I can't just let it down!"

"I didn't figure you for a girl who cared what people think," he said, looking around.

"I'm not, but one has to have some standards," she replied.

He stood up, walked around behind her and smoothly pulled the tie from her hair.

"What are you doing?" She started to raise her hands to her head and he gently pushed them back down.

"I got this." And he slowly ran his hands through her wavy brown hair from the roots to the ends, pulling it out of its previous state. She leaned in toward him slightly, taking in the musky scent of his sweat, fighting her body from going limp. *Damn those pheromones!*

After running his fingers through her hair several times, lulling her into a hypnotized tranquility, he abruptly stopped, letting her hair drop to just below her narrow shoulders, and sat back down across from her.

"There. Lovely."

In the background, the moving waterfall mural was replaced by a flash of light, followed by the Orbis symbol rotating around in a circular motion announcing a message from the President—they didn't notice.

- 27 -

Orbis's global spinning earth insignia flashed on billboards and halo-visions across America broadcasting that there would be a presidential announcement.

EPAN news channel's Julie Schiffer and Ted Bertrum announced that America's President would address the people in a brief news update regarding the mass short expiration dates. They reviewed, for those "living under a rock," what had been happening with the recent surge. As the President approached the podium, they cut it short.

"Okay, here we see President West is approaching the platform, we're going to go live in Washington to hear the announcement," Julie stated.

President West waited for the word to go on cue. Presiding at the podium, he leaned in, looked directly into the camera, and began to speak, his deep authoritative tone reaching through the crowd of reporters and halo-vised audience.

"Every country and region is addressing their people, simultaneously with what we have concluded after careful, extensive research."

He looked down to the group of reporters, gazes fixated on him.

"I ask the media to please hold all your questions until we are through here." He folded his hands and continued to look into the camera with sincerity.

"There's been a growing concern about what appears to be an epidemic in the recent months of an increase in infant death rate, due to expiration dates which are as short as three to seven days.

"Firstly, I want to say that we, Orbis, I, and everyone who have been involved in trying to find answers, hear you and are every bit as concerned about the well-being of our children, and in fact our future, as you are. Let me assure each and every one of you that we have enlisted the most prominent scientists, biologists, doctors, and theologists to investigate the troubling and unexpected devastation that has taken place here."

Following John's advice, he cited almost verbatim John's own convincing speech with him in their meeting at the White House.

"Our specialists have done blood tests on mothers, fathers, and babies. They've tested the soil, water, vegetation, and animals, while researching many other avenues, and what they've concluded in all of their thorough research is simply that this is an anomaly. A hiccup in our genetic material. There have been many examples throughout history where we as humans have *mutated,* if you will, in ways that could not be explained. Such as conjoined twins, pituitary hyperplasia, being born with additional limbs, the list goes on.

"There are many conditions and situations throughout history that we really don't have one definitive answer for in which we, as humans, have genetically gone off-course and done our own thing. As expiration dates did more than a hundred years ago. I'm afraid that this is one of them."

His hands had now moved to the sides of the podium and he continued to stand with confidence. "We have faced many adversities in our history, and yes, this will set us adrift for a bit, but we will continue to thrive as a world nation, as our ancestors before us have. Thank you."

A flurry of hands went up, each one wanting to ask the first question. Reporters chattered among themselves and into their own news cameras. The president stared out at the faces that carry a voice of the people and to the people. *Tell them what they need to hear and maintain the peace. I hope you're right, John.*

- 28 -

Ashlei, almost drooling, picked up her napkin and tried to wave it inconspicuously, attempting to cool herself down after having her head massaged by Claude.

Get a grip, he was just helping you relax! she told herself. Dale was just placing their drinks down on cocktail napkins. *Perfect.* She grabbed her glass and took a gulp.

"Have you decided what you'd like?" he asked.

Ashlei had decided at that moment what she'd like, her head still tingling, but she was sure he was asking about their food orders since they hadn't entered them in yet.

"Yes, umm," she stammered, "I'm going to choose the chicken quesadilla with guacamole and sour cream," she said, selecting her options on the table menu which were sent directly to the kitchen.

"And are there any special considerations with your order?"

"No, thank you."

"Claude, the norm?"

"No, think I'm ordering the French onion soup, steak tips, steak fries, mild wings and… mac and cheese." He pushed each option as he called it out. "Thanks."

Ashlei jerked her head back while Claude rattled off his order.

"Great, I'll be back with that order when it's done."

"Wow, you can really pack it away," she said when Dale walked away.

"Probably not." He chuckled. "I think my eyes are bigger than my stomach right now. I'm just hungry."

Claude cleared his throat and looked up at her.

"You really should wear your hair down more often, you seem more relaxed. That little stress line that's between your eyes is already gone."

She blushed and swiped her hair behind her ear. "That's great. I didn't realize you noticed the age lines in my face."

"I'm very observant. I noticed that you don't wear makeup, that I've ever seen. Not that you need it, you have a natural beauty that shouldn't be covered up. You carry yourself in a way that appears you're not confident enough in your talents to raise your head a little higher. You begin to sip your coffee when it's fresh, but by the second hour you're gulping it." He chuckled.

"I see," she said pursing her lips, realizing that he'd checked out every detail about her.

She took her glasses off and set them on the table. "Did you notice that these weren't really prescription?"

Taken aback he said, "No. Wow, why would you hide your eyes, they're exquisite!"

She laughed embarrassingly. "That's extreme!"

"Really." He flinched his head back slightly. "You're beautiful, why would you wear glasses if you didn't have to?"

"Same reason you seem to keep people out I guess, I want to be taken seriously."

She rushed to change the subject. "Let's analyze you now."

Leaning back, he stretched his legs out and put his hands behind his head. "Have at it."

"Let's start with our earlier conversation about the effect you have on people. Why you feel you have to be so tough when clearly you have a personality."

"Oh, rumors are going around that I don't have a personality?"

"No, that's not what I meant!" she retracted. "I just mean, like I just said, you keep to yourself and don't always seem approachable at times."

He continued to grin at her.

"You're the one who said that you have the kind of effect on people that make them want to trip you!"

"As I recall, *you* wanted to trip me." He was amused that he had her flustered.

"Why?" she asked.

"Why what? Why do I have that effect on people or why do people feel they want to trip me?"

"Why do you isolate yourself from the people that you spend the most time with, since you're always working."

"I don't really spend that much time with anyone at work because, other than you, they don't have anything to offer."

He leaned forward. "And in this field, like you," he pointed out, "not everyone takes me seriously. Look at me, I look like a beatnik."

Ashlei narrowed her eyes. "A beatnik?"

"A non-conformist," he chuckled. "So, most of my peers assume I am either unintelligent or naive. Basically, I'm a farm boy who was lucky enough to have parents who taught me all the right things, allowing me to go on to university, and meet a great professor who exposed me to a whole new world of science. Right out of school I was recruited into the military, and then I eventually landed a job where I feel I can do the most good."

"I feel like there's a lot in between that you left out."

"Okay. My family were farmers for generations. My parents both inherited land and were ingenious in their ability to stretch and make the most of what they had. We farmed the land—my parents, my brother and me. My mother sold the plants and vegetation we harvested, while my father sold land and taught those purchasers how to cultivate it. I flew crop dusters for not only my family's land, but for the neighbors too. That's actually what put me on radar of the military recruiting scouts. They had been keeping an eye on me during their monthly patrols since I was a kid. 'Strong, hard-working farm boys are the best soldiers!'" he said sarcastically.

"And I flew a crappy old duster, so I was the icing on their cake. They gave me the usual chunk of land for my service, and allowed me to stay the course and go to school first. I managed to get a scholarship to

Harvard, which was a huge change from my small farming community, but I made some necessary adjustments to fit in. After that, I was theirs to fly jets, choppers, and fighters for the next three years. But technically, I'm theirs for life."

"Well that explains some things," she said. "You said you have a brother?"

"Yeah, younger, Pipa."

"Pipa?"

"We traveled everywhere we needed to go by bicycle, like most, unless we were transporting a large harvest. Each bike had an extension attached so that my brother and I, when we were little, were pulled behind my parents when we went anywhere. As we got older, I upgraded to my own bike, but my little brother, Miles, still had to ride behind my parents in the extender." He chuckled. "I called him, 'pipa pipa', for many years, after the South American toad that hatches its young from its back. Eventually, that got shortened to Pipa and he still goes by that today."

She giggled. "Did he decide to go into the scientific field as well?"

"No, he stayed in farming and was able to obtain a small amount of land next to my parents. Anyway, I eventually ended up at the Bureau of Population Control and Statistics. When John recruited me to join Mike in Albany, he had already made up his mind within the first five minutes of meeting me that he didn't like me. From that point on, it's been a struggle to win his approval on anything. Not even sure I want it, but this is my first opportunity to prove that I have something to offer as a scientist, so I'm determined to suck it up and stay focused."

"But you have one of the most coveted positions in the company and your work speaks for itself, who would think you incapable?" she asked, baffled.

"There are many, like the dweebs I've pointed out at Exylon, who begin their careers with their heads up their asses thinking that they are the cream of the crop. They have no original thoughts, come in, tweak some buttons, pat themselves on the back and go home, proud of their accomplishments that day. Maybe they'll even write a paper to 'prove' how great they are. They are ants who don't really make any real contributions, just maintain what's already been put in place. Everyone needs an ant, I suppose, but it doesn't mean I need to boost their already inflated egos."

"*Now* who's hardcore?" she asked.

Her question reminded Claude of Ashlei's phone call.

Dale arrived with the food, asked if there was anything he could do, and departed.

"So, can I ask what that phone call was about? Clearly not good news," he stated, pushing the cheese down in his onion soup.

Ashlei was reminded of that phone call from her mother. *"Lydia died—she went skydiving."*

She winced and drooped her shoulders, slumping back in her chair. "Tuesday was my best friend's expiration date." She corrected, "We used to be best friends. We haven't really spoken in years, which is what made it even worse. The two of us were so close growing up and when I went away to school, we had a hard time trying to fit into each other's schedule." She sighed. "Knowing her expiration date was going to cut her life short, I promised her we would be together that day, so I could try and prevent it. Ya know, kid stuff. Do you remember that kid's game, 'Guess my death?'"

He nodded.

"So morbid, when you think about it. We are so desensitized to our demise. Anyway, we would play that for hours, trying to figure out how it would happen and then how we would prevent it." She smiled at the memory. "We acted out the scenes and I would come in and save the day. So morbid," she repeated sullenly.

"I regret letting our friendship fade. I regret forgetting about her day. I regret not coming through on my promise." Her face reddened and she blew out a breath.

"I'm so sorry," Claude said. "How did she go?" She sat up and said, "In a blaze of fire apparently." Claude stared aghast.

"No, no, not literally!" She was quick to correct. "She went skydiving and jumped without a parachute. If you knew her, you'd know this was no surprise, she lived her short life living!" Ashlei gave a short smile.

"My present love of neuroscience and genetics came from Lydia, I guess, who sparked my initial interest of wanting to change the course of expiration dates. I had this crazy idea as a kid that *I* would be the one to figure out why they exist and correct our natural course."

"You don't believe expiration dates are our natural course?"

"How can they be? We didn't start out this way. Something changed our path and ability to naturally pass on without a date already in place."

"Some may say that with all evolution comes mutation—change. Maybe expiration dates were our predicted path all along."

"Are you that 'some?'"

He grinned, "I don't know, the verdict's still out."

"My parents didn't allow us to know our dates." She displayed a mischievous grin. "But when I was thirteen, I snuck a peek. It wasn't that easy, I had to do some twisting and contorting to eventually find it on the back of my head."

Claude liked hearing about this defiant side of her. "Why were your parents against you knowing?"

"My mom believed that you shouldn't base your life on that number. You should live every day to its fullest, be the person you want to be now. Live *every day* like it's your last."

She hunched back in her chair again. "As soon as I looked, I wished I hadn't. They were right, there's something about not knowing the day you're gonna go that allowed me a freedom that I may never get back."

There's an awkward moment of silence.

"I had a friend that died recently," Claude began. "Well, he was more of an associate, Derrick. He worked at the Nutriment facility in Washington D.C. and suddenly just dropped. They said it was his expiration date. I'm not so sure though, if he had something physically wrong, his life monitor would have picked up anything unusual long before it had the opportunity to kill him. Yet, there are rumors that his life monitor could have been defective. Have you ever heard of that ever happening?"

She shook her head. "No."

"None of it sat well with me," Claude shared.

"Why is that?"

"Because, when I was down at the plant on business, we'd have lunch with a couple of other guys. He was a young guy and new employee, so

I took him under my wing. One day, I don't remember exactly what we were talking about, but he joked about probably losing all his hair and teeth before his expiration date took him out. That would put him well above the age of seventy at least, wouldn't you think?"

Ashlei nodded.

"And another thing, he ate like a horse at lunch, was acute—lucid. I didn't see any signs of diminished health that you usually see in someone the weeks and months before their expiration date."

"Why would his cause of death be reported as his expiration date if it wasn't?" Ashlei asked. "It's near impossible to go before then unless there's been some sort of freak accident, right?" she asked rhetorically. "Or… perhaps there *was* some sort of malfunction. There's a first time for everything."

Sitting unsettled in the back of his mind were questions—hints of suspicion Derrick had confided in Claude regarding Mike, suspicions Claude had dismissed.

Ashlei was already feeling a little lightheaded from her first drink when Dale returned with fresh ones. She took a long sip and this time she was the one who broke the silence, taking the opportunity to start a conversation she'd been wanting to broach.

"You talk a lot about Mike's passion over his VM9 project and spend a great deal of time working on it, but what about *your* passion?"

"I'm kinda in-between human and plant genetics. A crossbreed, if you will." They both chuckled at his corny joke. "Agriculture being my heritage, I was raised to appreciate the complexity of growing and nurturing vegetation, though I am currently working on a project that's geared toward human DNA. I hope to present it soon."

"Ah, mislabeled naive *and* interested in human genetics. I guess we're not so different after all," she pointed out.

They continued their conversation long after many other patrons had left. Realizing the time, Claude paid the bill and walked Ashlei to her car.

With Ashlei's hair down now, the light breeze blew the wavy strands in her face. Claude reached up to swipe them behind her ear and without a word did not hesitate to wrap his other hand around her waist, pull her close and kiss her.

-29-

JACK FOUND ELISA AT THE door when he answered it.

"Thanks for having me over."

"Oh, did we arrange this?" he asked, stepping aside as she walked past him.

"Sort of. We talked about regrouping after that one a.m. call at the hospital a few days ago."

He rolled his eyes, though happy for the company. She threw her jacket on the chair.

"I was gathering information…" She trailed off looking around his condo.

"Umm, why does your house look like you've just cleaned up a crime scene? It's so white and sanitized!"

She began writing in her phone: "clean and white with only splashes of personality."

"Are you making notes about my house?"

She giggled. "Yup! I can use this anomaly somewhere, this is too good!"

"It's not *that* unusual to be clean and neat."

"This is beyond clean and neat. This is sterile!"

There's nothing here, a nearly bare apartment. She stopped giggling and paused.

Maybe there's no mess, because there's no one else here to make it.

"Sorry, you're right, it's clean and neat and unobstructed. And I don't recall ever meeting a guy whose place smelled so good. You are a rare bird, my friend. Though… maybe you need a woman to sprinkle some color in your world."

Jack shook his head and offered her a cup of coffee.

"Please," she accepted, admiring the photos of his adventures on the wall.

"I'm a busy guy and it's not fair to someone when I'm not around. And I like being a bachelor, it has its perks. No one to nag me about my white walls."

Wondering which Adirondack mountain he was standing on in the photo, she studied Jack's face. His green eyes seemed absent of the joy he should feel conquering such a feat. Empty maybe. His slightly scruffy beard hid a partial smile. In the last few years that she'd known him, Jack had never really committed to anything more than a hearty smile or a shallow laugh. Perhaps he was holding back. Now that she knew about his past life, it all made sense. She frowned.

"Have you ever noticed that the nutriment injections—which on a side note, are shipped out from here in Albany at Exylon as well as in Washington D.C, —and expiration dates started about the same time?"

"What are you getting at?" he called from the kitchen.

"Well, expiration dates were documented as starting with Owen Cross in 2068, right? But if you think about it, there are many regions that are off our radar that could, technically, have had the first expiration date. A date that would correlate a little closer to the mandatory injections that began in 2067."

"You've really gone off the beaten track here," he said, handing her a warm cup. "Now you're delving more than a century into the past and trying to correlate it with the present situation."

"I was thinking more along the lines of maybe the injections containing a contraindication of sorts, causing our bodies to shut down and die. I mean is that so crazy to believe?"

"Yes, it is! Scientists, physicians, whoever, would have picked up on that immediately, a long time ago, if the injections were harmful to our bodies.

And also, how could a serum plaster a date on our bodies?"

"I don't know, how can everyone born have a birthmark of their expiration date! Nothing makes sense!" She shrugged. "I suppose it sounds absurd when you say it out loud. What do you think about them—how they began?"

"I guess I think it was a bit of evolution mixed with a bit of divine intervention."

"Yeah, me too," she agreed, situating herself in the brown leather chair.

He added, "I mean, certainly there's an explanation no matter how bizarre for the strange things that occur. Like, in Venezuela, at the intersection of two rivers, there is a nine-hour light show each night considered to be the highest concentration of lightning on earth. There's a couple theories, wind and terrain—uranium and methane deposits… Still, I strongly believe that there is a higher power. Not exactly holding strings and making us dance around like fools—people do that of their own accord. But I think that we have a course that we are on that was set in motion, not by chance. This course can shift based on the information we come across along the way or what obstacles may be thrown in front of us—but there is a course set nonetheless. Our fate is not determined until we get to the end."

Elisa gave thought to what he said.

Changing his perspective, he squinted his eyes, leaning back on the couch.

"I can see what you were saying though, about how evolution takes so long to kick in and be what it is meant to be. Perhaps expiration dates started out subtly with only few people here and there and escalated at some point until we were made blatantly aware of them."

She nodded in his direction. "Which speaks to my theory about maybe expiration dates starting before we knew about them. Who knows, maybe a century before that and it just caught up with the rest of the world at the point it did. But I also don't think things happen without a reason—without a purpose from a higher power."

"I still don't think you'll find your answers looking centuries into the past," Jack said.

"I'm just fishing, eventually something's got to bite, right?"

"You just used that analogy because I like to fish and you want me on board with your crazy idea," he said, pointing his finger at her.

She sipped her coffee and grinned. "Whatever it takes."

"And what does that have to do the current surge of deaths anyway?" "Probably nothing, but it was something that I think I'll look into more.

Though I came up empty, there is still the possibility of a recent contamination or virus," she said, refocusing.

"I ran it by Reed and he said there was always a possibility that anything can be contaminated, but the chances were very slim. Said he'd look into it further and that I should probably stick to hearts and not worry about it." He locked eyes with her. "I couldn't agree more."

"I can't let this go, Jack. I feel like Jessica's death could have been prevented. And with the reports of all these "abnormal" expiration dates… I just can't let it go."

"Do you think that maybe you are just so torn up about your family member's death that you don't want to let *that* go? And maybe this sudden rash of deaths is just what you needed to cast suspicion and redirect your focus?" he reasoned.

"Perhaps, but I need to follow this through. Even if I find nothing."

"I think you're just torturing yourself, but I understand." He sighed.

She glanced over at the side table with the photo of the young woman holding the baby, suddenly feeling his loss. "They are both beautiful."

He fixed his stare on the photo of his family. "Yeah, they are."

Elisa picked up a little knife next to the frame. "Is this a *Jack* knife?" she teased.

"Ha, yeah. My wife thought that was funny too, which is why she gave it to me."

"So, nutriment is made at Exylon? I thought they were all made in Washington," he said, changing the subject.

"Not made, but distributed. I asked Ash about it and they have a sister site here in Albany run by her boss, Mike. They continue to do studies, so he oversees that and distributes those from there."

"The Bureau of Population Control and Statistics in New York City is where I will probably need to get any questions answered, since that's their main hub. I'm thinking maybe I'll need to go down there and talk to someone—start asking questions, because they're not just going to answer them over the phone. Ash said security is tight."

"You know there was just a press release where the top scientists were brought in from *all over the world* and examined this thing thoroughly right?"

"That was bullshit! Did you buy that crap?"

"Well yeah! Why wouldn't I?"

"Come on, Jack. Let's just accept this as our next step in evolution? This is not like the anomaly of growing two heads! They either already know something they don't want the people to know, or they are just throwing crap at us because they don't want to continue to look into it. So, what if babies are dying at an exponential rate? Paul was right, Orbis doesn't care, so someone has to."

Jack sat up and moved to the edge of the couch across from her.

"First of all, what are you going to do there? Walk in and ask for the injection formula so you can analyze it? I'm pretty sure that's not on the tour. Second, let's say there is something wrong with it. Like you said, they may be trying to cover it up. Again, not volunteering information to the girl who showed up and said 'pretty please.' Do you even have a plan?"

"You know, you're right. I should try and get in there unnoticed and do a little investigating myself."

Jack stared for a moment. "You realize how crazy that sounds, right?"

"Yeah, but that is the only way I'm going to get answers. You said it yourself, they are not going to hand them to me."

She put her cup down and moved to the couch, snuggling her head in his shoulder. "Will you go with me, please? I may need someone to decipher the medical stuff, if need be. Or at the very least, to witness my incarceration if I get caught."

It's been so long since Jack felt the warmth of a woman so close. She smelled fresh. Like clean laundry hung out to dry. He softened a bit and took it in.

I'm just a doctor, what am I supposed to do there? "You're my friend, I want to help, but I'm not exactly Kojak," he reasoned

Lifting her head, she raised her eyebrows. "Really, that's your go-to? That guy's like two hundred years old! There are much more prominent officers today like, 'Wilson-detective-at-large' or 'Criminal-slayer Mark Talbut'."

"Okay, I get it. You're not a fan of Kojak."

"I didn't say… ughh. Whatever," she said, rolling her eyes. "You *are* a friend and that's what I need, someone I can trust to help me. Please."

He considered the repercussions.

"I could lose my license sneaking into a government agency."

"I doubt it. Unless they slap a malpractice suit on you for performing an unnecessary procedure on someone. You don't plan to do that, right?"

She hoped his silence meant he was contemplating.

"Please," she begged. "You need to add a splash of color to your life, don't you think?" she said, looking around his house.

"Stripes aren't my idea of a splash."

"Well, you need to get out more."

"I've been getting out! Reed and I did have plans this weekend," he mumbled. "Though he did cancel on me to go home for a few days. He usually jilts me for a girl."

Elisa frowned inwardly. She had no right to be bothered by that thought. "Ah, you see, your calendar is clear."

He shook his head, thinking of every reason he shouldn't go. "Alright, but seriously, if I feel I may be heading to jail at any point, we abort!"

She hugged him. "Thanks, Jack!"

"It's kind of a moot point anyway, like you said, serious security."

"Ash works at a government building; I'll ask her if she knows anything about security down there."

"And she'll just score you security tags, huh?"

"Maybe she could borrow a swipe or key or whatever they use to get in there for the day. I'm sure no one would even notice it missing."

"So, you're making your sister a thief and accessory to your crazy idea."

"She'd be *borrowing…*"

"And what if security is in the pupil or something, someone's definitely going to miss an eyeball for a day, don't you think?!" Jack joked.

"Oh my gosh, *you* have watched too many old movies!" she laughed.

- 30 -

THE FULL MOON SHONE DOWN on dozens of hover cars crowding the circular driveway at John's Boston estate. The cool summer breeze cut through the last of the expected guests as he pulled his collar up around his neck and scurried up the stairs and in the front door.

The crackling of the fire provided a calming atmosphere in the firebox room. John's intention was to settle any uneasy unrest over recent events. He motioned to a seat for the late arrival and began.

"Welcome, fellow Restituere members. Thank you all for traveling and taking the time to come to this meeting on such short notice. For those of you conferencing in on speaker; London; Madrid; Tokyo; Cairo; Berlin and the many others—welcome."

The room was filled with men and women dressed in everything from suits to jeans. Most were older, with a few members in their thirties. Some were talking quietly among themselves and the others were intently holding their gaze on John.

Mike was grateful that John was conducting the meeting in the firebox room—his comfort zone. He kept his stare on the paper before him, avoiding eye contact with the other members. *If they only knew that I am indirectly the reason this meeting is required.*

"I am happy to announce the success of Restore in its initial stages. The shipments sent out to their allocated destinations have been successfully distributed. However, there were some additional shipments sent out to regions not on our original list of selections. I have been getting some communication from many of you regarding the inquiries and news reports about the accelerated death rates around the globe."

Beads of sweat formed on Mike's forehead when John glanced over at him. He'd shrunk a bit in his seat, feeling as though everyone in the room were staring at him, cursing him; but of course, there was no way they could know that he was, indirectly, the cause of their dismay at the high-profile blunder that caused the world to take notice of the results of their actions. Actions that could end with undesirable consequences for them if discovered.

Mike had let John know that Derrick used Claude to send those shipments out and that Claude had no idea he was sending out the Restore nanobyte injections. He didn't let the opportunity escape to remind John of a conversation they once had. *"I think I mentioned to you long ago that the young and immature are not ready for Restituere. You may want to keep your eyes on the others."* It was a jab John didn't appreciate.

Mike shifted and straightened in his seat again. *They're not looking at you, keep your cool!*

"I understand the concerns brought forth and would like to assure you that this was an isolated incident. Without getting into too many details, there was an outside source who was responsible for the confusion. This matter has been personally handled from the lowest level to the highest."

A professor from Howard University lifted his hand. "How can we be assured that something like this won't happen again? I mean, do you agree that the spotlight shone on Restituere and hence any one of us," he waved his hand around the room, "is cause for speculation amongst our peers or worse? I think I speak for everyone when I say we cannot afford to have that happen." There was light chatter and nods around the room.

John raised his hand to the member in acknowledgment, while assuring all the affiliates, "I can guarantee, there will be no other incident like this again."

He motioned to Mike now. "Mike is handling all of our shipments out of his Albany site and will personally verify each shipment's destination."

Mike looked up at the members and with a nervous smile he nodded, pulled a handkerchief from his jacket, wiped his forehead and returned it to his pocket.

"I can also guarantee that the identity of each member of Restituere is kept confidential. We are a brotherhood and as such need to be able to feel comfortable and have trust within our group."

A tall gentleman with salt-and-pepper hair and an oversized mustache stood. "You'd better be right, or else, as much as I believe in what we are doing, I, along with my check, will be withdrawing my affiliation with you immediately."

He grabbed his Stetson cattleman hat from the table as he stood and headed towards the door.

Again, light chatter and nods among the members.

John looked at the departing member and paused. "I don't think there is any other new business, so if there are no other questions, we can conclude this meeting."

The activity picked up in the room and the other members began to rise, exit, and disconnect from the conference speaker.

John waited for the others to move away and as Mike got up to leave, he gently grabbed his arm and placed a small quarter-size device into his hand.

"I need you to upload this onto Claude's VCC. And don't make me a liar, Mike, I'm counting on you to oversee this thing a little more tightly on your end."

Mike acknowledged him with a nod and walked out.

- 31 -

Ashlei pulled her shoes off at the door of Claude's place, scanned the wide-open room, and found him on the VCC. "Hi, nice timing, I was just finishing up."

"Great," she said. With no walls within most of the apartment, eliminating the barriers of traditional rooms, the loft allowed her to feel unconfined and unrestricted. The same kind of floor-to-ceiling windows that brightened the lab were unobstructed here, looking out over the river. As the daylight faded, the few boats that sat on the water had their lights glowing while their owners entertained for the evening.

The last few weeks Ashlei had spent with Claude outside the lab were like a whirlwind—most of her nights spent at his apartment.

Just inside the door, on the wall, she was immediately faced with the same canvas black-and-white periodic table that she noticed the first time she came to his apartment. The night they had dinner at Vintage. She smiled warmly, taking in that entire night with one deep emotion.

They had burst into his apartment, entangled in one another. She didn't recall how they got there from the restaurant—perhaps the several drinks she had during dinner had something to do with that. Claude's apartment smelled like a much more potent version of him. It was intoxicating to her. They were not wasting time on formalities, giggling for a moment while Claude struggled to get her bra unhooked, followed by an intense drive to shed everything else covering them. It had certainly been a while for Ashlei, she had almost forgotten what it felt like to be aroused. Their actions were primal, rough. He knew exactly what she needed and where, as if he'd explored every inch of her before. He held her tight, she gripped his back, his arms—his muscles contracted. Their bodies moved as one. Just a few hours before the sun rose, exhausted, sweaty, euphoric, sheets half draped across them, they lay wrapped around each other like pretzels; without either saying a word, they fell asleep. In the morning, they took their time and enjoyed each other again on another level. Ashlei dozed off again, waking to the smell of fresh brewed coffee and bacon. Dressed in only a sheet, she'd made her way into the kitchen. "Good morning."

Claude smiled at her. "Good morning."

"Umm, I'm looking for my clothes." She smirked.

He handed her a cup of coffee and motioned to the couch. "I gathered your things that were so haphazardly thrown about the place and hung them there." He grinned, admiring her over the rim of his own cup.

She smiled and collected her clothes, noticing for the first time the enormous periodic table at the entrance.

"Wow, that's pretty serious," she stated.

"Well, sometimes I like to have a reference right at my fingertips."

"Surprised I missed that," she said. Though she hadn't seen much of any part of the apartment the night before.

The swoosh of the hover train could barely be heard in the distance.

Still clinging to the sheet and clothes, she circulated around his home, as if touring an art gallery, pausing in front of a framed painting of a human form, arms spread, made up completely of molecules tapering down from the waist to a double helix—the backbone of DNA. She raised an eyebrow in admiration.

She continued on. Positioned on a stand was a lone four-dimensional halo-sculpture of concrete rubble transforming into a rebuilt city in a continuous loop. *It crumbles and rebuilds itself.*

"Fascinating. It's like a hologram, but it's tangible," she said to herself, examining the structure from all angles.

"It's called Odbudować, created by Aleksander Kocienski."

He startled her from behind, while she was transfixed by the restructuring of the buildings and trees surrounding it.

"It means to reconstruct. My favorite period in history. It describes the resilience of mankind to rebuild in the aftermath of disaster." He sipped his coffee. "But that's not why it's my favorite era. Prior to the war, the world was so tied into gluttony, greed, and power—self-indulgence. Everyone using a vehicle, polluting the air and water with oil, meals that produced themselves from the push of a button, communication through implanted chips, waste everywhere! There was no accountability, no cares other than one's own comfort—making every step forward as easy as possible. Pretty much one of the reasons the war occurred. I'll admit that I'm in the minority believing that the greatest thing that came out of the Transitional War was leaving all of that stuff behind. Learning to take care of ourselves without the high-tech gadgets wiping our asses for us."

"I imagine there was one of those too." She smirked.

"This was a gift from my mother when I graduated the University."

Ashlei continued to explore. Against the wall, below the photo of a pair of crossed lacrosse sticks, sat a machine that caught her interest.

"What's this?" she asked, bending down to get a closer look. "*That…* is a record player, my pride and joy." He beamed. "Okay, what's it… do?"

He didn't wait for her to ask before he pulled a black, round, flat object out of its sleeve, and after lifting a plastic cover, placed it on the machine. From the speakers in each corner of the room there was a crackling sound and then music filled the air, reaching the high ceiling.

"It plays music," she acknowledged, nodding her head, impressed.

"Not just plays music, but involves you in every aspect of it. The sound is so intense you can feel it from within."

"It sounds like a bad recording of what is probably a great song," she said, arching an eyebrow.

"Give it a chance, eventually you'll learn to appreciate it. It's been in my family for generations. I found it packed away when I was a kid and though some of the albums were scratched, Pipa and I would listen for hours. This one's one of my favorites—Led Zeppelin."

Claude's voice pulled Ashlei back from her thoughts of that night. "Glass of wine?"

"Mhmm."

As with previous visits, she went straight to the carefully stacked albums—choosing a new one to play each time. Tonight, she chose Santana. The music filled the apartment with the sounds of Latin rock. She lifted her head, moving it back and forth, swaying her hips to the beat.

Claude poured two glasses of wine and smiled, appreciating her enjoyment.

"Ya know," she said, looking around at the disheveled apartment with clothes on the floor and dishes on the coffee table, "I guess I hadn't really noticed that you're not as neat and orderly here as you are at work."

"Well, maybe that's because you've had your eyes on other things when you're here. Maybe you should appreciate all that is me and not just my body," he teased.

"Ha." She considered this. "Okay, you got me there. Though I do appreciate your mind as well. And also, that thing you do that makes me care a little bit more about your body."

He laughed.

Settling in on the couch, curling her feet underneath her, she accepted a glass of wine from Claude.

"Or perhaps, you are so wound up about your work that you feel the need to just let loose here at home," she suggested.

"Are you saying I'm uptight?" he asked, sitting next to her.

"No, I just think you work a lot and it seems to consume you. You have a lot going on between VM9 and whatever else you're working on. What exactly is this other project you're working on?"

"Not something I'm ready to talk about. I'm currently pulling together my presentation. Soon."

"Well, is it something I can help with?"

"If I don't give you enough to do on VM9, I can arrange to load you up with more," he teased.

"Umm, no. You know I'm quite saturated with all I have to do. I just thought that maybe I'd be able to alleviate some of your stress."

"Do I seem stressed?"

"Sometimes, actually. You tend to tap your pen incessantly when you seem to have an issue or something to work out. Or when Mike's around."

"You have me all figured out, huh," he stated.

"Well, not completely, but I have a pretty good handle on some of the things that make you tick. Like, you are not the tough guy you like everyone to think you are."

"Old news, continue," he said.

"You bite your bottom lip when you are onto an idea. You scratch your head and entire body when you are overtired. You like your coffee black with one sugar.

"How am I doing?" she asked.

He smiled in defeat, grabbed her hand, pulling her up to move her toward the pool table.

"I bet I could even guess one of your most coveted secrets. Perhaps… your password," she said, smirking.

He chuckled. "Take your best guess."

"What do I get if I guess correctly?" she asked.

"You get to go through all my most coveted things." He grinned slyly at her.

"I see."

"And if you don't," he grabbed her waist and pulled her to him, "I get to go through all your most coveted things."

"Game on." She began with, "Arrogant!" and laughed out loud. Claude was smiling through this while he set up the pool table.

"Prove, triumph, VICTORIOUS, control, VM9. Your military number, whatever that is."

He chuckled. "Where did you even get that idea?"

"It sits at your station."

"Nice guess, but no."

She frowned and continued as they played their game, "Prevail, succeed… Eight ball right corner pocket," she called out. The black ball shot at high speed into the corner pocket as planned; she paused to do a victory dance.

"Nice," he said.

"Let's talk about VM9 for a bit," Ashlei said.

"Okay, what do you want to talk about?"

"Well, we've been working on it together for about two months, right?"

He nodded.

"And this technically is Mike's baby, right?" He nodded again.

"So why isn't *he* actually working on it? Not that I'm complaining, I like the work we're doing and the experience, but it seems to me if he is so passionate about it, he would be involved somehow."

"You are correct, he is very passionate about it, but he has been called away to another, apparently more important project. He would much rather be working on this I'm sure, but we are still pawns that don't always have a say."

"I see." She paused. "But, aren't you even a little curious about what he would be doing that would pull him away from such important, life-changing experimentation?"

Claude grinned as he saw she was about to get worked up over this.

"I mean, if VM9 showed results—*when* it shows results, this will be revolutionary for agriculture. Well, you know." She motioned toward him. "We are so close; I just find it so strange to have a dream that you worked on for so long finally come to fruition and not be an intricate part of that at its completion. He'd be missing out on the reward of that breakthrough. So… what would be so important he'd neglect to be a part of that?"

"I get what you're saying, I just think his business is his business."

"Okay, enough said," she replied. Then added, "I think either your ego is loving that he has to check in with you about VM9's progress, or your need for his approval is loving that he has to check in with you. Either way, I believe you are happy to be in charge of his baby, and therefore, have not questioned his motives to put you in charge."

"Ha, ha. So enough *wasn't* said!"

Now cuddled on the couch, she giggled in agreement and laid her head on his chest.

Claude didn't let on, but he had been having those same thoughts about what could be more important than a person's life work, and if it was connected in any way to Mike's outrageous rant about the shipment.

Her eyes heavy, undaunted by her futile task, Ashlei continued guessing his password. Twenty minutes later, as she dozed in his arms, she sighed and made one last-ditch effort to guess. "Pipa." She felt his body stiffen.

She smiled and fell asleep.

- 32 -

CLAUDE SAT ALONE IN THE LAB, the bright rays of the sunset rapidly beginning to fade away. Taking a drink from his mug, he scowled at the coffee that had gone cold.

He continued to type. "Jerry Turner, expiration date 2086—age 9. Mike Turner, expiration date 2086—age 41. Lisa Turner, expiration date 2086—age 66… In conclusion, I strongly believe that if something is not done to rectify this new turn of events, there will be dire consequences for the human race."

He finished putting all his data into its final report and was ready to present it to his mentor.

Staring at the proposal he'd just spent hours putting together, wording and rewording, he slid his fingers down the pen in his hand, flipping it from tip to bottom, touching the desk each time. Claude considered the reception he'd get from John and the members of the bureau. He frowned, concerned. *This is too important not to be taken seriously.*

He leaned back in the chair for a moment, incessantly tapping the pen on his leg. He thought of Ashlei and smiled.

Considering the conversation they'd had the night before, he glanced over at Mike's desk. *What are you working on that would require you to put aside your own research?*

Once again, he thought about the day Mike went on his rant. The first time and the last time Claude had ever been a victim of his tirade. He thought about the conversation with Derrick. *"What would you do if you thought someone wasn't benefiting the work you were doing? What do you know about Mike?"* A subtle way of saying Mike was doing something outside of proper practice? *Could* the injections be contaminated? Claude wondered. *Could* Mike be contaminating them? He shook his head at the notion—that sounded crazy, he brushed off the thought. He sat forward and pushed his current proposal, which was floating before him, to the background and pulled forward the list of addresses he'd sent the nutriment injections to months ago. He scanned through quickly. *I'm not seeing anything unusual here.* He looked to the door behind Mike's desk. It had always been locked as far as he knew. Mike said it was just storage and archived studies. More secrets? Claude poked his head out of the lab door, looked around and closed it again. He tried the closet door, not really expecting it to be open. That would be too easy. This is not my forte, he thought, while rummaging around Mike's desk looking for a key. He stepped back. "If I were hiding a key, where would it be?" he asked himself. He rubbed his hand back and forth on the underside of Mike's desk, hoping Mike didn't have an affinity for sticking gum in odd places like he and his brother did as kids. He grinned as he slid his hands across a taped up flat card. He retrieved it. *Looks like a passkey to me*—he hoped. He slid it against the door lock and the heard a click. The closet was more like a small room, and with no windows it was dark and musty. Claude felt for the switch on the wall and turned on the light. The room was filled with boxes, all labeled RESTORE. No piles of old study files or discarded lab materials and equipment as Claude had expected to find. He moved in further, sliced a box open with the key that let him in the room, and opened the flap to find carefully packaged nutriment vials. He looked around the box, at the others. They must all be nutriment vials. Why were they kept locked up in this musty room and not with the others? Maybe they were old or contaminated, meant to be discarded or something, he guessed. He heard the lab door jostle and leapt over to turn out the light and shut the door, and stood backed against the wall.

He heard footsteps. They stopped, continued and stopped again.

Somehow over his heart racing, Claude could hear Mike's muffled sounds. "Boy left his VCC on. Of course."

He continued on with some other discernable sounds. After twenty minutes, just when Claude couldn't take the hot, stale air in the room anymore, he heard footsteps and the door to the lab closed. He took a vial from the open box and re-sealed the package as best he could, locked the door and re-taped the key under the desk.

He slid in the chair in front of his VCC, taking another quick look at the door, his heart rate finally began to slow. Flipping the vial around in his hand, he continued to wonder why nutriment vials were kept in that locked room. After feeling a bump on the bottom several times, he flipped it over to discover an embossed R on the bottom. He pulled his head back and squinted before moving to the lab counter, taking out a glass slide, pulling the contents from the vial with a dropper and sliding it under the microscope. He jerked his head back abruptly. "What the… "

- 33 -

Dr. Troy Ali sat his desk, debating whether to contact someone regarding his unsettling suspicions of Dr. Persaud. He realized that now would be the perfect time, while Dr. Persuad was busy at the hospital with a delivery, so Troy retreated to his office, which he called the Dungeon. The only available room left in the two-story building that had been converted into an obstetrician clinic for the impoverished communities in the area, happened to be in the basement. He shared this space, just outside his office, with the boiler, unused miscellaneous equipment, and furniture left over from the previous use of the building. In spite of the boiler whistling and clanking and it being a bit drab and drafty, he didn't mind the chill, since he spent most of his time in the clinic.

He shivered, shaking off the chill running up his spine. He stared at the number of his mentor, Dr. Leland Carter, the head of Obstetrics and Gynecology at Johns Hopkins Hospital in Maryland, whom he trained with for three years. *Leland is honorable and I trust his judgment. Where else can I turn? This could mean my job, my career, my short-lived reputation,* he reasoned. *Never have numbers been such a burden,* he thought, as he decided on the right thing to do.

Troy had worked with Dr. Krish Persaud for the last six months, returning to his country after medical school and fellowship in America to practice medicine in some of the poorer, under-served districts. He felt honored to be chosen by Dr. Persaud, as his reputation for being an outstanding physician and humanitarian had preceded him. Troy's new colleague had started and championed most of the under-served maternity clinics in this area of Guyana. But he had learned pretty quickly that not all things were as they seemed. Troy had witnessed Dr. Persaud's disregard for the mothers and families that had come through his clinic. He showed a caring facade, but behind the scenes Dr. Persaud was loathing each one.

While Troy pondered his course of action, his thoughts carried him to a community event where families come to the clinic and learn about healthy eating habits, the immune system, the importance of birth control, hygiene and many other topics. Troy enjoyed these events, they gave him a chance to meet more of the local families, speak to parents, and figure out their needs in a less intimidating climate.

"Docta Ali!" The husband of one of Dr. Persaud's patients approached with his wife by his side. The woman was carrying their swaddled baby against her chest, who a few short months ago had entered the world with a deformity to both her legs and arms. He shook Troy's hand and the woman nodded.

"We want to thank you, docta, for the care you give to us."

He had thanked Troy at each office visit; the people in the small community were always grateful to receive anything.

"Still my pleasure, Mr. Singh. And how is little Natalya?" he asked, pulling the blanket back and taking a peek.

"Good, docta." Her mother lit up.

"Docta Persaud!" the man called out as his doctor approached from behind Troy.

"Thank you, docta," he said, reaching out his hand to shake Persaud's. Persaud did not extend his hand in return.

The man pulled his hand back undeterred. "We are tryin for anoder baby. Maybe a baby boy!" the father said enthusiastically.

Persaud smiled, looked from the woman to the man and said, "My recommendation is that you do not have another child. I fear with your genetic make-up, you will most likely have another deformed child. It would only be a burden."

The woman immediately teared up and began to sob. Holding his wife as she wept into his chest, the man stared after Persaud as he walked away and engaged in conversation with a clinic staff member.

Krish Persaud would be considered handsome, and though in his sixties, had the physique of a much younger man. He was a strong believer in eating healthy and staying fit. He diligently ran at least three miles most nights and maintained a regular exercise routine. Though just five foot ten, he towered over the petite parents, making his crude remarks only more intimidating.

Trying to shake the memory, it still sat uneasily with Troy. He was appalled and humiliated that Krish would behave in such a way and immediately had escorted the tearful woman and her family to a quiet area, apologizing for his associate's behavior.

When confronting Persaud about his disregard, he was reminded that he was fresh out of fellowship, new here and, especially in communities such as these, had a lot to learn.

I feel he champions these people, so in his sick way he can persecute them. His motives for this clinic and humanitarian work are far from noble.

Troy tried to avoid unnecessary interactions and didn't question him again until he had inquired about the nutriment injections.

"Krish, why do some of these nutriment injection bottles have a raised 'R' on the bottom?"

"Oh, um well, we are a clinic that does not have the luxury of affording anything new, so we receive our glass vials and much of our equipment from recycling centers. Most everything here has been re-purposed. We discussed all this in your interview, remember?"

"I suppose we did," he replied.

I have a feeling the "R" means something more. His explanation is valid, but I'm sure it isn't an accurate one.

Troy slid his finger across his band and it illuminated around his wrist. He began to press the numbers into the keypad, just before his head slumped to the desk next to it. A black gloved hand swiped again and the lighted numbers retracted back into the black band.

~

Persaud handed the new baby to her mother. She looked at him as he lowered his eyes. Lifting the small foot in her hand, she whispered, "Only two days."

Though he portrayed himself as a man who grieved for this young mother, there was no remorse in his eyes. Persaud reflected back to five months ago when he saw her in his office.

~

"Hello, Mona. How are you feeling today?"

"We're fine tuday docta," she responded, rubbing her belly. "See, I tol ya I make all my appointments. I'm eatin all da right foods an I dunt work too much. I been doin all da things right fo my baby."

"That's great, Mona." He smiled. "Have a seat."

She pulled herself up on the exam table, crinkling the white paper that extended the full length, as she positioned herself, legs in stirrups.

Persaud pulled out the vial labeled Nutriment and flipped it up, making sure it had the embossed R on the bottom. Mona tensed and retracted back as he pulled the sheet to her torso.

"Mona, I realize you lost your first baby early on, but remember it was *you* who hadn't seen a doctor prior to that point. And in fact, you only came to me now because you would be arrested if you didn't get the injection. Isn't that right?" She didn't respond.

"Your baby was so undernourished and feeble then due to *your* lack of nutrition and care."

She did herself, the baby, and the world a favor when she miscarried, he thought. *These mothers cannot take care of themselves, much less a baby.*

"I kept my promise when I'm gonna 'ave anoder baby I took da vitamins, made my visits, and 'ere I am, 'ere fo my injection."

"Very good. Just relax." Directed by ultrasound, Persaud injected the contents of the syringe directly into the fetus. He followed with a probe and clicked the trigger. Mona winced.

"All done. I'll see you next visit."

~

After delivering Mona's baby, Persaud left the maternity ward at the hospital and made the short trip across the road to his clinic. He walked down an aged hallway and entered a room with the same dingy floor flowing into it. It seemed that only the black checkered tiles amongst the white were broken and edging their way up, with several others missing. He greeted the man waiting with a smile and handshake, embarrassed to meet his guest in such conditions, but this matter couldn't wait for more pleasant circumstances.

"Hello, my friend. Good to see you. How was your trip?"

John returned his smile. "Long, but comfortable."

Persaud gestured to the chair. "Please."

"No thank you, Krish, I won't be staying long. Just thought I'd stop to say hello while I was here."

"Won't be staying long? Pardon the confusion, but we still have the matter of my young colleag—"

John raised a hand to Persaud. "All taken care of. No worries my friend."

John lifted his Brooks Brothers black scarf off the chair, draped it around his neck and straightened his collar. "Mr. P found a solution to your problem."

"Mr. P... is here?"

"Here and gone." John put his hand on his shoulder. "I'll see you next week at the next meeting, Krish." He exited the room, leaving Persaud's mouth gaping in awe at the efficiency of his cohorts.

- 34 -

Elisa took a country drive out to visit her grandfather, figuring who better to question about the expiration dates than someone who was around, though young, when expiration dates were fairly young as well. *He may have heard talk as a child about this somewhat new "occurrence" and have some insight.*

Elisa relished the drive to her grandfather's farm. The road was full of twists and turns and more greenery than she could find in any one place in the city. Surrounding old abandoned huts that could hardly be called housing, remnants of an overpopulation era, buds of trees were growing. To Elisa they looked like little children compared to the very few several-hundred-year-old trees she'd seen that were fortunate enough to be left alone, further north in the Adirondacks. She opened her windows, allowing the fresh air to filter through her nostrils, cleansing her lungs.

In the city and most surrounding areas, the landscape was dull and brown with the exception of certain patches of land that were preserved as protected parks. When real estate was being ravished and plundered, these pieces of land were declared government property and protected to maintain acres of grassland and trees. After Orbis was formed, there were committees set up around the globe to replenish the earth by plant-ing vegetation everywhere possible. There was still a concern about the issue of overpopulation and crowding into limited space, but working with geologists and botanists, they determined that in the time it would take for vegetation to grow and replenish, they would have gotten the population crisis under control, making room for new growth. Elisa often dreamt of a time long ago when everywhere you turned there was an abundance of food, water, fuel, land, fresh air. But she shuddered, imagining the early days of turmoil when there were such extreme restrictions on those essentials. There were still many restrictions, but for her—in her lifetime—the rations were so much greater and a bit easier to come by. Though, the law required that any kind of waste come with a heavy fine.

Ashlei decided to tag along, informing Elisa that she thought she was in love.

"You've been 'in love' twice before."

"Seriously E, if I'm wearing pigtails it doesn't count," she said. "Love takes on a whole new meaning when you're an adult."

"Oh, you're an adult now?" Elisa teased. "Ha." She curled her lip.

"So, isn't Claude one of the guys you claimed was a little strange when you started working there?"

"Yes, well, I was thrown into working pretty closely with him and he was every bit as weird as I had said, but in a good way."

Her eyes soften. "He makes me laugh, he listens and is interested in my theories and where I want to go with my work. He's a little hard to figure out if you don't know him, he can be serious and silly all in one moment. He's like a hot nerd." She laughed.

"Anndd, there it is! I was guessing he was probably hot or I would only see half as big a grin."

Ashlei smiled even wider. "Umm, yes! His beautiful light brown eyes are so deep I felt as though I could fall right into them and his hair curls right around my fingers—not that it's too long. It's just right," she sighed.

"All jokes aside, I'd never thought I could feel this way about someone," she said thoughtfully. "His smile makes my heart melt."

"I'm happy for you, Ash," Elisa said genuinely. "When do I get to meet this guy?"

"Come to Exylon for lunch, you can meet him then."

The car in front of them gradually began to lower to ground and the wheels pulled down from their wheel wells. They passed as it moved off to the side of the road and Ashlei watched from her mirror as the driver got out, kicking her car.

"Shoulda *chaaarged* your hover," Ash said, amusing herself. "So, what exactly do you think you're going to get out of grandpa?"

Elisa sighed. "I don't know, a different perspective maybe. I just want to pick his brain. He's been around a lot longer and has seen much more than us, maybe there's been deaths like this before?"

"Well, if there have been, he'll have a story about it." Ashlei chuckled.

"I still think there may be something to my theory about a contraindication between the nutriment injections and expiration dates, despite Jack's dispute."

"It could hold some validity. But why only those areas, and why just now? If it were a true mutation, the way you portrayed it, it would have spread out over years and regions. These deaths are too precise. I think there's something going on specifically in those areas that is changing their expiration dates."

"Which then brings us back to the virus or contamination theory," Elisa said.

As soon as she saw the sign that read, "Welcome to Voorheesville," Elisa's spirits lifted the way they always did when she'd visit her grandfather. All the problems in her world would fade away with his hugs.

As they pulled up to the old farmhouse their father grew up in, Sean Quinn exited through a squeaky front door to greet his granddaughters with arms wide.

"Oh, my girls, so glad you could come visit an old man," he said, leading them into the house.

At eighty-one, Sean still had sprigs of his natural Irish red hair mixed with his nearly full head of gray. No longer running the farm, he spent his days repairing broken fixtures around the house.

The old home had an abundance of reminders of their grandmother, Cara. Her favorite sweater still hung over the arm of the bench that sat in the entryway, eleven years after her expiration date.

"I swear I can smell Grandma's perfume," Elisa whispered to Ashlei. "And you'd be right! I spray it every so often to keep her scent around." She winced, bringing her hand to her mouth.

"Oh, it's alright dear. Nothing wrong with you knowing I miss your grandma. Or that your old grandpa can still hear like an eagle."

Elisa kissed his cheek. "I get it, Grandpa."

"She used to fuss about the house and over me, everyday making sure she did the things she enjoyed—the 'silly little things' she'd say that she'd miss, smelling fresh flowers in the house, listening to the crickets at night, your dad and you girls! She'd often have me complain about the tractor not working. Ha, ha, can you believe that. She took nothing for granted." He stared off for a moment.

"Iced tea, lemonade, coffee?" Sean asked.

"Sure, I'll have some lemonade," Elisa said.

"Me too, Grandpa. Let me get it," Ashlei said, reaching for the refrigerator handle.

He tapped her hand away and ushered her to the kitchen table. "You're some of the only guests I get out here now, let me serve you."

"Okay." She complied.

Elisa jumped in right away. "Grandpa, I wanted to ask if you remember anything about expiration dates from when you were younger."

Sean poured the lemonade in the glasses Ashlei placed on the table and paused.

"Sure! Remember that guy, Michael Farmer?" he asked.

Michael Farmer was sort of an urban legend in town. He was no longer a person, but a verb or an act or an object—a cliché. Elisa had heard her grandfather tell his version of this story many times before, but Ashlei had only heard this story told in school and by friends. This wasn't what she had in mind, but Sean was willing to forget he'd told it before and began to tell it again.

"It was an unfortunate, tough lesson taught to many people, which tested what most felt was God's will. Michael Farmer was a college student studying at a small community college in Sullivan County, downstate New York. He was an art major, which according to his parents meant that he really didn't know what he wanted to do with his life. For Michael using a pencil or other medium was an extension of himself and he was really good at it. Good enough to be able to make some sort of career of it, he felt. He would fall into this world of lines and detail," Sean waved his hands around in the air, "so much so, he became part of his subject. Of course, there was no use for that sort of thing then—not with the world being what it was. Anyway, Michael also liked to have a good time, as most college students do. So, he and a couple of his friends were drinking, smoking a few doobies."

"Doobies?" Ashlei repeated in a surprised giggle.

"Yeah, you know, joints," he replied. "The one thing that *did* seem to grow abundantly at that time."

"Yeah, *I* know, grandpa, I didn't know *you* knew," she said with one eyebrow raised.

"Well, I'm old now, but I wasn't always," he said, winking.

"I know," she said, glancing at Elisa who was giggling too. "This is just a crazy side I hadn't known about is all."

"Can I get on with my story?" he asked, raising his hand out in a gesture requiring approval.

"Absolutely." She gestured that he had the floor.

"So, they're pretty high," he cut them a look, "and they're bored because this was a pretty small town. Not just that, but being high can make you think some awfully strange things and make you come to some awfully strange conclusions. Some very *stupid* conclusions! These boys had what they thought was a deep discussion, about their expiration dates and what would happen if they challenged the date that had been on the sole of their foot, head, whatever, since they were born. Probably since they were first conceived!" he pointed out. "So, one of them, his name escapes me, decided well, why don't we test it and see what would happen. The other idiots decide nothing will happen.

"'We can't die until our expiration date,'" one said.

"'Let's do it then,'" Michael encouraged.

"'Do what though bro, like jump off a building or something?'"

They found it funny that their grandfather was throwing in a little character acting.

"And what do these bone-heads do! They go find a road, lie down in it and wait for a car to come and run them over. In their intoxicated minds this made sense! Can you believe that! What happened was the first to get run over was Michael. He was in a position where the tires went over his head and he was done for immediately. Squish!" They both cringed.

"That's harsh, grandpa." Elisa flinched.

"Yeah, well, the whole thing was stupid and senseless and another reason that youth is wasted on the young," he retorted. "The next jackass managed to escape with nothing more than a twisted ankle because after hitting Michael the driver swerved and missed that kid. The twisted ankle came from him getting frightened and jumping up to get out of the way. The next unfortunate idiot was hit when he got scared and leaped off the ground, but right into the car when it swerved. He ended up a quadriplegic. Broken back, neck, you name it. So, in the end they proved that yes, although we have expiration dates, if you're stupid enough to get run over by a car, you can make that date a lot sooner. Or, you can make the rest of your days here on earth pretty darn miserable. Michael should have died at the ripe old age of seventy-six."

"I'd never heard the story told like that before," Ashlei said, a little disturbed. "Shouldn't they tell that *whole* story in schools or something to ward off other curious adolescents from doing something stupid? I mean I knew that Michael Farmer died that way but the whole story put it in a different perspective. I pictured this talented guy just experimenting with an idea. Granted it was a stupid idea. This would be a good lesson on the effect of drugs and alcohol. I don't know, I just think the whole thing might have more of a positive effect if it were known."

"Well it's not like it's a secret," he said. "You can look it up on virtual cybernetics computers anytime. Anyway, as you know there's been other idiots out there who have done similar bonehead moves. That's one of the reasons your father was always so determined to teach you girls those lessons. He's seen a lot of bad and stupid things out there as an officer of the law *and* as an everyday citizen."

He stared intently. "You don't ever want to know the things people will do for greed—or out of desperation. When you live through the most desperate of times, you get it all. He made sure you girls will never be victims! You can think," he tapped his head, "and fight like a Quinn!"

They nodded their heads while Elisa refilled her grandfather's glass with lemonade. "What I had in mind, Grandpa, was, do you remember anyone talking about expiration dates and nutriment injections?"

"Oh, we didn't usually talk about our dates outside the house like you kids do today. It was more of a private thing—dignified. But I'd heard the adults talking about it here and there. My parents would threaten me, that if I wasn't a good boy, *"God will shorten your date!"* they'd say. I was a rambunctious boy, always into some kind of trouble." He burst out laughing. "As a matter of fact, my older brother, your great uncle Paul, took a pen while I was sleeping, parted my hair and changed the year of my death! He got in a lot of trouble for that!" he continued to laugh. "I thought I was going to die the following week!"

Ashlei laughed along with her grandfather.

Elisa realized it was hard to keep her grandfather focused.

"What did people say about where expiration dates came from?"

"Oh, evolution mostly, damn chemicals in the water. Some believed they were caused from the power plants that went up so quickly and exposed everyone to an abundance of dangerous radiation; others accused foreign nations of planting something during the war that took years to take effect." He throws his hands in the air. "There were all kinds of crazy ideas that floated around. God's will, alien DNA. You'd probably know something about that Ash, wouldn't you?"

"Not really, grandpa, I didn't study that." Ashlei glanced at Elisa and grinned.

"Oh. Well, to your previous question, nutriment injections are the reason we have endured the chemicals, radiation, malnutrition from hunger and the lack of ability to sustain our own health. They have supplemented what women are not able to provide to the unborn child."

He sounds like a public announcement, Ashlei thought.

"Most of the deaths before these dates came about were caused by disease, ailments that are now predicted by our life monitors, pollution, selfishness—many other awful ways to go that I can't think of right now. I'm not so sure I wouldn't rather just… go."

I am no closer to an answer, Elisa thought.

"Maybe I'll stop in and see Reed," she said to Ashlei on the way home. "Perhaps I can probe him a little more than Jack did, about the nutriment injections."

"Reed huh, I see." She raised her brow and nodded.

Elisa gave her a dismissive look, though turning away, she grinned ear to ear.

- 35 -

Meeting Ashlei at Exylon for lunch, Elisa was taken by surprise by the amount of security she had to go through just to have lunch with her sister. Ashlei came to the door after receiving a call from the security booth. She waved to the new smiling security guard for Elisa's release.

"Yeah, I forgot about that, sorry," Ashlei said.

"How do you forget about that? Just to get through the gates, I promised Diego there, that anxious security guard, my first born, while the other has dibs on my puppy!"

"You don't have a puppy."

"Nor do I have a child, but he doesn't know that. I had to offer up something."

"You're overreacting." She chuckled.

Elisa chuckled too. "Well, a little, but not by much. He only let me through when he saw you. I think he likes you."

Ashlei rolled her eyes. She guided them from the large lobby through a long wide hall, which displayed huge windows allowing the sun's rays to illuminate the entire space. Scientists, researchers, and other employees walked among them, some with a destination in mind and some in deep conversation with others.

"Down the hall, there," Ashlei said, when they got the second floor, "is the lab I work out of." They continued up a couple more flights of stairs leading to the fourth floor. "I usually eat lunch in the lab, but I thought you'd like our cafeteria. Claude had to go to a meeting and then take off for the bureau in New York. I told him that I am having lunch with you if he wanted to join us before he left."

"Would he have anything to do with you not wearing those stupid non-prescription glasses you don't need?" Ashlei only grinned at her sister's observation.

"I certainly will have worked up an appetite by the time we get there."

"Well the alternative was the elevator, and I know you would have wanted to opt out of that option."

"Yes, indeed!" she agreed. "Wow!" She took in the brightly lit cafeteria, its cathedral ceiling which opened up into a skylight, along with the many vendor choices ranging from sandwiches, pizza, burgers—all the normal lunch fare to high quality restaurants.

She looked around like a kid in a candy shop. "And why don't you eat here?"

The cafeteria was filled with plants, flowers, artwork on every wall, as well as employees. Soft music was piping from speakers hidden within the plants, as far as Elisa could figure.

"Sometimes I do, but honestly I'm usually too busy to make the effort to come up here."

Elisa followed her nose to the steakhouse option simply labeled Steak House. She ordered rare prime rib, brown rice, grilled squash and zucchini. Ashlei settled on a salad.

"Really? That's all you're getting?" Elisa asked, raising an eyebrow. "I'm not up for a heavy lunch today. Not feeling well."

Elisa lifted her wrist, looking for the pad to swipe her bracelet to pay. Ashlei said, "Oh, this is all free, company perk!"

Elisa's eye lit up. "Bonus!"

"They try to make the work atmosphere as pleasant as possible so the workforce will be more productive. There's a whole algorithm on how to keep your employees producing. Along with the obvious skylight to brighten the room and music in the background, you'll find Exylon's mantra on the walls, scattered throughout the building; 'Accelerating innovation, taking future generations of humanity into leaps of discovery,'" she mechanically chanted. "And, every so often, throughout the building, a soft melodic voice will pipe in telling us how great we are and what a positive and essential contribution we are to the company. I do find I'm sleeping better at night."

Elisa chuckled.

Ashlei waved Claude over when he entered the cafeteria.

"This is my sister, Elisa. Elisa, Claude." They shook hands and exchanged pleasantries.

"Excuse me, but I'm starving, I'm just gonna to grab something quick and I'll be right back." And he darted off in the direction of the steakhouse.

"The steakhouse," Elisa observed. "I like him already." Ashlei smiled at her approval.

"How are Shauna and David doing?" Ashlei asked. "I've called a few times, but she's not up for talking."

"I'll go see her on the weekend," Ashlei said. "Maybe make them a meal."

"Good idea."

Elisa pulled out her phone and began to note all of the sights, sounds and smells that made her feel welcomed in this place.

"What are you doing?" Ashlei asked.

"Notes."

"Are you still doing that?"

"Careful, or you will end up in one of my books in a not-so-flattering light."

"I didn't say anything negative about it, I actually think it's a great idea and pretty cool that you still do that."

Claude returned to the table with enough food on his plate to feed four. The women noticed and smirked, but said nothing.

"So, Elisa, what do you think of our facility?"

"Well, so far, the cafeteria is my favorite sector. Aside from security, that was actually the best part of my visit thus far," she said sarcastically.

He chuckled. "Yeah, they're pretty thorough. For good reason, though. There's a lot of research that goes on here, and since we're not a closed facility, there needs to be safety measures put in place making sure none of that is compromised."

"Yeah, I get it. I was just a little thrown off."

"Still, it's pretty light compared to other government facilities," he added.

The Orbis news conference replayed in the background on a distant screen.

Elisa huffed, "I call bullshit! I'm not buying that answer." The others turned to see what she was responding to.

"Did you hear the news conference the other day?" She didn't give them a chance to answer. "An anomaly! A hiccup in our genetic material! They either haven't done their homework or they're not telling us exactly what they figured out. They're not telling us everything—they never do."

"The government have a lot of resources at their disposal, I'm sure every avenue was investigated," Claude said.

"I have some theories about that."

Claude sat back and listened, while Ashlei thought this was not how she wanted lunch to go.

"What if the nutriment serum was tweaking expiration dates? I mean I understand the serum is made up of nutrients that are supposed to be good for us. But, since the beginning, when women were first injected with nutriment, has anyone looked into whether something has changed in our genetic makeup because of the formula? And before you say I'm reaching," she said, restating Jack's response, "I'm just saying, has anyone looked that deep into it? It seems as though Orbis didn't spend much time investigating. Or, maybe the serum's been infected with a virus."

"I can tell you we haven't had any complications at the Nutriment facility."

"In Washington?"

"Yes."

"Can you give a tour of the nutriment plant?" Ashlei narrowed her eyes at Elisa.

She ignored her.

"It doesn't work like that. We don't do tours, but with your being in the medical field, I could probably pull some strings to get you a first-hand look at the way things are done—maybe ease your mind."

"Hello," a shaky voice came from behind them.

Claude turned with an incredulous look and slowly greeted Mike. "Hello," Ashlei followed, quickly glancing at Claude.

She introduced Mike to Elisa while he positioned himself at the table next to Claude, uninvited.

His plate was just as full as Claude's, which surprised Ashlei, because with his small frame, she didn't picture him as a huge eater. Though it was filled primarily with vegetables and fruit.

"Mike, didn't think I'd be seeing you so soon," Claude said.

"I heard you mention you were going to the cafeteria after the meeting, so I thought when I finished up, I'd join you. I didn't realize you would have company."

Ashlei and Elisa exchanged glances, continuing to eat their lunch.

In the meeting, Claude noticed Mike's usual attire of khaki pants and button up shirt had been replaced with out of character jeans and a polo, so he figured he'd use that to break up the awkward moment. "Golfing today?" he joked, assuming that Mike wasn't a golfer.

Rubbing the back of his neck, Mike smiled, appreciating his joke. "No, just thought I'd change it up a bit and dress down today."

He glanced around the cafeteria, fidgeting with the carrots on his plate. "The food looks good here, I don't really get up here much." He turned to Ashlei. "I hear from Claude that you are doing exceptional work on VM9. He said he had high expectations of you from the start and that you have met everyone."

"Thank you, Mike," Ashlei said, blushing. She glanced at Claude. "And thank you too." She addressed Mike again. "I am learning so much, having the opportunity to work on this project."

"Hear you've had some good insight as well. Keep up the good work."

"I will, thank you."

Ashlei didn't recall him ever dressing down. Though, occasionally he got crazy with the colors of his button-up collared shirts, sporting a yellow, blue, or green instead of his usual white or gray. Still, he was very predictable in his routine. At five minutes after eight, he was usually walking down the hall with black coffee in his white mug on the days he came to join Claude and her in the west wing lab. He said his hellos, activated his VCC and then went to the shelf and chose a binder to work on. He sat at his desk and usually didn't say a word until he left.

Resting his chin on his hands, Mike revealed a tattoo peeking out from the edge of his sleeve that she couldn't make out. *So, Mike has a little bad ass in him!*

He addressed Elisa. "Are you as smart as your sister or have you chosen some other walk of life?"

Elisa sat back.

"I've chosen some other walk of life. I chose to save lives!"

"I see."

Wow, not sure whether to consider that a compliment of my sister's intelligence or be shocked that you completely offended a total stranger without the bat of an eye!

For several moments of awkward silence, the four pushed their food around their plates.

"Don't you think that there are enough lives on the planet without us saving them *all*?" he asked her.

She hesitated, waiting for him to chuckle at his own absurd comment, but nothing followed.

"I don't even know what to say to that," Elisa responded. "You would rather we didn't save lives?"

"I think we need to be socially conscious of the consequences of our actions."

"Actions? What actions? Saving lives?" She sat forward, her tone sharpened.

"Well, yes. The world is saturated with so many people that it is difficult for us to comprehend or remember the amount of consumption by each individual during one's lifetime. It will be only a matter of years before we are depleting our resources again."

Elisa consciously contained herself in her seat. "I'm confused— aren't you a scientist? Don't you work for a company which is based on discovering new ways to improve well-being and make life easier?"

"We do, actually," Claude interjected, glaring at Mike. "That is exactly what this company, our profession, and our research are about. We are always looking to discover new ways to improve humanity." He switched his sights to Elisa.

"I think sometimes in our quest to save the world, in the way we feel is just, we may not relay our intentions the way most may consider reasonable."

Mike cut back in, hand extended toward her. "Young lady, are you aware that only a short time ago, our planet was on the verge of extinction because there were *too* many people exhausting every possible raw material they could scavenge? I don't blame you of course, you cannot possibly appreciate the vast devastation the thoughtless acts of the many have brought and will bring. Consider no more natural resources: fresh water, fuel, minerals, AIR!"

Elisa felt the hairs on the back of her neck stand up. "I'm well aware of our history, but it seems extreme to want to annihilate everyone on the planet!"

He chuckled. "I'm certainly not suggesting we annihilate everyone on the planet, but we're only beginning to recover from the devastation still seen only seventy-five to a hundred years ago. We are not seeing fast enough results. And yes, while scientists," he glanced at Claude, "are making great strides to find ways to improve the quality of life, I have to wonder if we aren't digging a deeper hole to jump in. Radical change requires radical solutions."

"There are other ways to assure the continued existence of the human race rather than simply writing them off and not trying to help them." She squinted her eyes at him. "How about I'll keep doing my job, helping to save lives and the scientists," she waved her hands at Mike and Claude, "can find a way to do theirs and sustain them!"

Mike took his cue that he had said too much, stood, and said his goodbyes. "Hope to see you again, young lady." He nodded. "Claude, Ashlei." And walked away with his tray.

His polo sleeve slightly rose and Ashlei made out his tattoo: Restituere.

"Well, it's been an enlightening half hour," Elisa stated to no one in particular.

"Not sure which is making me nauseous, this salad or his demeanor, but I need to use the restroom," Ashlei said, as she dashed off.

They both looked after her, concerned.

Elisa returned to Claude. "Is he always such an asshole?"

"Yup, that about sums it up." He shoveled a forkful of steak in his mouth.

When his mouth was empty, he added, "He's a really smart asshole though. I tolerate him while I need to. We all do." He waved his hand slightly to include the entire cafeteria of employees.

Ashlei returned to the table looking flush. "You okay?" Elisa asked.

"Yeah, you don't look good, babe."

Ashlei fought a smile through her nausea, *he called me babe.*

"I'll be fine, stomach bug or something."

"You should have gone with the steak," Elisa joked.

- 36 -

Mike stood over Claude's desk, flipping the small gold storage device between his fingers, not sure if he had done the right thing. He didn't know what was on the disk and didn't want to know, but he had his suspicions. It had been weeks since John instructed him to upload the file, but he wasn't comfortable involving anyone else nor was he comfortable lifting Claude's prints and passcode to break into his VCC.

Though my work with John is so very important to our future, it continues to take me further and further off my projected path.

Mike's parents had moved them from Lebanon to London, England hoping to find a better life. Growing up in an overcrowded neighborhood in the city, they found the same struggle people faced everywhere: overcrowding, poverty, hunger, and lack of opportunity. Mike, an only child, had very few friends and spent most of his time in his family's one-room flat reading. Outside of his books, he enjoyed caring for the vegetables they were able to grow. At that time, each family was allotted a five-foot by five-foot patch of earth. This was a prized possession and needed to be kept inside the family home—functioning land was rare. Most families only had the food they grew, usually fruits and vegetables, since meat was inaccessible due to lack of land and theft. Livestock was under the control of the government, as was most everything at that time. Mike had his first piece of meat at Harvard with his professor—

he was sick for two days. He watched his mother cross-pollinate fruit and vegetables to create something new, maintaining variety. He became enthralled with this mutation process, which was where his fascination with genetics originated. He dove in to create his own "Frankensteins," as he would call them. Most failed when he started, but he was persistent and became successful, eventually selling his creations at the local markets and on the streets. Taking the academics test earlier than most, and with his almost perfect score, he won a scholarship to Harvard University, where he studied human and plant genetic modification, broadening his scope to entail the human genome. His goal was to try and mutate vegetation to find a solution to feed those who were malnourished and create a more sensible way of life.

The door to the lab opened and Mike quickly stepped away and returned to his own workstation, realizing the blue beam had only just receded back down into the silver disk on Claude's desk.

"Done with lunch and assisting with saving the world already?" he asked Ashlei.

"Well, I don't want to anger the boss by extending lunch too long."

She narrowed her eyes, observing a blue flash on Claude's desk and then nothing.

Mike took a huge gulp of water, picked his bag up and headed toward the door, brushing past Ashlei. Hand on the door handle, he paused and turned toward her.

"You and Claude have been spending a lot of time together."

Slowly pulling the sleeve to her lab coat on, she redirected her attention to him. "Of course, we work long hours."

"Do you think that maybe you should spend some time away? You know, get a break from each other."

She pulled her head back.

"Just to let you know, it is frowned upon here at Exylon for employees to fraternize with each other outside of this facility."

"People can't hang out together when not at work?"

"Dating, Ashlei, dating is frowned upon."

Standing tall, she crossed her arms. "Well, with all due respect, my personal life is my personal life."

He opened the door and without looking back said, "Miss Quinn, my business is not only plants, but women too, their maternal cycles. You may want to get yourself tested." And he closed the door behind him.

The blood rushed from her face. "How can he…" She shuddered at the thought of him in her personal realm and then covered her mouth.

The nausea, the running to the bathroom… What if Claude noticed too? No, he would say something—wouldn't he? I need to find out. She called her doctor's office and made an appointment, but not before calling Elisa and making plans to meet later.

- 37 -

Elisa saw Ashlei right away, sitting at one of the cafe tables against the wall when she walked into the Vintage House. She recalled a few visits with her coworkers for Tuesday night specials, buy pretty much any drink get one free, and that was a deal she couldn't refuse.

"Hi E. I took the liberty of ordering you white wine," Ashlei said, sipping her water.

"Thanks." She hung her bag on the back of the chair. "You okay? You still look kind of piqued."

"Yeah, stomach bug or something. I think there's something going around."

"No, there's nothing going around. Ash, are you pregnant?" Ashlei's expression didn't not change.

"So, I assume you've suspected this?"

"I don't know. I guess I've been in denial and afraid to find out." "Ash, this is a big deal. You have to find out! Make an appointment, I'll go with you, okay?"

"Actually, made one earlier today."

"This isn't what you wanted to talk to me about though, is it?"

"No. I need to bounce something off you—get your advice. When I returned to the lab after lunch, I walked in on Mike hovering around Claude's workstation. The VCC disk at Claude's desk was illuminated for a moment like it had just shut down, which meant that Mike was probably on it. I'm not sure what else Claude is working on because when I've brought up the subject in the past, he didn't volunteer any information, so I didn't press it. But he's been working really hard on something that is clearly very important to him and I'm afraid that Mike, being the creep that he is, may be stealing his information or sabotaging it or something." She took a breath and a sip of water and continued.

"Back story—Mike doesn't appreciate Claude and is condescending when dealing with him. I don't understand what his problem is with him, but I don't trust him."

"I met the guy, remember. I just think he's arrogant, misguided, and self-absorbed, AKA asshole." She sipped her wine.

"So, why don't you go to Claude with this?"

"I feel he'd think I was being silly or ridiculous and I don't want to be wrong and make us both look like idiots confronting Mike."

"I think you're going to need to talk to Claude. You can't let it go, right? Go with your gut."

"Well… " She gave a mischievous look. "I'd been thinking that I could look into Mike's VCC and see if there's anything relating to Claude's work on there. I mean if he's stealing something, he'd need to put it somewhere, like his own VCC. And if I'm right I can tell Claude and if I'm wrong—no harm, no foul."

Elisa was baffled. "Number one, you don't know what Claude's working on to recognize it. Number two, I'm pretty sure that will get you fired if you get caught. And number three, do you have Mike's handprint or password to get into his VCC?"

"Come on, E, don't you recall I was able to break into all of your password protected journals!" she laughed. "I am a genius at guessing passwords!"

Elisa rolled her eyes with a grimace. "Yeah, I remember." "And his print?"

"I'll figure it out." She finished off her water. "And, I'm sure whatever it is I'm looking for will stand out. Can't hurt to browse."

"Umm, yes it can! But I can see you've made up your mind, so be careful. Next time, if you're going to solicit advice, you should take it!"

Elisa quickly added, "Oh, by the way, I wondered if there's something you can do for me. Hopefully, I'll be able to go to the nutriment plant with Claude, but I also wanted to head down to the New York City bureau and see if I could get answers there. Though I probably wouldn't be able to get through security without some sort of clearance."

"Ya know," Ashlei lowered her head and softened her tone, "I understand you wanting to know more about what's going on, but, E, this isn't going to change the fact that Jessica's gone and Shauna hasn't come back yet from her depression."

"It's not just about them anymore. We're talking about the deaths of so many! Where does it end? Another 'tweak' in our genes fifty years from now! You of all people should know where I'm coming from. You've wanted to study this stuff for years. Did you agree with the conclusion of that investigation from Orbis?"

"No, I guess not, but what're we supposed to do?"

Elisa explained her plan involving Jack and asked if she could look into the security issue with Claude.

"I mean since you're already in stealth mode, which you must get from dad, maybe you can scrounge us up a couple security tags or something." She grinned.

"I don't think it works that way, but I will look into it and only if it doesn't put Claude's job at risk."

"And by the way, this doesn't seem like a sound plan—maybe you should take your own advice."

$$-38-$$

Ashlei returned to the lab after leaving Elisa at Vintage. Just as she opened the door, she ran and gripped the trash can, taking deep breaths in and out. Though she didn't get sick, she brought the basket with her to keep nearby.

She dropped her purse and keys on her desk and made her way over to Mike's desk, watching the door the whole time.

"This is probably a bad idea," she said to herself.

Normally, an action like this would cause her to worry about getting fired, but there was something about Mike that made her think her punishment may be a bit more extreme.

Using a trick she saw in an old movie, she ripped a wide piece of tape off the roll and wrapped it around the glass Mike had left on his desk earlier. *This will be amazing if it works!* Slowly pulling it back off the glass, she placed it on the silver disk on his desk and a blue ray shot up from the disk.

"Hello Mike." The Mike look-alike head greeted her. Ashlei let out a breath. "Hello, Mike," she whispered and grinned, psyching herself up for the rest of her task.

She stared at the floating yellow panel in front of her. *This is different. Okay, you are the master at this password game.* She typed, "asshole," smiling to herself. The letters, still in sequence, scattered. "Hmm." She typed again. "Vegetation," "Exylon," "VM9". *Why are they scattering? E's right, what are you even doing, it can be anything, in any variation!* She glanced at the door every couple of minutes. This was the night Mike needed to stay late to attend the monthly corporate meeting. It usually took a couple of hours, but she thought, this would be that one time they got everything worked out in a half an hour. *Perhaps.* She held her breath and typed. "Restituere." The letters scattered. *Damn.* She let her breath out, stopped and stared at the yellow panel again, for what seemed like forever. *Why aren't the letters staying in sequence?* Her leg bobbed incessantly, but it wasn't something she was in control of. She thought of Claude tapping his pen. She stared some more. She glanced at the door and could feel her opportunity fading away. Her leg bobbed. She tapped her finger on the desk. Think. *They're not in sequence, because you're doing something wrong, genius. Mike is a little different, a bit odd. So, it's fair to say he does odd things. Like have an unusual way to access his computer.* A smile rushed across her face. *This is not password activated.* She recalled in disgust how Mike would lick his thumb, before typing in his password, like someone would do before turning a page, but he wasn't typing in a password at all, he was using his saliva. It's his DNA!

"Gross and weird, but clever!" She slumped back and flung her hands in the air. "I'm done!" She started to get up. "Unless… " Ashlei picked up the same glass she retrieved Mike's print from and looked around the rim, scrunching her face in disgust at the mark his lips left.

She pressed it against the yellow panel. Nothing. She swiped it several times. Nothing. She rolled it slowly back and forth: a full screen appeared in front of her. "Bingo!" she whispered triumphantly, rapidly scanning through all of his icons looking for something that may connect him with Claude. She went to "files" and found a folder that read "Restituere." Curious, she started there. It appeared to be a contact list.

Cuba: Yanet Fernandez, PhD.—Lead geneticist. Ambrose Technologies. Avenida 21 yO, Miramar Plaza, Ciudad de la Habana, Cuba Zona Postal; 10400. ph- 0111+53+7 848 7896

Guyana: Yannick Persauds, PhD. MD—United Medical Center. 1207 Brickdam, Georgetown, Guyana. Ph-592-383-7998

Somalia: Aaden Tahiil Gulêtt, PhD—Lead geneticist. Banadir Hospital. P.O. Box 6524 Mogadiscio ph:(525 1) 86 21

South Korea: Kim Hanja, PhD. MD—Bioinformatics Research Scientist. Seoul Technologies Sajik-ro-5-54 Jongno-gu, Seoul 30174 (South Korea) ph-+850 2 18111

Afghanistan: Aryo Zubair, MD—Biomedical Science. District No. 10 Zone 44, Road Mark Jeem House No. 58 P.O. Box 636 Kaboul ph-+93 67 512 0098

Yemen: Ahmed Khouri Al Qurashi Tamim, PhD. MD—Pivotal Systems/Biomedical Research Lab P.O. Box 16609 Sana'a Republic of Yemen 01-610-567/280/281 ph- +967-1-776-632

Ethiopia: Ebo Neigusse, PhD. MD—ABABA INNOVASION K. 4 W.67 house no 546 1000 lADDIS ABABA ETHIOPIA ph-+251 91 456 7685

United States of America:
Boroughs of NYC:

Veronica VanHuesen, PhD. MD—PRODIGY Medical, Inc. 64 W Broadway, New York City, NY 10013 ph- (212) 675-5676 Mike Khoury, PhD. MD—Exylon Pharmacuticals Corporation Rte 9 and 20 Albany, NY 10671 cell (518) 546-5623

She illuminated her band, put it up to the list and took a picture, then continued to go through the list of folders. "Bureau, plant configurations, budget, VM9… Ashlei Quinn." Her heart raced. Everything else faded away when she pulled the file forward; she looked up at the door and then back at the information in front of her. *My profile of demographic information, education, and resume. Why does he have information about my family? My parents, Elisa, their occupations, and addresses?* She pushed her file to the background and all the other files reappeared. Claude Monark. She opened the file. *Claude's personal information.* She pushed the file back. *As well as other employees' demographic files.* The lump in her throat faded, feeling a little relieved that she wasn't singled out.

Ashlei continued on and pulled forward the Documents file, coming across a folder simply labeled "Restore." "Or Restituere," she mouthed.

She froze when she heard loud voices outside the door, which faded as their owners moved away.

Mike's unopened blinking emails drew her attention. Refocusing, she pulled forward "emails" careful not to open the unopened ones. Paging down the list, not completely sure what she was looking for, an email dated seven months prior caught her eye. She recognized some of the same names from the contact list she'd just opened a few moments ago. She clicked on the email and read.

Fellow Restituere members:

Per our last gathering, duties and responsibilities have been assigned to those who are able to participate in operation "Restore."

We have been given a gift. An opportunity to create a world as it was before—better! Each and every one of you, whether you have a direct part in Restore or not, are a great asset to Restituere. You carry on our mission—our message, so that others, like us, will eventually see the greater good. Our brilliant physicist/geologist, John, will be overseeing "Restore" along with Mike, Krish, and myself of course. We have created a contact list of who is to receive each shipment.

I know we speculated briefly about to whom and where these shipments will be dispersed and you have each given a list of who you personally think should receive them. We are taking all options into serious consideration. But keep in mind, we are not heartless. We are not in this for our own personal agenda. Do not forget Restituere's beliefs! That we should reclaim a world of purity. One where the strong minded shall endure to create and further our species development. To help those who are a benefit to our society. To support those who help our world thrive and grow.

We only eliminate the opportunity for the weak and diseased to fester and continue to contaminate our planet. Those who, though not always through fault of their own, pollute our world and utilize resources needed for the few who are to evolve and advance our people. Now, thanks to the insight of John, we have an invaluable opportunity to do just this through the technology already at hand. This is all for now, there will be further updates as we learn of further developments. It is our destiny for our intention to be realized. Transcendent em illume!

*Regards, Mr. P - *R**

Transcendent em illume? Huh, and what does the 'R' stand for, a symbol for Restituere?

She glanced up at the door again, getting increasingly paranoid and queasy; she snapped pictures of the email and discontinued her connection. She took the first good breath she'd taken since opening and invading his virtual computer. Grabbing her belongings, she headed out the door.

~

"Did you get in?"

"Of course I did," Ashlei answered.

"Did you find anything?" Elisa asked.

"Nothing about Claude's projects, but I did find this." She followed Elisa into her kitchen and showed her the photo she took of the email. "Mike is in some sort of club or something, called Restituere, that's Latin for restore. I noticed a tattoo of the same name on his arm at lunch."

"What kind of club do you think this is?" she asked, reading the text.

"Not really sure, but they talked about restoring the planet to 'the way it was' as it says. I wonder if he means before the Transitional War; perhaps utilizing VM9?"

"Wouldn't Claude be involved in that?"

"No," Ashlei scrunched her face up. "You would most likely never see them engaged in anything together outside of work."

She pointed out, "See how he goes on to talk about the weak and diseased festering and contaminating the planet? Right in line with Mike's attitude—not something Claude would ever be a part of."

"Hard to believe there are more people out there that think like that," Elisa said.

Transcendent em illume. "If I recall that means to make greater or surpass. Something like that," Ashlei said.

"I wonder if the shipment and addresses are maybe set up to try to recruit more pathetic followers by sending out pamphlets or something," Elisa speculated.

"Well, I just stopped by to give you that info, I'm on my way to Claude's. I'm gonna to talk to him about all this when he gets back from New York."

"Okay, see ya later."

- 39 -

For weeks, preparing his report, Claude feared John and the BPCS executives and geneticists wouldn't take him seriously, and he was right. He had a two-hour drive back home to run it through in his head, trying to figure out what he should have done differently. He stood before them in the conference room to discuss his revelation about the evolution of expiration dates. He laid out everything he had been working on over the last two years—the research, the field studies, the calculations, and the facts.

"A mutation or variation of expiration dates is prominent in several generations of injections, simulating or replicating the parent's expiration date," he informed them.

John shuffled the papers that Claude had presented containing his facts and statistics around on the conference table.

"Claude, I don't think a random study in these remote areas can really determine a shift in the genetic makeup generated by expiration dates. I think you're reaching here."

"I stand by my data, sir. This is not random. This is a developing issue that I think is going to escalate if we don't investigate and address it."

"What do you suppose we do, stop the injections?" a BPCS exec chuckled, looking around for support.

Claude stepped forward, "If that's what it takes."

The exec's lips tightened. "Look here junior, you are embarking on a road you may want to reconsider traveling. Expiration dates are what keeps us all sustained."

"Are they though?" Claude interrupted. "There are potentially other ways to tap into resources, some we've looked at, some we haven't."

An older geneticist, arms crossed, asked, "Such as?"

"Such as our oceans."

"Young man," an exec sighed and sat forward, "don't you think that avenue has been ventured? Many years before you were born. You are not the first to theorize numerous ways to find additional resources. It's been tried and failed."

"Exactly, many years before I was born! It's been tried by traditional methods and failed and thought impossible. But there are other ways to skin a cat and I've figured out a few."

The first BPCS exec to speak stood. "Okay well, I think we're done here."

The rest of the group stood and follow behind.

John put his hand on Claude's shoulder. "I like your enthusiasm, keep it up."

~

Claude couldn't think of anything better than to come home from the bureau and find Ashlei waiting in his bed. She stirred when he turned on the lights.

"Well, this is a nice welcome home," he said.

"Did you just get in?" She turned toward him and stretched.

"Yup." He stripped down to his underwear and climbed in next to her. "How was your meeting?"

"Not sure, my boss wasn't exactly impressed with my report. I'm going to go above him and report to the Executive Officer in Washington D.C. You can tell Elisa she can come with me. I'll have some of the pharmacists there answer any questions for her."

"Are you sure?"

"It's fine. If it's gonna help her to heal, I'm happy to help."

She slipped behind him, positioning herself to rub his shoulders. "Listen, I know you think that Mike is just a jerk and that I shouldn't concern myself with him, but after lunch, when I returned to the lab, he seemed on edge and he was suspiciously moving away from your VCC."

She conveniently omitted the conversation about his suspicions of her possible pregnancy.

"He looked even more nervous than his usual awkward self. I was afraid that he may have been trying to, I don't know," she speculated, "steal what you've been working on or maybe even sabotage it."

"Why would you think he'd want to do that?" Claude eyes were closed, his neck sinking into Ashlei's soft hands.

"What other reason would he have for being on your VCC? He seemed to be resentful of you working on VM9. He clearly has unsubstantiated issues with you! Maybe I'm grasping, but I know what I saw."

"Why didn't you mention this to me earlier?"

"You were busy in New York and I thought you might have thought I was being overly paranoid. Soo... I... got into *his* VCC." He pulled away and turned to look at her. "And looked around to see if I could find something," she continued, she held her breath, waiting for the backlash.

"Seriously?!" he paused. "And what did you find?"

Still unsure if he was angry, she told him of the email and contact list she found. "It appears that Mike is involved in a club or association of some sort. The email talked of an Operation Restore, have you ever heard of it before?"

Claude shook his head.

"It's affiliated with a group called Restituere. In any case, it was a very uncomfortable read. Mr. P, the author of the email, seemed to have the same disturbing concepts as Mike. I'm assuming that goes as well for the rest of the recipients."

"As far as... ?"

"As far as his superior "godlike" complex that he feels gives him the right to berate others! It goes beyond that though. There's something eerie about the way he projected his opinion."

Hesitant to let Ashlei know that he didn't trust Mike either, Claude didn't tell her about the boxes with the vials or what he found inside them. Not yet.

Not until he learned more.

"I think maybe you're reading too much into this. He's a little different, but I think Mike's harmless."

Ashlei grimaced and leaned back against the wall.

After a moment of silence, Claude asked, "Find what you were looking for? Anything associated with me?"

"No. Just our resume info."

"So maybe he just happened to be just standing by my computer."

"I don't think so, your VCC disk was illuminated for a moment when I just walked into the lab and he had just walked away."

"I see."

"Something just didn't feel right." She defended her intuition.

His face softened. "Ha, crazy girl." He grinned. "You would do well in espionage."

Ashlei decided to let it go for now and cuddled beside him when something caught her eye.

In his peripheral vision Claude could see her reach toward his ear and he pulled away. "What're you doing, Ash? Do I have a pimple or something?"

She pulled him close again. "No, come here, you have something in your ear. It could be a bug or something, let me save you!" She teased.

"Oh," he chuckled, "that's not a bug. That's my security clearance to get into the bureau. "He reached up and extracted it from his ear, placing it on the nightstand.

She pulled her head back, eyebrows raised. "First of all, that is a very cool security tag and second of all, why would you need that kind of security at the Bureau of Population Control and Statistics?"

He casually answered, "It's a government agency. Most federal buildings require some sort of security."

"Exylon is a government-run facility, we don't have that kind of cool security."

"Exylon doesn't hold government secrets," he teased.

"Ahh, of course, the lower end of the government spectrum. How do you even get that in there?" She tried to probe his ear. "Is that like a bar code?"

"I actually do it myself using a code gun." Ashlei winced.

"It's not painful. Actually, it tickles a little. I can feel it in my nose when I do it, usually makes me sneeze."

"Do you have a number or something that identifies you?"

"Not a number, but everyone has a special code linked to a blood sample."

Again, she raised her eyebrows.

"Trust me, in the government, that's not as weird as it sounds."

"So, are your codes all loaded in the gun?"

"No, I load it, but I'm only given three at a time. I have a couple more visits to a bureau office before I need to refuel."

"Are they only good for your agency in New York?"

"No, but *I* am limited."

"That's pretty high-tech stuff."

"Does that turn you on? Because I can produce many other high-tech gadgets if you're interested." He pulled her down and kissed her.

- 40 -

REED'S OFFICE DOOR WAS AJAR, so Elisa gently knocked and pushed it open. He got up from his chair and walked around to the front of his desk.

He smiled warmly at her. "Hi there, in my neck of the woods again I see."

"Hey yeah, I actually wanted to ask you about something." She paused and Reed sat back against his desk ready to listen.

"I guess I'm grasping, but as an administrator of the nutriment injections, I thought… maybe you had some thoughts about what's going on that could potentially explain these deaths. I'd been thinking that maybe contamination or a virus could be a potential factor?"

"Jack came to me with that same question." He crossed his arms and gave her a sympathetic look.

"Elisa, I am so very sorry about what happened with your cousin's baby, but it was her date—like any other. Trying to search for a reason is only going to drive you crazy."

"I understand that, but with what's going on with the rash of deaths, I thought that I could try and figure some stuff out for myself."

"I'm not completely sure there is anything to figure out. There's a bunch of random clusters of deaths and everyone is getting excited." Recognizing his callous tone, he softened his approach. "Don't think me insensitive, I'm just as disturbed as you, but I've seen a lot of things over the years that have come and gone that just don't make sense and I don't think this is any different."

He stared at her for a moment and sighed. "Listen, when I was a kid, about nine or ten, there was an underground tunnel I used to play in that ran from my family home out onto the neighbor's property. I kept going through it even though my mother banned me from playing in there. One day there was a torrential rain causing a flash flood and water filled the tunnel quickly from the nearby creek. I barely made it out and my mother made my father block it off. Point is, for lack of a better phrase, you're going to drown yourself if you keep going down that road, or tunnel, whatever—block it off! With… whatever you need to block it off with—you're going to make yourself sick."

"That was an awful analogy."

"It's all I had." He chuckled and moved in next to her, gently squeezing her arm, his button up shirt clinging just enough to reveal his chest muscles. He stood so closely she could see the soft freckles that faded into the background of his cheeks. *My god, he smells so good.* The flutters in her stomach were overwhelming, a sensation she'd become accustomed to when he was around. She gazed into his pale blue eyes and gravitated to the low tone in his voice.

"We've probably seen all we're going to see and this surge will go down as, what did President West say? 'An anomaly,' like so many others in history."

Never did a sentence with the words, president, and anomaly sound so seductive, she thought.

Her heart pounding, she reached in to receive his kiss.

A resident knocked on the door, peeking his head in. They separated quickly. "Dr. Frederick, hi, sorry to interrupt, but can I ask you about the patient in Room Nine on maternity?"

"Sure." He turned to Elisa. "I'll just be a minute." And stepped out of the room.

Elisa let a deep breath out. 'Okay, that guy sucks! That was really bad timing!"

Reed and Elisa began on a friendly basis, sharing an affiliation with

Jack, but more and more they'd enjoyed quick hallway conversations, tedious hospital luncheons, and silly inside jokes outside of their Jack connection, which eventually led to secret rendezvous around the hospital and more intimate sessions at her place. She did relish the little teases they shared during their random trysts. But even when they weren't sharing intimate moments, they kept their conversations shallow. She knew as much about Reed Frederick as everyone else.

She could hear the two speaking outside the door.

"I understand your concern, Dr. Pin, but looking at the big picture, this will be better for her and her family in the long run. Maybe see what we can do to make this transition tolera…"

She backed away from the door, feeling guilty for eavesdropping. Pretending not to have heard any of his conversation, Elisa reached up to look a little closer at a photo on the wall of Reed and a couple of other men on what looked to be a golf course, knocking his satchel to the floor. Embarrassed, she quickly gathered the contents, shoving them back in the bag, and replaced it on the desk, pushing a cluster of nutriment injection packages against the back. Without giving it a second thought, she didn't hesitate to slit the side of one of the packages, grab the vial, and replace the package as if still unopened. Nervously looking back at the door, she dropped the vial on the floor, quickly picked it up and pocketed it. She met Reed at the door on his return.

"I can see you're busy." Her heart was beating so fast she had to take in a deep breath—disguising it as sorrow. "You know you're right, I'm having a hard time getting over her death. I'm just trying to find some sort of closure, I guess. I'll talk to you later."

"Okay, well, any time you feel like you want to talk about it, I'm here."

"Thanks." Walking away, she turned and gave him warm smile.

- 41 -

Ashlei entered the foyer of her small one-bedroom apartment, located not far from Exylon. Unlike Claude's apartment, everything was neat and orderly, nothing was out of place—the way she liked it. However, since spending so much time with Claude at his place, it no longer felt like home to her. It lacked the subtle scent of Claude's sweet sweat that stayed in her nostrils after being with him, and the warm sensation that swirled around her stomach when she entered his place. She plopped a packet full of information down, scattering the contents on the small round table in front of the sofa, sat down, and pulled her feet up.

I'm not exactly sure what I'm supposed to feel, she thought, exhaling. Currently, the feeling was nausea. She brought her knees to her chest, wrapping her arms around them. Sprawled across the table was the sheet with her next appointment on it, a pamphlet that read "Now that you're expecting, what next?" and another explaining the nutriment injections with ultrasound that were to follow. Sitting on top of all of them, staring back at her, was the paper with her due date on it.

Her face softened a bit and she smiled at the notion, but that was immediately followed by a nervous chill. *How will I tell Claude?*

- 42 -

Elisa practically ran to the cardiology clinic attached to the hospital, where Jack was currently seeing patients.

"Hi, Shelly," she greeted his scheduling coordinator. "Is he with a patient?"

"Yes, he is."

"Mind if I wait?"

"Be my guest. You can wait along with the other seven people waiting to see him." She motioned to all his patients in the room.

Elisa waited impatiently.

Jack made it a practice never to look at the expiration date of his patients, a condition he made clear to all new patients. He wanted no predetermined outcomes or expectations when he was working on someone's heart.

"So, Mr. Davis, we'll see you same time next year," Jack said, making a notation in his chart.

"Oh—nooo, doc!" the seventy-seven-year-old said, exaggerating his words. "This day next year is my expiration date. You're not getting your hands on me that day, buster. Maybe I'll see you in six months or maybe not at all. I mean, you got me this far and I thank you for that, but with any luck, I'll be in Bermuda this time next year," he said this with an acceptance that Jack admired.

"Mr. Davis, it has truly been a pleasure." took his hand in the kind of shake he would extend to an old friend.

Mr. Davis was one of Jack's favorite patients. For the last six years he'd had the pleasure of treating this gracious man who, in spite of serous stent procedures, painful disfiguration of his hands, and family tragedy, stood tall, always an optimist; he was the kind of man you liked right away. He carried himself with dignity and class and had nothing but good things to say about the staff, from the physicians to the house-keepers. And he'd never left the office without telling a humorous story.

"Pleasure's all mine doc," he said, returning the hand shake.

"Okay ready, last one," Mr. Davis announced. Jack stood, arms crossed, leaning against the exam table, while Mr. Davis stood by the door. He nodded in anticipation.

"So, I'm talking with a lawyer friend of mine who had taken on this case from a woman that was up against the company that makes those chairs." He snapped his fingers in Jack's direction. "You know the one—that makes the chair that gradually elevate us old folks into a standing position."

Jack, smiling, shook his head no.

Mr. Davis hastily went on with his story. "Well anyway, he was representing her because she claimed that—Netco!" he yelped, startling Jack. "Netco, that's the name of the company. Netco! What a stupid name for a medical equipment company. Sounds more like a candy company if you ask me. Anyway," he continued, "she claimed that she pushed the button and the chair didn't go up. She pushed it again and nothing. She pushed continuously and then zoom." He slapped his hands together and slid one up to the air as if he just launched a plane. "She's catapulted across the room like a rocket." He roared and slapped one hand on his knee. Jack couldn't help but laugh, picturing this poor lady go flying across the room. He remembered the chair now. He'd seen the commercials and remembered thinking, *I know it's mean, but wouldn't it be funny if they were just launched across the room.* He couldn't believe it actually happened.

"Is this a true story, Mr. Davis?" he asked, catching his breath.

"Absolutely! My friend said the company examined the chair and then replied to him, 'It's impossible for that to happen.' So, my friend said to them, *"Come on, you mean to tell me that that eighty-year-old lady broke her hip doing calisthenics?"* Needless to say, they settled." Mr. Davis opened the door and turned to walk out; Jack placed his hand on his shoulder.

"Thank you, I will certainly miss your stories." He was still chuckling.

His patient lingered in the doorway. "We've eradicated deadly diseases, we can regenerate limbs like flatworms, systematically detect a problem before it's a problem." He flicked his right upper chest where his life monitor was implanted. "But yet, you manage to keep yourself a job."

"Ha, well, the body is not perfect. The heart is still a muscle—muscles get used—used things wear down. Though we have definitely come a long way, I think I'll always have a job."

"Good, we need good people like you looking after us!"

"Enjoy Bermuda, Mr. Davis." Jack waved as he started walking down the hall.

"It's George, doc," he called back without turning. "You've been calling me Mr. Davis for six years, it's just George."

Jack found Elisa in the waiting room and waved her back to his office.

"Hmm. You've rearranged your credentials on the wall. I like it!" She waved her finger around at his display of degrees from the Hellman Center and Tufts University.

"To what do I owe this visit?"

Hesitantly, she informed him of how she obtained the nutriment bottle from Reed's office.

"Um, I'm not sure I want to be an accomplice to your felony."

"What crime, I picked it up off the floor? I thought it was garbage, looked for a wastebasket to toss it, couldn't find one so I've held onto it until I do."

His dumbfounded expression said it all to her.

"I thought maybe you'd have access to a lab where we could run our own test on it."

"I don't know how to do that! Isn't that something your sister can do at her lab? She's more of an expert in that field anyway," he suggested.

"You're right, I don't know why I didn't think of her first."

"Don't you think he's going to miss that vial when he opens the package at his next appointment?"

"Maybe. Probably. But I'm sure he gets damaged packaging all the time, and it could have fallen out of said damaged package easily enough. If I hadn't seen it fall, he'd still be missing it."

"Wow, you're good."

She smiled slyly.

He stood to walk back out with her and sighed. "You're not gonna let it go, so yeah, take it to Ashlei and see what she says, if only to eliminate that option. All of this stuff in the news, these deaths, speculations, have been sitting on my mind too. It's unnerving to know that any child, at any time can be born with an immediate expiration date. The roulette of our dates is tough enough, but when those odds are raised…" He paused. "The implications aren't just losing a precious child so soon, we're talking about the fear and anguish of new parents, expectant parents, and families who feel helpless and wonder, 'is this our new reality?'"

"I'm sure, much like the first expiration dates," Elisa added.

"Parents who are defending their young can be like caged animals. If an answer isn't found soon, who knows what will follow."

She waited.

"I guess like you, I don't want to just sit and do nothing. Not sure what we can possibly find out, but we'll feel better trying, right? I'll go with you to Ashlei's and see if she finds anything, okay?"

Elisa wasn't sure Jack would ever feel better, but she had a suspicion that he was doing this for Peter and Miranda.

She called Ashlei on the way out, then called Jack.

"She can't let us in the lab while Mike's there, she'll meet you at Exylon first thing in the morning. Your first procedure is at eight-thirty, so be there at seven."

"Me?"

"Yeah, Claude's taking a last-minute trip to Washington tomorrow and said I can come along. I already switched my shifts around and got someone to cover me. Thanks, Jack."

- 43 -

Turning away from the small airplane window, Elisa nudged Claude's shoulder with hers. "Feels like a fieldtrip. Thanks for bringing me along."

"Yeah, just don't be that one kid who always throws up."

"That's why we left Ashlei home," she joked.

She startled when the engines roared.

"Who are these other people?" she whispered.

Three other people dressed in business attire were spread about the eight-seater plane.

"People who have quick business at the plant, like me. Most of the time federal employees, but once in a while, outside physicians, pharmacists, some lay people—like you. Sometimes the plane is filled and sometimes there's just five, like today. We'll be heading back about noon."

She tried to refrain from tugging on her ear, gently pulling down on her lobe to satisfy the itch. Just as Ashlei described, Claude's security tag gun had tickled her nose and she sneezed when she impressed it in her ear. She wore her hair down to keep it hidden. She had no intention of letting Claude know it was in, unless absolutely necessary. He most likely would not have approved of Ash giving it to her. However, if she were able to get away and look around without him, it might come in handy.

"I'll give you a quick rundown of how all the branches work. BPCS, being the first global organization after Orbis was formed, has not changed much since its inception. It's set up in a similar fashion in all countries with the exception of America being the only country with sister sites."

Elisa gripped the arms of her seat as the plane crept higher into the air. *Just focus on his words and not the fact that you are trapped in a metal box thousands of feet in the air!*

Claude continued, unaware of Elisa's anxiety.

"The bureau's main administrative building is housed in New York City with a sister site in Washington D.C., headed by John Vanburen, and the other in Albany, headed by Mike. Most countries' Bureaus are divided into several different divisions. There is the division that crunches numbers for keeping track of the quantities of people in the country, divided up by state, city, and borough."

Number crunchers, got it, she thought, desperately trying to focus on his words.

"These statisticians calculate how many people existed, exist, and will exist. The research center is committed to finding ways, in alliance with The Bureau of Agriculture, of balancing the food rations in each community."

A finely polished woman looked on, annoyed by the additional chatter.

"The Washington facility, the nutriment plant, AKA the division of Women's Health and Obstetrics, produce, nutriment injections, which are shipped to all the states or regions, then reallocated to the smaller sectors or cities. They are then, in turn, distributed to government clinics in accessible areas to be delivered to every woman in her fourth month of gestation. Exylon is the only exception—we study a certain amount of nutriment and distribute it as well. This division is responsible for following all pregnancies and issuing warrants to any woman who doesn't comply with their injections and follow up."

When Claude was done, they rode in silence for the remainder of the trip. Elisa was grateful to be on the ground again. She reached forward, picking up Claude's blazer from the table in front of them, slipping his access key from the pocket and then handing it to him.

"Thanks," he said.

~

They landed a half a mile away from the facility, a car hovering just outside the doors to bring them the rest of the way.

The five of them piled in and the car sped off toward the facility. They approached a sign that read, "Danger Electric Fence." The driver opened his window, allowing in a silver ball about the size of a golf ball. It scanned his left retina, then the right, and retreated.

Jack would love to see this. "Does it need to scan everyone?" she whispered.

A gate lighted up and an automated voice announced, *"Gate deactivated, it is safe to enter. You have three minutes to enter before electrification will re-activate."* The car jetted forward, the repeating announcement fading in the distance.

"No. We'll have our security tags read ahead. John should have notified the officers that you are with me and have temporary access. It pays to have friends in high places."

The group approached the military officers at the entrance.

"Private Brooks," Claude greeted him.

Private Brooks stepped forward. "Lieutenant," he said. He raised a thin gray box to Claude's ear and a green light flashed on—across the screen read "Claude Monark" accompanied by a head shot of Claude underneath.

"John Vanburen approved this site visit." Verifying their notification, Elisa showed identification and they nodded them through.

"Lieutenant! I'm impressed," she teased.

He chuckled. "Don't be, I'm glad to be out, haven't been active in a few years."

They were scanned inside the door by fluoroscopy for weapons and then went straight to the glass dome in the center of the lobby. The doors slid open as they approached.

"Here, put this on." From a panel of hooks, just inside the door, were hanging a number of blue lab jackets. He handed her one with a tag that read "Nutriment Division."

"There, now you're official."

"Fancy."

"I have to run and meet with the plant manager."

"I assumed you were taking me around."

"Monica," he pointed to an administrative assistant who hadn't noticed them, "will walk you around and I'll see about getting one of the people who handle the injections to talk with you, okay?"

"Sure. I'm good. This is great. Thanks," she said sincerely.

Monica was an older woman riddled with wrinkles. She greeted Elisa with a smile that pushed the old woman's high cheek bones up just under the rim of her very outdated glasses. She assumed she must have worked here since the plant opened, a hundred or so years ago. But that's not the first thing Elisa noticed. The numbers 5212173 ran across her forehead, just at the hair line. People like her had inherited the name "MODs"—"mark of death." Though technically, everyone carried a mark of death—their expiration date—these were the unfortunate souls who had their expiration dates displayed for all to see. On their forehead, their ear, the top of their foot. That they carried a special name at all was cruel. Fortunately, it was rare to have it exposed, but you couldn't help but feel an empathy for those who had to endure the looks of pity throughout their lifetime. Many people chose not to reveal their expiration dates. It was poor etiquette, like asking someone's age. She didn't have much longer—five years.

Monica led her to one of four halls that were behind the dome. They reminded Elisa of one of those games that challenged you to choose a path. "Where do the other halls go?"

"The middle one is where you'll find the conference rooms and the other is our store and cafeteria. Too bad you won't be here for lunch, the food is very good around here."

Monica took Elisa through to the different labs that manufactured the formula for nutriment injections and worked with the nanobytes. All behind glass windows that she got to look in.

"Can we go inside and talk to the lab assistants?" she asked.

"Well, no. They're all working, honey," Monica croaked behind her yellow tinged teeth. Elisa sighed heavily.

They watched through the glass as the lab technicians transferred nanobytes from one canister to another. Elisa thought she was going to fall asleep right then and there.

Monica gave her the history of nutriment injections. *She knows about as much about nutriment injections as me.*

"So, how do the nanobytes work in the nutriment serum?"

"Well, they are like tiny robots that are the size of a biological cell. Microscopic machines that perform certain functions within the body. They're actually used in medicine, assisting with regeneration and certain injuries among other things—and of course nutriment injections. That's all I can tell you, honey; I don't understand all the technical stuff."

Elisa could tell she'd had that speech down for years.

Another woman from the office approached quickly, citing a problem with an order.

"Oh dear. I'm sorry, Elisa, I need to handle this, do you mind hanging here for a moment while I take care of this?"

"That's fine. Actually, I'm gonna to use the bathroom."

Monica was off and not caring before Elisa finished her sentence. "O…kay then," she said to herself.

Grateful for the blue jacket that helped her to blend in, she smiled and nodded confidently at the couple of workers who briefly glanced her way as they passed. She genuinely could use the bathroom, but wanted to use her time more wisely.

Standing in front of a random door, she pulled out the flat key she'd taken from Claude, hoping since he was well known here that he'd find another way around. Still, she felt guilty. Looking around first, she stood to the side and slid the card across a small round pad on the wall. It opened onto a room full of people who immediately looked her way. She quickly backed away out of sight.

As soon as the door slid shut, she continued to walk down the hall. *I'm on limited time. Well, I'm just gonna go in one of the labs and talk to someone without permission.* Ready to enter into a lab, she noticed an elevator, tucked away in the darkness at the at the end of the hall. It read, in unmistakably large bold letters, 'Restricted'.

"Tag, you're it." *Restricted. Let's see how far you're able to go, Claude.* She swiped the pad and the doors opened. "I'm already on the Main level, so level G it is." She pushed the button, but the car sat still. *Why aren't we moving?* She held her breath, quickly second guessing her decision to snoop. Seconds felt like an hour when a small silver ball uprooted itself from a socket above the keypad and levitated toward her head. *Oh god, it needs to scan my eyeball.* It glided around to her left ear and scanned the tag.

"Claude Monark. Welcome." The elevator jerked, then descended.

She stepped out, taking in a deep breath. Looking left and right, the hallway was empty. She crept to the left where there was at least light down at the end of the hall. She stopped halfway down. This door didn't require swiping. Elisa slowly cracked it, held her breath, and looked in. She recognized the same white sterile jump suits hanging that the hospital used in the operating room, complete with a hood. There was a small window into another room. She looked through. *No one there.* Gnawing on her lower lip, she paced the small space. *This is crazy!* She stopped, gripped the door to go back out, turned and quickly put on the suit. *You won't get another opportunity!*

~

Claude reached into his pocket searching for his key card to swipe into the conference room. He pulled his blazer off, frantically looking. Woodworth Porter stepped up next to him. Embarrassed, Claude couldn't let the Executive Officer in charge of overseeing all the government facilities in this part of the country know he misplaced his key card.

"Sorry, Mr. Porter, I just need to use the rest room, I'll be back shortly."

Woodworth swiped his card, opening the door to a room of five other people, including John. "I suggest you handle that now then."

"Yes, sir."

Claude hastily made his way down the hall. "'I have to go to bathroom'—that was so stupid!" *Way to think on your feet, now you can't get in. I need to get that key, it has access to everything!*

"Dude! Claude in the D.C.!" His energetic co-worker grabbed Claude's hand in a shake.

"Hey, Miguel," Claude said, distracted. "Sorry man, I'm in kind of a hurry."

"Gotcha, another time," Miguel called after him.

Claude stopped and turned. "Actually, Miguel." He grabbed both of Miguel's shoulders. "I need a huge favor. My key pass is on the plane, Porter happened to be standing there when I couldn't get into our meeting."

"Wow, that's bad, man."

"Yeah, I know! I don't have time to run out there and get it. He and five others are waiting on me to get back there and present my material. Loan me yours?"

Miguel hesitated.

"What the hell, you've saved my ass more than once."

"Thanks, I owe you!"

"Yes, you do!" he called after him as Claude ran towards the conference room.

Claude wiped the sweat from his forehead and threw his blazer back on. He swiped in and the door slid open to the six faces in the room staring at him.

"I apologize to you all for the wait."

"All good, I trust!" Woodworth said.

"Yes, sir."

Claude glanced at John, his face stone. He jumped right in.

"In my research, while I was searching for my own way to preserve resources, I discovered that expiration dates are evolving."

Woodworth asked, "What do you mean evolving?"

"Travelling all over the world for my research, I hear all kinds of stories from the locals. One particular account that kept presenting itself was too coincidental for me to just chalk up to human interest stories. I continued to look into any other similarities in these accounts and discovered that they are much more prevalent than are known. The research I've done shows that a mutation is kicking in within several generations of injections, showing several expiration dates mimicking each parent's life span. Here," he slid his pad to the center of the table so all could see. "Let me show you."

Motioning for them to lean in to see, he began to make a chart.

"For example," he continued, "Mary Turner procreates with John to create a daughter who at an appropriate age procreates with another."

Mary Turner b. 2101—expiration date 03/5/2189

John Turner b. 2100—expiration date 08/20/2185

Daughter b. 2131—expiration 11/27/2217—86yrs expected expiration date—11/27/2217

(daughter's husband exp date 2171)

Son b. 2156—expiration date 11/27/2217—61yrs expected expiration date—8/17/2225

(son's wife exp date 2192)

Son b. 2188—expiration date 11/27/2217—29yrs expected expiration date—8/17/2248

(son's wife exp date 2254)

Daughter b. 2216—expiration date 11/27/2217—1yr expected expiration date—12/1/2301

"Notice the expiration dates of the parent compared to the child. All expiring on the same day!"

He took a breath. "They all trace back to Mary and John Turner. This has taken me all around the world over the last two years. I have found dozens of instances with familial proof of expiration dates mutating into generational mass deaths. I realized that it's not specifically a mother or father thing, it all seemed to be just familial. Children are born with their own expiration dates, but surpass or die before in accordance with their parent's expiration date. They are somehow bypassing the nanobytes' programming or the programming is being reconfigured. I don't know, I have to continue to explore this until I can figure it out. But I will say this, nature, or should I say evolution, is going to really kick our ass on this one! This can wipe out whole families! And this is only what I've begun to find out. Who knows what else these nanobytes could be doing to our DNA. In the world of evolution, this is an awful quick response to change!"

Claude received the same results he got in New York. "What would you have us do, stop the nutriment injections?" and "Keep up the good work!" Which basically meant to Claude, "We're not going to do anything about this."

He stood at the conference table as they all shuffled out of the room. John stopped.

"We're on the same team, ya know. This." He waved his hand over the table. "Going over my head. Unacceptable!" And he walked out.

Claude sat at the table, hanging his head, defeated. *Are they all so concerned over disrupting expiration dates that they are willing to do nothing?*

The door opened. "Oh, good, Mr. Monark, you're still here." Stewart entered, sashaying his way toward Claude; his bright blue suit clinging to his thin build. "I had them load some boxes on the plane that needed to go to Mr. Khoury at the Albany site. He's expecting them, but I need a release, can you sign here." He had his VCC out, illuminated invoice projected, ready to be signed.

"Sure." He sighed and looked it over. "What's this K level? Over here in the corner?

Stewart was patting the sides and top of his black, curly hair, which rose six inches toward the ceiling.

"Mr. Khoury's overseeing that research."

"K level? There's nothing down there."

"There is now, the other lab."

Claude looked up at him. "What other lab?"

"The government," he huffed. "Another classified project." He swung his hand on his hip. "Bottom-dwellers like me don't have access to anything but conference rooms. Couldn't tell ya exactly what they're doing, but word is it's classified because it has something to do with them messin' around with a nasty virus. I don't mess with them boys when they come up from down there to the lunch room. Thanks."

He shut down his VCC and left.

Should check in with Elisa, she's probably at max tolerance with Monica's nutriment stories. He looked at the time, then decided to head to the other side of the building. He took the only elevator that led to level K. It had been desolate for years, used for the medical records of all the women who had received nutriment injections when the building was constructed.

Those records had since been updated to VCC files, accessed at the tip of a finger. He'd only been down here once, rummaging for a part he insisted he could find in the old junkyard of forgotten equipment.

The elevator doors opened just outside the control room. It looked so much different now—a fully functioning lab.

White hooded jumpsuits hung on the wall, in the picture window Miguel's face lit up through the plexiglass shield in his hood. He took his gloves off and entered the control room.

"Bout time!" He playfully swatted Claude.

"You know how long Derrick worked on you to join, man. Poor sap. His own fault though, right."

"Right," Claude said, playing along.

"Anyway, I told him he should let me talk to you. You and I are cool." He tapped his shoulder again. "Put on a suit man, let's go."

Claude took his time suiting up, trying to reflect on the conversations he'd had with Derrick that meant him joining anything.

He entered the lab. Miguel had lowered the music considerably. A woman peered, alarmed, at him through her hooded shield, he recognized her from around the plant. He nodded. A man at the huge monitors turned to look as well.

"Your key. Thanks, you saved me." Claude looked around at the lab that was almost identical to the expiration date lab on Level G.

"Payback for the many times you've saved my ass, man," he said again, tapping Claude's shoulder.

"You should have let me know you were coming. Mike send you to get the lay of the land?"

"Had some business here, thought, why not kill two birds with one stone," Claude lied, trying to catch up.

"You know Jen." Her expression relaxed now. "And this is Charlie. Charlie, this is my man, Claude. The one I'd been telling you about that we wanted to get on board."

"Hey," Charlie said, uninterested, and turned back to his work.

"Well, we're just picking up the pace again, since that whole Derrick thing, but they're not interested in waiting till the news reports die down. Business as usual."

"Lab looks great, I remember when this place was pretty much a storage dump."

"Yeah, it's been up and running for almost a year now. Mike keeps the staff pretty low down here. Just those of us members who worked in the main lab upstairs," he motioned to Jen, "and two members who he brought in who he wanted more hands on. Charlie actually came to us from a tech company in Texas."

"How long have you been a member?"

"Of Restituere? Pretty much from the beginning," he said proudly.

Restituere. Mike's cult, Claude thought.

"What would you do if you thought someone was sabotaging the work you were doing? Wouldn't you try to get rid of them to protect that cause?"

Derrick wasn't trying to warn me about Mike, he was trying to recruit me!

"Well, there's not much I can really show you here, man. The layout is the same as upstairs with the exception of a couple things. Our dates are still calculated at random, however, they are carefully monitored to match up with what our other affiliates need. Where most of the work goes on is over here." He led Claude to Charlie at the control center. The huge screen had dots everywhere. "Our clinics, our Restituere guys all over the world, report all of their anticipated dates of birth. We send them the batches they need to inject their nutriment serum in the fourth month of gestation, but the dates they receive will guarantee expiration dates of seventy-two to a hundred and sixty-eight hours after birth. Sometimes, if gestation is longer than the projected date, the mothers miscarry."

Claude felt sick. He struggled to keep his tone calm.

"All over the world? Each country doesn't have a lab like this one?"

"Nah, we're still a small operation man. Our affiliates in other countries receive all their Restore injections from here and from the ones we send to Exylon first for Mike's research. Science first, right."

Restore, the label on the boxes of vials in Mike's back room.

"A lot of thought and work was put into this," he said, pretending to be impressed.

"Brilliant minds, man. Isn't that the point?" Miguel chuckled.

"Almost taken down by gung-ho, power-hungry Derrick." Miguel lowered his voice. "If he wasn't such a whack-job, sending out those Restore injections to high profile sites, he would still be alive. I mean, don't repeat that, but we all know what happened to him. Anyway, there's usually only a couple of us on a shift. Just making sure shit runs right, ya know."

"Thanks for the welcome, I still have a few things to do before my ride takes off."

"Oh, yeah sure." He lightly punched Claude's shoulder. "We'll hang for lunch next time."

"Sure thing."

Anxious to run out of there, Claude casually walked out to the control room and took off his jumpsuit. His pace picked up heading to the elevator.

"Hey!"

Claude's heart dropped.

"Dude, did you get your key card back?" "Oh, no, didn't have time."

Miguel swiped the elevator, when the doors opened, he leaned in and swiped again.

"By the way, this card is the only one that has access down here, get Mike to get you access. Welcome aboard."

Claude's fake smile fell as soon as the doors closed. He quickly hit G level. *I've got to find John.*

- 44 -

Entering the room, Elisa shivered as the temperature dropped about twenty degrees. The lab was set up much like any other lab she'd seen. This one was completely white though, *much like Jack's apartment,* she thought, amused. White counters, white walls, white instruments. *Large white drum! An incubator?* A large screen taking up half the wall displayed the spinning Orbis insignia. She moved in closer to the large drum. "Nutriment infused Nanobytes," it read. The exceptions to the all-white room were the five black mechanical arms encased in glass, busily working. Each arm had a window where red numbers were punching in at a rate of, probably, a number every five seconds. Too fast for her to figure out what they were doing. 12162179, 9182254, 922261, 5152242, 832203.

Within the encasement and slightly below the mechanical arms, long probes were quickly shifting into place, moving just as fast as the arms. At the end of each mechanical arm was a long needle. The needles injected the nutriment serum into syringes which were joined with the probe, packaged right away and pushed through a tube extended to what looked like a honeycomb—each team launched into its own cubby. When the honeycomb was filled, it moved out on a conveyer belt which led through a hole in the wall into another room. Packaging she'd seen before. *The numbers.* Numb, Elisa stood frozen.

All well-coordinated. Everything seemed to be in working in unison, the arms, the probes. *They would have to if the numbers were to match up and be imprinted. Expiration dates!* She hadn't taken a breath in what felt like a lifetime when she felt a jolt.

"Who are you? What are you doing in here?"

A hooded white suit swung her around by her arm—they stood face to face.

"I'm Elisa," was all she could muster.

The entire lab staff piled in behind him from the next room—their daily briefing since the increase in short infant expiration dates. "What are you doing in here?"

"Umm, I am…"

The control room door she entered through swung open.

"Dr., we're actually gonna be starting in the nutriment lab today," Claude called out. He waved to the guy in the white jump suit. "Sorry, Mo, first day."

"Hi, Claude," a couple of others called out.

"No problem." Mohammad slowly waved back.

"My first day," she repeated, stepping back and moving toward the door.

"Take that off, what are you doing?!" he demanded, once in the control room.

"Oh my god, Claude!"

"Just be quiet!"

He looked around as they approached the elevator, absentmindedly reaching for his card. Elisa pulled it out of her pocket. He shook his head. The elevator came immediately; as soon as the door closed, they shouted at each other.

"How did you get down here? Where is Monica? Did anyone else see you? What am I saying, *everyone* saw you!"

"This is the manufacturing and programming of nanobytes! They were numbered! Expiration dates!"

Claude stood silent.

She lowered her voice. "Expiration dates."

"Yes," he said.

The little silver ball emerged and levitated to the side of Elisa's head and scanned. "Claude Monark. Welcome." His lip curled.

"We have twenty minutes before the plane takes off. I need you to not say anything about what you saw right now. There's more going on here—right under the noses of John, Orbis, everyone."

She let his tone lead and realized it was probably in her best interest if she didn't say anything.

The doors opened and she followed close behind him. He popped his head in the office on the way out.

"Monica, have you seen John?"

She rose from her seat, looking confused, while Elisa hung her blue jacket back up.

"Oh, there you are, Elisa! Sure honey, he flew out as soon as you were done with your meeting."

"Okay thanks, see you in about a week."

"Well, okay, hope you enjoyed your tour." She waved to Elisa.

~

Claude pulled his blazer off to cool down as the car cruised four feet above the ground to the small engine plane, pulling up dust in its wake. There was only one other person from the original crew and three new faces that were returning. Elisa knew she couldn't talk to Claude now, in front of all these people. She stared out at all the faces wondering if they knew too. They didn't say a word while boarding.

The plane began to taxi, then slowed to a stop. They looked to each other and back at the hover car racing from the building to meet the plane. The car stopped abruptly as the pilot let the stairs down. Claude leaned forward, while Elisa couldn't take her eyes off the passenger car door. The door opened quickly and the same polished woman who arrived with them from Albany scrambled onto the plane, harried. The plane began to move again.

Staring out the small window of the plane, Claude said, "I'll explain. To you both. Together."

Elisa's head was reeling. For an hour she was alone with her thoughts. *This has been going on for a hundred years! How could they keep such a secret? Claude knew!*

- 45 -

Diego stood outside the security station, wringing his hands nervously. His eyes were glued to the stranger he was instructed to let through the gate, confident that joking around and making friends with the right people would help him to advance his career. Maybe to head security! Still, he was ready to run and tackle Jack if he made the wrong decision.

Ashlei met Jack at the front door of Exylon after calling security at the gate to allow him to drive through.

She noticed the guard standing outside the booth, gazing at them, anxiously waiting for her to give him the okay. She waved to him, he stood down, relieved, waved back and reentered the security booth.

"Sorry it took me so long to get down here, I was working on something."

"It's fine, I made a new best friend with Diego over there, he can appreciate a good joke," Jack said. "He mentioned several times how nice you were, I think he likes you."

"That's great," she said sarcastically. "It's been a while, it's nice to see you."

"You too, congrats on the not-so-new job."

"Thanks. It's still sort of new to me."

Following Ashlei, Jack listened in on the soft voice piping throughout the building from an unseen speaker.

"You are an essential part of our company. Your contribution to Exylon is what fuels our success. We need your ingenuity…"

Just before they climbed the stairs, a sentence was projected on the wall before them.

"Accelerating Innovation, taking future generations of humanity int leaps of discovery."

"Company mantra," Ashlei offered to Jack.

"Smells like lavender in here," he commented.

"They pipe happiness in from every corner of the building." Once in the lab, Ashlei held up the vial Jack handed her.

"Where'd you get this? These are only allowed to people with special clearance. *I* don't even have authority to get my hands on these."

"Let's just say your sister found it on the floor." She glanced at Jack while he rolled his eyes.

"Hmmm." She ran her fingers across the bump on the bottom.

"There's a raised 'R' on the bottom, any idea what that could mean?" He shook his head.

Moving over to the lab area she pulled out a couple glass slides and redirected the floating microscope in position, preparing to examine the contents of the vial.

"I'm not sure that I'll be able to answer any questions for you guys. I can probably tell you whether something is not right, but I am by no means an authority on the intricacies of particular viruses or whatever we may find here."

"Whatever you can find, which may be nothing, then at least Elisa can let that theory go and move on." *And so can I,* he thought.

Ashlei looked through the microscope, pulling her head away almost immediately.

"What the—" She looked again more intently, pointlessly shifting the glass slide.

They're moving so rapidly. That doesn't make sense.

Jack moved closer. "What?"

"This is insane. This can't be the nutriment serum? Where did you say you got it?"

She continued to look through the microscope.

"What are you seeing?" he asked impatiently.

"Well, they're nanobytes, but these ones are moving very rapidly. Too rapidly."

She invited him to look through the microscope, continuing as he peered in. "I'm not an expert on nanobytes, but I do know what they look like and I'm pretty sure I know how they are supposed to act and these are not like any nanobytes I've ever seen."

She examined the bottle, tracing the R on the bottom with her finger again. "This *is* a nutriment vial. Where did you get this?" she asked again.

"Your sister took it from the hospital." Jack was still looking in the microscope. His pulse was racing, he raised his head.

"Then this is it! It has to be the problem!"

He took another look, then turned to Ashlei. "So, why are these different than normal nanobytes?"

"The purpose of their use in nutriment serum and why it works so well in maintaining health is because these tiny robots literally carry the nutrients, fusing themselves at a molecular level. But these are not any nutriment nanobytes that I've seen before. There's no need for them to move this quickly. Again, I'm not an expert, we touched on it in one of my classes years ago."

"So, the injections *are* contaminated?"

Ashlei raised an eyebrow. "I don't know what you would call this." She paused. "I think we should talk to Claude about it when he gets back, he would probably know more about them."

$$- 46 -$$

CLAUDE SPENT THE TRIP trying to figure out how he was going to approach Ash and Elisa when they arrived—exactly what he was going to say and how much. *Elisa knows about expiration dates now; I've got to tell them everything. But how do you explain probably the best kept secret in our world history?* He paused behind her outside his door before they entered.

Elisa rushed in, barely allowing Ashlei to open the door.

"How'd it go in Washington?" Ashlei handed Claude the vial and began without waiting for an answer. "Jack brought the vial by the lab this morning. I'm glad you asked me to meet you here because I looked at the contents and I'd never seen nanobytes move like this. Have you ever experienced any abnormalities or malfunctions in *your* work or studies?"

Elisa turned to Claude. "Talk!"

Claude decided in that moment that he was relieved to finally talk to Ashlei. He'd been carrying a heavy load. The conflicting feelings about the knowledge of expiration dates, his suspicions of Mike, the mutations he'd discovered, everything.

One thing at a time. First things first.

"Have a seat, this may take a bit."

Ashlei looked to Elisa, slowly moving to the couch. "What's going on?"

"There's something I need to clarify for the two of you."

Elisa huffed. "I'll say."

Ashlei glanced at Elisa and back at Claude. "Okay," she said.

He suddenly felt like all the moisture was sucked from his mouth.

"Guess I'll start from the beginning. To answer your question Ash, yes, I have seen nanobytes like these. The nanobytes allowed for studies, research, and education are not the same ones delivered from the bureau for injection. They are simply nanobytes with a vitamin solution infused. The nanobytes that are actually injected, into a fetus, do contain the nutriment formula, but they are also genetically engineered. The reason they are moving so quickly is because they have a genetically altered timeline."

"What exactly are you saying?" Ashlei asked.

Arms crossed, Claude leaned back against the pool table.

"I don't need to give you a history lesson on the previous state of our world and the formation of Orbis, so I'll just jump right into their solution to the crisis they were faced with.

"Orbis began looking for solutions to the global epidemic all over the planet about a hundred and fifty years ago. You may or may not have heard of all the options that were explored. Habitation of other planets; restricting use of all-natural resources; rationing the use of water, minerals, et cetera. A bureau was put in place to monitor population. Still here today, of course, my division. Do you recall the period in history, about a hundred years ago or so, when families were restricted to just one child and women were forced to get mandatory hysterectomies after their first child?"

They nod.

"Of course," Ashlei said. "I can't imagine that."

"At the time, people were so desperate for a solution that they were willing to try anything. But after about fifty years of this, couples decided that they wanted more children and protested, eventually changing things back to the way they were. What they didn't know was that Orbis, though they put up a good fight, really didn't care so much at this time because the strategy of limiting children did in fact lower the population rate. Also, what the public were not aware of is that they had implemented something else at the same time they began the child restriction laws that they would continue to practice to this day.

"American, Swedish, and Chinese scientists worked together and came up with a solution that would change the course of mankind." Rubbing the back of his neck, he looked at the floor and back up at them. "Expiration dates."

Elisa, the entire trip from Washington, had been trying to figure out how such a thing could have begun. All of the things that were attached to expiration dates. The only thing she could think of was the stupid kid's game they use to play, "Guess My Date." *Who does this to children?! An orchestrated hoax! Playing with people's lives—we are expendable!*

Ashlei shook her head, trying to wrap it around what he was saying. "What do you mean, the solution?"

Claude shifted from one foot to the other before he continued. "Every child born would have an expiration date assigned randomly and so these dates would control the population's rate of growth. They are genetically engineered nanobytes to be time released—'atomic bombs' programmed to kill us at a specific time."

Silence. Ashlei scrunched her face and Elisa's mouth was ajar.

"The idea, of course, was laughed at and mocked by some, but representatives from Germany knew that there was research already being done that could be further advanced to create something that only sounded absurd, and make it possible. Scientific teams got to work on the project "Heal the Earth" or "HTE." In collaboration, scientists, biologists, and physicians came up with a formula using control over cell division with nanobytes. These nanobytes were preprogrammed, constantly working on cell death with a specific time calculated to end life. They were designed to work on the cells throughout the life span they were programmed for, placed early in the womb through injection. When the programmed nanobytes have destroyed the exact number of cells in the exact time frame they were designed to, they reach end of life and so do you. At the time of placement, dates are laparoscopically tattooed on the child's head or foot, the easiest accessed position of the child, to keep track for query."

Ashlei instinctively placed her hands on her stomach, curling her lip.

"The probes and injections are packaged together so the dates concur," Elisa verified, "I saw them."

"Yeah," Claude confirmed.

He took a breath and waited a moment for a gasp, questions, or for Ashlei to chime in. He almost wished she would.

"Orbis decided that HTE would be kept confidential. No one needed to know about this other than those who needed to be involved. They concluded that if the public knew, though this was clearly for the good of the world, there would be widespread revolt and thus no hope for the continuation of our life as we know it."

Taking a drink of water, Claude shifted feet again, uncomfortable with the silence in the room.

"All members of Orbis took an oath and they went forth deciding how to bring in the cooperation of those who they needed to run such a project, from scientists, biologists, to computer analysts—lay staff, such as housekeepers, maintenance, IT… would only know that this was a special division for the Bureau of Populations Control and Statistics. They took care to make sure every loophole was covered."

"Nutriment injections was the way they made sure every fetus was injected with the nanobytes," Elisa said, shaking her head. "And if you refuse an injection, you get arrested. Not for the good of the mother and baby, but so that 'every loophole was covered!'"

Ashlei asked, "How do you know all this?"

Claude cleared his throat. "I work for the division that is in charge of distribution of the nanobytes."

Ashlei was sure she was going to vomit. She felt paralyzed for a moment, then stood and looked in his eyes. "So, you're an accessory to murder?! Because that's what this essentially is! You admitted that these are atomic bombs, waiting to kill at the scheduled time!" Her shaky voice was rising.

Elisa gently pulled Ashlei's arm and stood in front of her.

"Claude, what I saw down there, you're saying expiration dates are a government conspiracy?"

He looked beyond Elisa at Ashlei's reddened face. "I didn't say I agree with what has been going on for the last hundred years. Clearly, I did not have a part in that!"

Ashlei stepped back in front of Elisa to face Claude.

"But you are in charge of the division that delivers death to babies!" Her voice cracked.

"When I was hired, I was selected to work with an icon in my field. He moved me into this position in which I was entrusted with this secret, an honor comparable to the changing of the guard at Buckingham Palace. I was grateful to be chosen for such a responsibility."

He saw her tearing up at the realization that her boyfriend was a baby killer.

Elisa had so many more questions but knew enough to give this a moment to unfold.

Claude moved in and tried to hold Ashlei's hand, but she pulled away. "The vital importance of not letting this be known was instilled in me, and the security behind it all. I never thought it was okay!" he said in a plea to get Ashlei to look at him again. "But I thought, in some arrogant way, that I could, maybe, find another solution."

Elisa spoke up. "Another solution… to… killing us all?"

He hesitantly stepped away from Ashlei and addressed Elisa. "I thought I could find another way to better utilize our resources to allow them to go further. And perhaps, come up with a plan to tap into landscape resources like unexplored territories beneath sea level and reevaluating uninhabitable terrain to make it inhabitable."

He turned again to Ashlei. "The work we're doing with VM9 can be a huge part of that! My own project, the project you thought Mike was trying to sabotage, is everything I just stated—finding a way to be able to eliminate the expiration dates for good; to maybe make them obsolete."

This time she let him take her hands. Sitting on the arm of the comfy, blue, oversized chair they loved to sit in together, the tears were now trickling down her cheeks. He squatted down in front of her.

"You know me. This was *not* okay with me, but in order to find a solution, you have to immerse yourself in the problem."

She sniffled and wiped her tears. "It's insane to imagine you being involved, but I trust your character enough to know you have a reason for being there."

He smiled, grateful for her acceptance, stood up, and kissed her forehead. "Thank you."

"How has none of this ever been questioned?" Elisa asked.

"Well, it was! For a while. There were a number of people who tried to prove conspiracy theories, but couldn't. You had the religious groups who, of course, declared 'This is an act of God!' After all, God is the only one who can create life and determine its course. However, the die-hard scientists and engineers would never be convinced that this is God's work at hand. 'There must always be a scientific explanation, mutation, natural selection?' Hell, they would even take aliens as an explanation over the idea that there is a higher power in control making all the decisions for us—an unseen force that manipulates us likes marionettes in a puppet show!"

Elisa realized she has been clenching her teeth as her jaw began to hurt. *Betrayed by our own government!*

"But remember, most of all," Claude pointed out, "the government had been in complete control of most things since Orbis was created. People tend not to question authority, especially those in despair. Only a select few were allowed to make and distribute nutriment injections—and they work for Orbis. Most people have been concerned with trying to survive over the previous hundred years. Things have gotten better in the last fifty or so years, but concerns were not about revisiting the origin of what is orthodox."

"Let's circle back," Ashlei said. "The mass deaths lately that have been happening, is this a government plan or mistake?"

"Well, there's something else. Something more disturbing than just expiration dates."

"What can be more disturbing than what you've just told us?" Ashlei asked.

"Elisa, just before I found you, I stumbled on another lab—run by Mike. He's got some of the employees at the plant working that lab, manufacturing these faster programmed nanobytes from seventy-two hours to a week expiration dates. Right under the noses of John and the plant managers."

"Derrick was killed," he said to Ashlei.

"You know that?"

"Yup."

She cupped her mouth.

"That vial you have there most likely came from a shipment that Derrick had brought to me to send out. Sounds like he went off on his own and used me to get the job done. Several weeks back, Mike went insane over those shipments. Said that I could have drawn attention to whatever we were doing. At the time, I assumed he meant government-run expiration dates, but then it was really strange the way he changed his demeanor and ended that conversation so abruptly. A couple days ago, I gained access into the back room in the lab, closet, whatever you want to call it, that Mike keeps locked."

"Behind his desk?" Ashlei asked.

"Yes."

"Gained access? You mean broke into? So, you didn't trust him either?"

"No, not after I started seeing all of these things add up. I heard everything you said," he emphasized. "Like handing off VM9, and you walking in on him, hanging around my computer. I had the same suspicions, I just wanted to collect as much information, without involving you."

She felt even more connected to Claude at this moment—knowing they were always on the same page.

"In that room I found the same vials of nutriment injections that you have there—with the raised R. I also looked at them under the microscope and found them to be way beyond the normal acceleration rate of any of the normal nanobytes. These are moving at a speed that will, well, attack and shut down all of your organs a lot faster than the government nanobyte injections, which work over time. At minimum, four to five months—the remaining gestation period of a fetus. The same serums are being manufactured in Washington D.C. and shipped out to clinics and hospitals all over the world."

"That vial, with the raised 'R' on the bottom, sent out from the Exylon site, why do you think Mike was so worked up when you sent those injections to the addresses that Derrick gave you?" Elisa asked rhetorically. "They were not his targeted regions! Ash, remember that email you found on Mike's computer talking about restoring the planet and how the weak and diseased were using resources needed by others? What do you remember about those addresses?"

"They weren't exactly vacation spots."

"No, they weren't. As a matter of fact, they were some of the poorest and uneducated areas around the world! Recall the speech Mike gave at lunch about not saving lives, because there's not enough resources?! Those injections ended up at hospitals and clinics that are higher profile then his intended targets—unintentionally getting immediately recognized by the world! It may have gone unnoticed for years, or forever."

"Even more concerning, there may be many more out there we haven't heard about—and many more to come," Ashlei pointed out.

"That encrypted file, you tried to access it this morning right, any luck?" Ashlei asked.

"Right and no," Claude confirmed.

He pulled the silver disk from his bag and handed it to Ashlei.

"Encrypted file?" Elisa asked.

"After Ash told me Mike had been hanging around my VCC, I searched it thoroughly to maybe find what he may had been looking for. Just when I exhausted my search and figured she was wrong, I found something that looked like a glitch, but I couldn't get to it. I'm pretty savvy on a VCC, but I couldn't even figure out where its source was. I called Ash at the lab and she figured it was an encrypted file."

"Let's see what we can bring up," Ashlei said.

-47-

ASHLEI SAT AT CLAUDE'S DESK, sliding the disk down. Claude placed his hand on it and a blue ray shot up before them displaying a keyboard; he typed in his password and a three-dimensional image of his choice of welcome presented itself.

"Hello Claude," the virtual head of an owl greeted. Elisa snickered.

Ashlei watched him type. "Hmm, I thought I guessed your password? A certain frog…"

"Ha, no, that's only part of it."

She pursed her lips. "Let's look at this on flat screen, shall we." She pushed a button, the owl image shrank down and a wide screen image appeared.

Right away a folder with the image of a lock on it appeared.

"Wow, that took me like an hour to find," he said.

"This is AES. It's a really old type of encryption. Advanced Encrypted Standard. It is a symmetric encryption algorithm. You need a key or a password to access the file."

She typed again. Nothing.

"How do you know so much about old encrypted computer programs?" Elisa asked.

"I needed a minor."

She continued typing.

"What do you want to bet that Mike isn't very creative when it comes to passwords?" She typed in Restituere.

The images in front of them quickly flashed numbers and letters out of sequence.

Password declined.

"Uggh, I was sure. It's trying to unscramble my code." She typed in "restore."

The images of numbers and letters flashed again.

Password declined. "Caps?" RESTITUERE.

Password declined.

"Didn't you say you needed his DNA to get into his computer?" Elisa asked.

"That was *his* computer. And like I said, this is old technology, it's not that complicated."

She typed in "vegetationmutation9."

An image came alive. She pulled forward the only file in the folder displayed.

"And neither is he. Bingo!"

"That looks like another language. Or gibberish," Claude said, leaning over Ashlei's shoulder.

"It looks like gibberish, but it's meant to be deciphered."

"Like another code?" Claude sighed.

"Precisely."

Claude tilted his head back. "Great!"

"But sometimes all you need is a password to decipher it. Let's try one of the others that failed the first go around," she said optimistically. She typed in different lab codes and anything she thought Mike may have thought was significant to Claude. All denied.

Claude and Elisa called out random passwords. "Exylon, nutriment, nanobyte, project, VM9…"

"Stop! You're distracting me!"

She placed her hand on Claude's arm. "What's your military number?"

"What? Why?"

"Let's try it."

"Why would he…"

"Just… what is it?"

He rattled off his identification. She typed, 1LTcmOAF1222235 and the gibberish turned into a readable file.

They gathered around the computer. "My military number?"

"Yeah, it made sense. Your tag is placed right above your workstation. He didn't have a lot time at your computer, he'd need something quick. And would *you* have ever thought to access this file with your own number?"

"It looks like an outline or agenda," Ashlei said.

She clicked on an attachment. "It's the list of names and addresses that I found on Mike's computer! Plus, hundreds more."

"Go back to the first page again," Claude said.

It read:

To continue on this way would be insidious. There's no reason the rest of the world should suffer as I do and tolerate the incompetence and inferiority of the other half. I feel it's my responsibility to rid us all of those who have nothing to contribute to our society. And with this I will take it upon myself to use nanobytes to extinguish the regions of leeches saturating the earth.

"What the hell does that mean?" Claude asked.

"'*The other half… my responsibility of ridding us of those who have nothing to contribute.*' I think it means that he wants to wipe out anyone he thinks shouldn't here!" Ashlei answered.

Elisa plopped down on the arm of the chair. "Whoa, I was exaggerating when I accused him of wanting to annihilate everyone on the planet that day at lunch. He can't be serious!" Elisa said.

"And he's planning on setting you up to take the blame!" Ashlei said, turning to Claude.

"All he would have to do is point the finger at you and any federal agency can decode this old encryption. These passwords were meant to be easy. *Meant to be yours!* He made it just out of reach, but attainable."

"I know the guy doesn't care for me, but I would never have guessed anything like this! I don't even talk like that!"

"This is crazy, he went from accelerating the deaths in a couple regions to planning to cleanse half the planet! How can he even do that?" Elisa asked.

"Only a couple of regions *that we know of,* but again, who knows how many people he's reached. Remember half the planet is off the grid. Those addresses I found were from poor uneducated countries—would anyone even notice right away?" Ashlei said.

Claude paced the room, contemplating. "This seems like an impossible task. How can he reach half of the world with nanobytes? I think he's just deranged!"

Ashlei added, "I don't know, he found a way to cause all of the accelerated deaths. He reached all *those* people!"

"We have to go to the authorities!" Elisa said.

"No, we can't do that!" Claude said.

"What!" they said in unison.

"Right or wrong, expiration dates are classified information. We cannot run around sharing that information with everyone."

"Well, it is wrong and people should know!" Ashlei said.

"Perhaps, but not this way. You can imagine the chaos this information will create. We need to stop Mike from what he's planning and then worry about informing the world."

"Okay, so how do we do that?" asked Ashlei.

"I don't know. I'll go to New York and talk to John. I trust him and he'll know how to handle this."

"I want to go with you," Ashlei said.

"Me too," added Elisa.

"Ash, I know you want to go, but we're going to need to get a flight out and with you not feeling well I'm not sure if that is going to work for you, babe."

She would have liked to protest, but the queasy feeling in her stomach was telling her not to rebel. "Okay, you're right."

"There's a flight out in one hour. If we leave now, we can get to the airport in time. We should get to New York by about five."

"Wow, alright," Claude said, impressed with Elisa's efficiency. Ashlei got Elisa's attention and motioned her eyes toward the door.

"Okay, well I'll wait outside for you, Claude."

Ashlei turned to Claude. "Hey, umm, can you sit with me for a minute before you go?"

"Sure," he said apprehensively, afraid she was still not okay with his involvement in the bureau.

She motioned for him to sit in the big chair while she sat on the coffee table across from him. She needed something hard and stable right now to give her support.

"This is probably not the best time to talk about this, but I've been holding this in until we could talk and then… well, then all of this craziness happened. And it's so important that you get through to your superiors because well, now we have a vested interest…" she nervously rambled.

He looked at her, sliding his hands up and down her arms to calm her.

"What are you trying to get at, Ash?"

Alright big chicken, she thought to herself, *out with it.* She took in a deep breath and blew the words back out. "Well, there's no other way to really say this. I'm pregnant."

Seconds ticked on. The silence was deafening. She couldn't recall how many seconds had gone by before she last took a breath. *If he was happy, I'd see some sort of a reaction, but he's just staring at me.*

The pressure in her eyes began to build, ready to gush. "I'll take any kind of reaction at this point," she said, her voice cracking.

"I'm sorry, honey, I just, I didn't expect to hear that." He pulled her in to him and hugged her.

"Oh, baby, I was just waiting to hear you say you didn't want to have anything to do with me because of my job." He pulled back and cupped her face in his hands.

"I am surprised, yes, by your announcement, but I am not disappointed!"

She breathed again. "Really? Because it just looked like you were trying to figure out the quickest way out of here."

"Don't be silly, this is my apartment." He chuckled and hugged her again.

"Ha-ha. Jerk." She snuggled in closer.

"We'll talk later." He kissed her long and hard before rushing out the door.

- 48 -

"Change of plan. John informed me he's in Boston, wants us to meet him there. He's sending a pilot over to Exylon, we'll take a flight out there."

"That should get us there quicker."

"You know Ash is pregnant?"

"Of course." Elisa smiled.

"No matter what happens, she does not get a nutriment injection!" he said.

"That goes without saying."

She stared out the window for a bit. "Those people at the nutriment plant, do they all know that the nanobytes are programmed?"

"Most."

"Monica?"

"Yes. BPCS Nutriment Plant falls under a Central Intelligence division called Special Activities Center. Each country's main branch is Expiration Dates. Employees are tight, as needed. Everyone goes through the same rigorous training as I did. And we all know, you don't talk."

Elisa felt a chill.

"Like I said, the statisticians that keep track of the population numbers that calculate how many people existed, exist, and will exist," he reiterated from earlier, "it's all a balancing act preparing them to run to the powers that be if the scale is tipped a little and there's a small surge of growth somewhere. And if there's a threat of too much growth in any one area, hence a potential to grow the country, they tweak their expiration dates to keep the balance."

Elisa scrunched her face up in disgust. "Barbaric."

"Yeah," he agreed.

"Of course, it's unknown that these injections each carry the date of their child's demise which is then branded with the ultrasound probe. There are other minor departments and subdivisions within the building. Also required is a department that remains in contact with the other members of Orbis, all making sure there is balance around the world."

"It takes a tribe to harbor and execute an atrocity," she said sarcastically.

"I would lie awake some nights wondering, how I would feel about it all when I had my own child on the way. Knowing that it's just a spin of the roulette wheel for how long my child gets to live. It's not something I want the government, Mike, or anyone else to be in control of."

The blades from the helicopter created a swirl of leaves, sticks, and dirt. Elisa clasped her sweater, so it didn't blow off as they ran to get in.

Clouds rolled in and a light shower began to fall. "Strap in!" the pilot called back in a monotone manner.

- 49 -

THE TAPPING OF RAIN on the roof had progressively increased to a steady flow. Elisa wiped the occasional splatter from her face that had managed to make its way back from the slightly opened window in the cockpit. Arriving by air gave them an impressive view of the grounds they were hovering above.

The New England property spread out to a hundred acres or so with the house being the focal point. The well-manicured garden took up an acre alone and led into an elaborate maze carved from tall hedges. Beyond that, a veil of trees surrounded the property on all sides, with the exception of the entrance, which was met by a long, welcoming road leading to the front of the house.

Elisa couldn't help but smile at the geese frolicking in the fountain located in the center of the circular driveway. The two struggled over what she assumed to be lunch and, in their battle, dropped the prize, allowing a third to come in and snatch it up. "Touché," she said lightly.

They descended next to another government helicopter with the large initials BPCS inscribed on the side, though this one was not as decorated as the powerful government machine they were currently in.

"Clearly John gets to play with the all the government's toys."

"Mr. Vanburen called ahead, he said he'll meet you in the library," the pilot called out over the slowing whopping blades.

"Oh, the library!" Elisa mocked. "Where are we supposed to find that?"

"John has a flare for the dramatic, you'll find. And etiquette is important to him."

"A good host would have met us at the door," she mumbled.

A six-foot-five man approached wearing a blue uniform unique to BPCS at the bureau. *Geez, it's a Guardzilla.* Elisa couldn't help but notice every muscle trying to escape through his shirt.

"Mr. Vanburen wants to meet you in the library. I'll take you there." His tone as brutish as he looked.

Elisa glanced at Claude, raising her eyebrows.

She whispered, "Is he supposed to be his butler?"

"He works for the bureau—don't know what John would be using him for here. Other than as his door man."

They quickened their pace, attempting to escape the now pelting rain.

The mini-mansion greeted them with long wide stairs leading to pillars at the top of the entrance. As they ascended, Elisa stumbled and grabbed onto Guardzilla to keep from falling. He didn't budge. *He's like a rock!*

"Sorry," she said, and they continued into the house.

The enormity of the house, with a ceiling that seemed to reach to the sky, was overwhelming to Elisa. When they ventured further into the foyer, she could only see a bit of a room to the left, but the large room to the right held a table that was almost as large as the room itself.

With the sound of the rain falling, the house is beautifully eerie, she thought. *Something from a gothic tale.*

"John obviously has an affection for art," she said, passing artwork lining the walls on either side of them. "This house is an architectural treasure," she noted, appreciating the eloquently clustered embedded roses, leaves, and grape patterns as well as cherubs adorning the borders of the room.

"That painting there," she pointed to a painting of a woman surrounded by children, "is The Virgin of the Rocks. That's a Leonardo Da Vinci painting."

"I never took John for a religious guy."

"You don't necessarily have to be religious to appreciate the beauty of religious art."

The guard led them to a bridged walkway, beyond the foyer, which connected to another wing of the house. Windows made up the majority of the walls on either side, though the rain beating down on the panes clouded their view.

To Elisa it was a comforting hum, but it hadn't always had that effect. She remembered a day, when she was very young, when her father had her and Ashlei practicing defensive skills in the rain.

~

"It's cold and the rain is in my eyes," Elisa complained.

"Good, perfect conditions for our lesson today."

"Daddy, can we just go inside, I'm cold too," Ashlei whined.

"Look ahead, what do you see?"

"Rain," said Elisa.

"Nothing, it's raining too hard!" Ashlei said.

"What do you hear?"

"Rain!" they said in unison.

"Listen again. But this time I want you to listen beyond it, tune out the drops of rain. Take some time and listen."

Ashlei dropped to the ground, her raincoat rode up to her waist. "Hhhmmm!"

Elisa listened intently. After several moments she said, "I hear the squirrel scurrying up the tree to get out of the rain."

Ashlei giggled.

"That's great, honey, nice job! And you Ash, what do you hear?"

"I hear the rain pounding on the ground!"

"Try again," he instructed.

After several moments of pouting and swirling the puddle around in front of her with a stick, she became still.

"I hear a bird. He's in that tree," she said, pointing up to the tree five yards away, just as it swooped down and grabbed a field mouse, taking it back to the tree.

"Aghhhh, that poor mouse!" they cried and began to hop around in the puddles.

Killian Quinn laughed and settled his daughters down. "Did you see that? That hawk depended on his super hearing to be able to find his prey, so he can eat. He tuned out the sounds around him in order to hear beyond any distractions to have the advantage. You need to see and hear what your opponent doesn't—this gives you the advantage."

The girls looked up at their father in awe.

He patted them both on the butt. "Now, go inside and get dry—Mom has cake."

- 50 -

THEY WERE SURROUNDED by floor-to-ceiling bookcases when Guardzilla left them in the library. The room was cluttered with literature spread throughout, covering the large oak desk, the floor, and the lamp tables. Each chair had reading material on it.

Though John didn't seem too interested in Claude's theories or data earlier, he was hoping that John would take more of an interest in what he had to say now. Lives would depend on it!

John entered from a passage behind the bookcase.

"This is Elisa Quinn. You'll understand why she's here in a moment," Claude spouted, responding to John's raised eyebrow at her presence.

John extended his hand. "Yes, Ashlei's sister, the cardiovascular specialist. How was your tour, my dear?" He feigned no knowledge of their motive for being there.

"Interesting!" John looked familiar to her, she thought they'd met.

He sat on the edge of the desk, folding his hands. "Okay, what was so important that you couldn't tell me on the phone?"

Elisa sat on the divan, while Claude paced in front of John.

"I have reason to believe that Mike is planning to do something horrible with the expiration date nanobytes. He's responsible for the recent mass deaths, as is a group he's involved in called Restituere. He's been using a lab he secretly built at the nutriment plant to manufacture nanobytes for the injections to reach end of life in a matter of days! He ensures that these serums go out to his designated regions through the nutriment plant and also by having them sent to Exylon. Derrick was involved too. All these deaths in the news, were his doing!"

Claude was charged up and could barely take a breath before getting out all he has to report.

"Mike reamed me a new one for sending out a shipment a while ago, that Derrick had actually gotten me to send out. It was stupid and I shouldn't have, but I believe that shipment was supposed to go to the addresses from the list we found within an encrypted file. Instead, Derrick had redirected them."

"Encrypted file?" John asked, continuing his charade.

"Mike put an encrypted file on my computer, incriminating me as the executor of this crazy plan he's devised; if it weren't for Ashlei, I would have taken the fall. The few regions on the list are only the beginning of his objective."

John threw his hands up. "Okay, slow down. What plan is this that you are to have executed?"

"Taking out, like, probably half the population, if it was up to Mike. He's an egotistical introvert who thinks that he's superior to most anyone he comes in contact with!" Elisa blurted out.

"We'll need to track down all the shipments Mike and the others have sent out. Here's a good place to start." Claude pulled the list from his pocket and handed it to John. "It's a list of the contacts Ashlei printed from the encrypted file."

John took the list and looked it over, then Claude watched as he tossed it on a table.

"John, he left his signature on my VCC. It said exactly what his plan is, minus it's execution!"

"If that file is on *your* VCC, then it's not his signature, it's yours. You can't trace that to him." He paused.

"Was Mike there? At this lab?"

"No. His name was thrown around as being the one in charge."

"I can't crucify someone based on 'your guess' and assumptions of someone you didn't even witness being there. It's speculation. These are incredible accusations; you need to be prepared to back them up."

"Guess! This was a real lab, with real nanobytes being manufactured for the purpose of a personal agenda!"

John stood. "Okay, well, we don't need the local police or curiosity seekers poking around asking questions. You understand that!" He stared firmly. "What it could mean for the stability of the future. Are we clear on that?" He looked to Elisa as well.

They both nodded. Now was not the time to challenge him on what the future should hold for expiration dates.

"Good. That said, you will make that clear to Miss Ashlei and I trust you adhered to your oath and kept this all confidential?"

"Yes, sir, that's why I came to you. I knew you would know how to handle this without divulging expiration dates to local authorities."

John smiled. "Good. I'm taking this very seriously, but Mike has always been a good guy and an asset to the bureau. I'll have to make some calls."

Claude grabbed John's arm. "He's doing this all behind your back, don't let your friendship with Mike cloud your judgment! I'm not sure what kind of time we have here. I have no idea what Mike's strategy is to execute his plan, but I'd say you need to stop him now before he hurts anyone else. And maybe use your authority to find out about Restituere!"

John shook him loose, his tone deepened. "I'm going to assume you're just anxious and not questioning my ability to handle my responsibilities! I will address Mike myself about the Restore injections."

"Not questioning at all, sir."

"Then let me handle it!"

Elisa stood and grabbed Claude.

"We never said Restore was what Mike had called his nanobyte injections. John is probably also with Restituere!"

"And what do you know about Restiturere?" John glared at her.

He rapped on the door. Guardzilla, and what looked to be the sidekick to his much larger balding partner, came in already prepared for their requested services.

Alarmed, Elisa and Claude stepped back. "John, what is this, is that true?"

The guards, harboring no appreciation for literature, tipped two chairs allowed the books to slip to the floor and brought them for Elisa and Claude to sit on.

"Careful with those!" John yelled.

Both guards maintained their silence, while Guardzilla grabbed hold of Claude's hands. Claude stiffened, clenching his fists, but he saw the gun holstered on the other's hip and thought of Elisa.

"Don't!" Guardzilla warned. His look was enough for Claude to hesitate any attempt at fighting. He was pushed into the chair and held down, while the other tied his hands.

The smaller guard turned and tied Elisa, slipping the band from her wrist, then taking Claude's.

When they were done, without making another sound, they left the room.

John shook his head. "I really was hoping you'd be on board with us. That Derrick could interest you in our cause. I left it to someone more your age—thought that would encourage you. My mistake. I hate to say it, but Mike was right on this one. You couldn't just let it be. Did you think that I wouldn't hear about you down on K? That idiot, Miguel, thought Mike had gotten through to you and you'd joined Restituere."

He turned to leave. "My plans are much too important and bigger than either of you to have them jeopardized."

"What's your plan for us?" Elisa called after him. He ignored her.

"Claude said etiquette was important to you. I've yet to see that, but then again, I guess he was wrong about trusting you too! You're uncivilized! No different than what you say you despise in the very people you're trying to hurt.

"I'm an enthusiast and an optimist," John charged back, addressing her. "Everything I do or say is for a better me, a better you, a better place. It does disturb me to have to deal with these little unpleasantries along the way," he said, motioning to them, "but don't confuse my securing the safety of an ideal perspective future, for incivility!"

"Restituere is the future?!" Elisa spat.

"It is a brotherhood of great minds who believe that our planet can be better than it ever was. Renewed. Untainted. Unfiltered brilliant minds that can imagine, create, invent, solve! Half of the inhabitants on our grand orb are Neanderthals, really! Scavengers who exhaust the natural resources from those of us who really should be able to thrive.

So, what kind of world do you think it would be if these people didn't exist? We've been held captive by this primitive society because we must support parasites!"

"Wow, that sounds really crazy," she said flatly.

He grimaced at her remark.

"You're pathetic and I'm pretty sure this is all for naught! There's no way you can accomplish what you've set out to do. And if you've figure it all out, you won't get far without getting exposed and shut down!"

John slammed his hands down on the arms of Claude's chair, his face so close he could smell the onions from John's lunch. Claude pulled his head back.

"What's pathetic is that we've let this go on too long! We require the ability to come up with new ways to utilize the technologies we had to abandon due to our restriction of resources. We must advance with new technology and we need to be unhindered by obstacles! Orbis's vision cannot expand beyond *their* idea of what the greater good of all people is. They do not see that the inept among us cannot contribute because they lack the ability to think beyond what their familial genes have afforded them. Therefore, we have carefully chosen who will carry on and benefit our new world of advancements, and those who are inferior, well, they will expire prematurely." He smirked. "You wanted to know how this plan was going to be executed. A rebirth of an idea from the Transitional War utilizing germ warfare against our enemies—slightly altered, of course, in order to carry out the necessary distribution of nanobytes in selected regions around the world."

"You're planning germ warfare in the form of nanobytes?" Claude questioned.

"What does that mean?" Elisa asked.

"Precisely, Claude! And what that means, my dear, is that, when we are prepared to launch, thousands of nanobytes hosted by drones dispersed throughout the planet to their designated positions will be guided by infrared and one's good old heartbeat and released to find their target, each recipient expiring within minutes. There will be no exposure or shut down," he mocked.

Elisa's gut tightened. John beamed, proud.

"You're talking about murdering thousands of people?!"

"Millions, my dear."

"When did you, as a scientist, stop trying to come up with solutions to help *everyone*?! The best part of what we do is the challenge of discovery and solutions!" Claude said.

"How do you know that generations down the line, one of these 'Neanderthals' will not produce a descendant that will colonize on another planet or find a resource that hasn't been discovered yet? Now you are depriving your 'great new world' of all of its possibilities!" Elisa argued.

"I do still live for those challenges, but this *is* our solution. We have a greater chance of success when we have command of our choices," John rebutted. "What better way to control chaos than to control the population?"

"You're insane!" Elisa said.

"Insane is not fixing a problem if you have the ability to do so!"

Elisa scrunched her face in disgust.

"Oh," John stopped and turned to them on his way out, "I am well aware of Miss Ashlei's involvement as well. I'm sorry, but she will have to be dealt with too."

"No, please!" they both called out as he exited through the door they were brought in.

"How could I have been so stupid!" Claude said.

"How would you know? We have to get out of here!"

~

Just outside, John made a call. "Unless he's lying to me, and I don't think he is, Ashlei Quinn is the only other person that is aware of the situation. As soon as I have located her and have her taken care of, I'm sure I'll no longer need them… Yes, though Mike may not be up for the task. I may need to go to Albany myself. My men will take care of these two here when I give them the go ahead. After I leave Albany, I'll be on my way."

- 51 -

CLAUDE WIGGLED HIS HANDS vigorously, attempting to loosen the plastic ties.

"Stop that! That'll only make it tighter," Elisa said.

"Well, what do you suggest?" He looked around the room for anything he could use to cut the ties. "We don't have a lot of time here! My guess is that he wants to make sure he doesn't need us anymore. Once he realizes that, Guardzilla and his sidekick will be back."

"I don't know, but that'll make it worse, I *do* know that."

She stretched her fingers trying to reach her back pocket.

"When they came in, I swiped the lighter that was on the desk. It was the closest thing I could get without them noticing. It's in my pocket, if I can reach it, maybe I can melt the plastic enough to loosen them."

"And severely burn yourself in the process!"

"I don't want to die—I don't care if I get burned!"

"Alright, can you reach it?"

Leaning down in the seat, she struggled, just able to touch the rim of her pocket. She paused, straightened and tried again. Squeezing her hand in the pocket, she reached the top of the lighter with the tips of her fingers, carefully pulled it from the opening and it dropped to the floor.

"Ugghh!" She squirmed around trying to see where it fell.

"I can't let anything happen to Ash or the baby!" Claude said desperately. He rocked the chair back and forth, still twisting his hands trying to break free. "Damn, they're getting tighter."

Elisa broke out in a sweat and started to hyperventilate. *I have to get free!* She began the breathing exercises she used when her claustrophobia kicked in, taking a moment to calm herself, she closed her eyes and began shifting her hands around.

"On my twelfth birthday, Ash thought it was funny to tie my hands and feet while I was sleeping, so when I woke, I couldn't get out of bed. The worst part was that I had to go to the bathroom so badly."

She winced at the plastic cutting into her wrist.

Claude watched as Elisa maneuvered her hands and fingers in awkward positions, as though they were dislocating.

"Arghh…" she cried out.

"What are you doing?" he asked, pulling and twisting, cutting the ties deeper into his hands.

She continued her story.

"I was yelling for my mom, but she couldn't hear me. I was so angry with Ash. I could hear her laughing and playing outside. My dad is a police detective, and he was obsessed with these 'life saving drills' he took us through. So, I calmed down, concentrated, used his relentless teachings to contort my fingers and hands in a way where I could squeeze my hands out." Her hand cut in several places and bloody, she worked it through the tie. "Ash thought she was helping me 'train.' Our childhood games were weirder than most."

She pulled her other hand free. "Remind me to kiss her later."

"You'd rather have set yourself on fire, then get out that way."

Elisa reached down and grabbed the lighter and melted the ties holding her feet.

"I wasn't thinking and I haven't actually tried it since I was a kid."
"Hold still." She burned the plastic from Claude's hands.

Blowing on them, he quickly wiped the melting plastic from his fingers, while she burned the ties at his feet.

"The front door may not be the best option. Let's try the bookcase," Claude suggested.

"Did you make it?" he asked, feeling around for a handle to the bookcase.

"Make it?"

"To the bathroom?"

"Oh, no, I didn't. Payback was in order." Together they carefully pulled on the bookcase, exposing a spiral staircase.

"I created a web of string just above her bed while *she* slept and poured water in her bed, so she thought she peed herself *and* she couldn't get out of bed."

"Harsh."

"Yeah, I guess I owe her."

- 52 -

Ashlei rehashed everything that had discovered in just the last ten hours.

Expiration dates are a government conspiracy! Mike is behind the mass deaths! And what if we hadn't found the encryption? Claude would have been set up to take the blame for this whole crazy idea of Mike's! What if we had never found out about his plan to kill all these people and he actually went through with it!

She counted sixteen times that she'd passed the same, nearly empty, glass of water that Claude left on the stand next to the couch.

Expiration dates are not just a phenomenon in nature. They should never have existed! What does that even mean for us? I guess, for starters, this means my research is unnecessary. She looked at the clock.

I wonder if those vials in the back room at the lab somehow made their way to the Hellman Medical Center. They could be evidence! She changed into her jeans, grabbed her sweater, and headed out the door to Exylon.

- 53 -

The opening behind the bookcase was deceiving, just wide enough to fit a large person. Claude ducked his head and descended the spiral staircase with Elisa close behind. It wound around tightly, giving the illusion it was closing in on them as they continued to descend.

"Do these stairs have an end?" Elisa asked rhetorically. "Can you go any faster?"

"They can't go that far down," he stated, just as they reach the bottom. The door at the bottom opened into a dark hallway softly lit with sconces on the walls. They heard voices coming from the other side of a door as they passed.

"This passage probably leads to hidden doors in many of the rooms, like the library," Claude said.

"Mahogany wooden doors. The house must be a few hundred years old at least, who knows what's down here," Elisa said.

Claude put his ear to the next door and opened it. "A lecture hall or auditorium." He shut the door behind him.

"Look at this one, painted metal, no character, unlike the others," he said.

"Never look for the shiny objects, the true treasure is usually hidden beneath the debris and soot," she said, quoting her father and moving past him. She listened, opened the door and was hit with soft rain, causing her to retract.

"It's the garden, the maze is on the other side. Think we can make it through, to get to the opening, without being seen?"

"It's getting dark now, so that will help, but I think we should go along the edges in case someone's around. We won't be obvious targets."

This time Claude stuck his head out the door to searched for the guards. They heard a creak from the hall, and quickly stepped out into the garden, softly closing the door. Behind them, the exterior of the door was covered in bush and vines, blending in with the garden.

"This way," he said, leading them around the perimeter of the garden.

"If I recall correctly, from the aerial view we had when we arrived, once we enter the maze, we should make our way to the right. That should bring us back around to the front helicopter pad," Elisa said.

She grabbed his arm. "Claude, how are we going to get back to Albany?"

"The chopper, I can fly."

She eyed him skeptically.

"It's the one thing I was good at when I served in the military."

"We're going to the east end, you two take the west!" voices called out from the distance.

"I think they've figured out that we're gone," Elisa said.

"Yup, let's go!" Claude grabbed her hand.

She pulled back. "This is not the right way!"

"Yes, it is!" He pulled her straight ahead through the maze, which was illuminated from lights below the hedges. Following the hedges, turning with each next crossroad, they exited into the woods.

"This is not good," he said.

"Shhh…" she whispered. They quickly hid, barely camouflaged behind a large oak tree.

A twig snapped, and Claude knew exactly where their pursuer was. He saw him, hand raised, ready to shoot. *Sidekick!* Claude slowly and quietly pulled up a large branch from the ground. Just a little closer… He came down on sidekick's arm with the huge stick, slivers of bark breaking off and hitting Claude in the face. Swiftly, he swept sidekick's legs from under him, and with all the force from the palm of his hand, he jammed it quickly and forcefully into his nose. With all the force from the palm of his hand he jammed it quickly and forcefully into the sidekick's nose. Elisa could hear the crack and threw her hands over her mouth. Claude picked up the gun.

"Others are coming!" he warned, detecting footsteps and shouting getting closer. Elisa pulled him back into the maze, taking the path they should have gone on earlier.

Each step created suction when their feet left the cushion of the muddy ground. Elisa's foot desperately tried to escape her shoe each time she lifted it. Using the coverage of the eight-foot juniper shrubs, they twisted and turned their way toward the house.

Elisa stopped cold when the next corner left them facing another assailant, his short stature accentuating his muscular build. From his belt, he confidently pulled a huge hunting knife, causing Elisa to stiffen.

"Claude, look out!" she yelled as Claude pushed her behind him.

He produced the gun he had taken from sidekick, hoping to deter the fight, but his aggressor rushed at him. Claude hesitated briefly and then fired one shot. The man collapsed to the ground at his feet.

Elisa ran to the crumpled man.

"What are you doing?!" Claude called out.

Reaching out to the man, she looked up at Claude. "I need a weapon too!" The dying man reached up and with the last of the fight in him, slit Elisa's side with the knife. She fell backward to the ground, crying out in pain.

"Elisa!" Claude yelled.

"I hear them! Over there!" The voices were closer.

"I'm fine, we have to go," she cried, grabbing the knife from the dead man's hand and holding her side.

They ran in the opposite direction of the voices, making left and right turns until they found their way out of the maze.

"There, I can see the edge of the chopper pad," Claude announced.

Skirting the side of the hedges, they moved toward the front of the house. Elisa was trying to step with a steadier stride, but the cut in her side was making it difficult to move quickly.

"The lights under the hedges are going to give our position away," Claude predicted. "We need to move faster to the house or get out of sight. How bad is your cut?"

"I don't know, it's bleeding through, but not gushing." She panted. Claude looked for an entrance back into the maze.

"How many do you think there are?" she asked.

"No idea, but they're security guards, albeit ruthless, but trained as security, that's to our advantage."

"Well, you took out two," she said, breathing through the pain. "And we heard at least two…" She stopped, put her hand up to Claude and listened.

They heard the sloshing of footsteps from the wet ground, getting closer as two men simultaneously appeared on either side of them.

Elisa stepped back. A man rushed at her and she jabbed her foot in the air attempting a kick to the throat, but he caught her foot mid-air and flipped her. She went down hard on her shoulder, momentarily taking the breath from her. He reached down to grab her and she kicked him as hard as she could in his groin. He wailed in agony and teetered back. She struggled to get up, with only a moment to her advantage, and using what little strength she had shoved him down, pulled the knife from her belt and jammed it hard into his groin. He let out another deafening wail.

Behind her, the other guard slumped down in Claude's arms. Elisa cupped her mouth. "Sidekick again! You strangled him!"

"No, sleeper hold."

"Oh. Drag him over here," she commanded.

"Why?"

"Quickly!"

She positioned her pale assailant's hands over his punctured artery, where he was rapidly losing blood.

"Put him on his leg, here." Claude did what she said and dropped the unconscious guard onto the other's groin. Again, he screamed in agony. *Hopefully the weight will provide enough pressure until someone gets him help.*

"I wouldn't move him or you'll bleed to death," she instructed the injured guard.

She responded to Claude's perplexed expression, "I don't want to kill anyone!"

"No, you're just maiming guys left and right." He looked around. "Come on, we can make it to the front."

"Wait!" Elisa ran back to Sidekick, rummaged through his pockets and pulled out their bands.

Two gunshots fired past them.

"Get back to the maze!" Claude yelled.

The swooshing sound of the bullets sped past Elisa's head—she braced herself.

"You're limping?"

"Sidekick came down pretty hard on my leg with his elbow." Hidden in the hedges, the voices were getting louder.

"You okay?" Claude asked.

Her heart felt like it was going to beat right out of her chest. "Scared."

"It won't be long before they find us, we need a distraction. Still got that lighter?"

"Yes!" she said, catching on to what Claude had in mind.

She shoved her hand in the branches of the hedge, stifling a moan, and lit it afire in several different places.

They moved through the maze, careful to stay out of sight, setting it on fire and distancing themselves from the lit hedges until Elisa, light-headed, fell to the ground.

"I tried to suck it up, but the pain is too much," she confessed, holding her shoulder.

"Yeah, I can see it, your shoulder is out of joint." Claude placed his hands on either side of her shoulder. "Ready?"

"Ready for what…"

He swiftly snapped it back in place. She almost blacked out from the pain.

"Sorry, you needed it. It's gonna hurt, but at least you can move it." He steadied her as she started to fall over. "You okay?"

She threw up.

He gave her a moment. "We need to move, stay low to the ground."

"I'm not sure if I can get *off* the ground," Elisa mumbled.

The voices were getting louder. "They're not on the south side of the maze, I'm going to check the woods—Joe, check the perimeter!"

"It's getting too hot and smoky in here, retreating, sir."

"Check the perimeter!" his superior demanded.

"There's no guarantee the fire will deter them from looking for us," Claude coughed, "but they will be just as vulnerable as we are. The rain has slowed, but there's also no telling how much of it is going to thwart the fire. We need to get to the helicopter, can you move?"

"I can move." *I have to move, there's no other option,* she told herself, holding the collar of her shirt to her nose and mouth.

"I can't keep my eyes open, the smoke is burning them," Claude said.

"Stay low, listen for a minute." She paused. "Follow the sound of the rain hitting the roof of the house."

"Footsteps!"

"I hear them," she whispered.

They rolled and tucked in as tight as they could under the hedge.

Elisa looked up to see Guardzilla stride by. They escaped being noticed.

"They're moving away," Claude said.

Barely able to open her eyes, as the smoke and fire continued to fill the maze, Elisa grabbed onto the first part of Claude that she came in contact with, his sleeve, and led him, crawling along the ground.

She stopped and listened again to where the rain was hitting the roof, worried she wouldn't be able to hear through the crackling of the fire. They continued on as it quickly caught up to the bushes next to them, urging them to get away from the blaze they created.

Bringing his face as close to the ground as he could, Claude desperately searched for fresh air.

"They're going to be checking the perimeter, I think it's just the two left, one's in the woods and Guardzilla can't check the entire perimeter at once. We have to take a chance," he pointed out.

Elisa finally led them to the outer perimeter of the maze with the blaze just behind them—the pain in her arm was consuming her. Still struggling to breathe and see, she stopped and listened again.

"I can hear the rain hitting the water in the fountain at the front of the house."

"Still best to stay against the house, we'll be harder to spot," Claude reminded her.

He followed her, fighting to open his eyes in spite of the sting.

Once away from the bulk of the smoke, they took a moment to breathe, then continued along the side of the house with the helicopter in view.

Peering around to the front of the house, Elisa scanned the area, instantly stepping back. "The pilot. He's on the front stairs, what now?"

From the waist of his jeans, Claude pulled out sidekick's gun. "I don't want to kill anyone else either, but I'll do what I have to do to save Ash."

They are overwhelmed with smoke when a shift in wind carried clouds billowing to the front of the house.

Still low to the ground, now coughing heavily, Elisa said, "We have no choice, we have to go."

They ran as fast as they could toward the chopper. "Look, he's going around the back to see what's going on! He didn't even see us!" she said.

Claude climbed into the fuselage after pushing Elisa in before him. "You don't look good, you're pale."

Elisa crawled onto the seat and laid motionless. "Yeah well, I'm not feeling so hot either."

In the cockpit Claude tried to wipe the sting from his eyes, quickly re-familiarizing himself with the flight controls. "Like riding a bike," he said to himself.

"I just tried twice to reach Ashlei, Claude—she's not answering!"

"Try again!" he demanded. The blades slowly begin to increase their speed.

Several rings later, she said, "No answer."

"We're not going to reach her in time, call Jack and tell him to get her to safety!"

Jack answered on the first ring.

"Jack, Jack," Elisa yelled into her wrist, then coughed incessantly. "I don't have time to explain, but Ashlei's in danger. I'll explain later, but you can't call the police, you have to get to her and take her to your place." She attempted to raise her hoarse voice to compete with the roar of the blades. "Please Jack, you have to get to her first. I can't talk. Please get to her," she yelled and disconnected, hoping he heard everything she'd said.

Elisa saw Guardzilla and the pilot running fast to reach the helicopter before it took off.

"They're coming! Get us out of here!"

Claude pulled back on the lever and they began to rise into the air as gunshots ricocheted off the side of the chopper.

She looked down in time to see Guardzilla shoot a few more rounds before he realized that they were out of range.

As they continued to rise, Elisa slid into the co-pilot's seat next to Claude. For the first time in hours the tension in their bodies released, if only temporary.

"Look down," she said, "Ironically, from up here, ablaze, the maze looks beautiful."

~

Looking down over the Hudson river from the co-pilot seat in the cockpit, John reached up and touched the device in his ear. "Yes. What?! How the hell could they get away from you? I don't give a rat's ass about the maze! I'm sure they're headed to Albany. No, but stand by."

He disconnected and made another call.

-54-

MIKE WAS FEELING RUSHED now after the night guard, Diego, kept him talking at the gate. John had given him and Persaud a task that required him finding Ashlei's address, which he kept on file in the lab. He reached for the handle, but the door opened from within.

Coming out of the lab, Ashlei gasped when she found Mike about to enter with a slightly taller man whom she guessed was of Indian descent.

"Hi… Mike."

She had a call coming in. "Excuse me."

"Hey, Jack, just leaving work." She glanced up at the men in front of her. "Can't talk now, though I'll call in just a bit."

"Ashlei, wait!" Jack called out, but she'd already disconnected. He called again. *Jack. I'll call him back when I'm away from Mike.*

"Miss Quinn, I didn't expect to run into you here, but, actually, you are exactly who I needed to see."

As uneasy as Mike usually made her feel, this was the first time she'd ever felt a chill rise up her spine.

"Sorry, Mike, I'm in kind of a hurry right now." She backed up, turned and walked away. "I'll see you tomorrow," she yelled back to him.

Just as Claude had said, the key for the back room was under Mike's desk, but the boxes he'd found labelled Restore were gone. Shipped out to be injected into unsuspecting women as it had been for over a hundred years. But this time, there was no chance for their children to live beyond a week.

Her dad entered her thoughts. She and Elisa were the only girls in town who could easily place someone in a choke hold. In his mind, he was preparing them for the awful things he'd seen, but she was sure part of that training was to prepare them for dating. She knew what to do if she needed to.

She looked around—after hours, no one else in sight. *They're probably waiting for me to get to a closed off place.* She looked behind her; they were just standing at the lab door talking.

"Okay, I'm being paranoid!" she said quietly to herself and chuckled nervously.

Ashlei stopped walking briefly and listened. *Footsteps!* Her whole body was trembling, but she continued on.

What if they have guns? A knife? Her eyes darted around searching for the best route for her to escape. She glanced behind her. *Now they know I know they're coming!* The footsteps quickened.

She took a deep breath and turned around. "Hey, Mike, do you need something?"

"Yes, I need you to come with me."

"Why?"

"I just have some questions for you regarding VM9. It shouldn't take long."

Not taking long doesn't sound encouraging.

"What did you need to know?"

"Let's go back to the lab and pull it up on the VCC," he said, gently grabbing her elbow.

She walked slowly. *Think!*

~

Jack was taking every shortcut he could to get to Exylon while continuing to call Ashlei.

"What the hell is going on?! Elisa's not answering. Ashlei's not answering. No police!" *She could have been a little more specific about the kind of danger Ashlei may be in.* He stepped on the gas. *What am I supposed to do when I get there, if I can't call the cops! Just tell her to come to my place and we wait—simple task.* "How am I supposed to get past security! Shit!"

- 55 -

ASHLEI'S THOUGHTS BOUNCED around her head as she tried to figure out what to do next. *Focus.* She took deep breaths in.

Just below them there was a door that led to a corridor and then another door. On the other side of that door there was a security guard station. *It's now or never.*

She slammed her foot as hard as she could onto Mike's. Then swiveled to her left, she jabbed her fist into Persaud's throat. He crumbled to the floor, unable to make a sound. She turned quickly back to Mike before he recovered, pulling her knee as hard as she could into his groin. Pulling away from Mike's loose grip on her sweater, she ran as fast as she could toward the staircase, her band sliding across the floor. She could still hear Mike yelp as she descended the stairs three at a time. Grappling for the security tag attached to her jeans, she wasted no time. She got to the door and nervously dropped her tag, picked it up, put it up against the lock, opened the door and felt an excruciating pain as the door slammed against her right arm and head just as she was about to go through. Persaud had thrown the weight of his body against the door. Fear soon masked the pain she felt as he grabbed her by the neck and threw her to the floor.

"Believe it or not," he said, looking down on her, taking in several breaths, "I was going to be the nice guy for once. I was with Mike on maybe trying to convince John to find another way to deal with this—

with you." He took another breath, leaning one hand on his knee. "But, fuck that!" He rubbed his throat with the other hand. "I don't care what he does with you."

Mike caught up with them, also out of breath. "Not smart, Ashlei. You just made this much more difficult on yourself. And look, your head is bleeding," he said, handing her a handkerchief. "That wasn't necessary at all—you have no idea what's going on."

He looked at Persaud. "Let's take her to the lab."

Mike struggled with his thoughts on the way to the lab. *Expiration dates were already a part of society, changing them wasn't that big a deal. I never agreed to harming anyone outside of the accelerated dated injections. But Ashlei may have tied my hands.*

~

Jack slowed down as he pulled into Exylon and was relieved to see the guard he'd joked with from earlier this morning at the booth. Rolling his window down he called out, "Hey, Diego, what are you pulling, an all-nighter?"

The guard struggled to recognize the face inside the car, making Jack nervous.

"Oh, hey, doc. Sorry, yeah, been here a while, double shift. Almost done though. Forget something?"

"Actually, I'm meeting Ashlei Quinn here. The biologist I met with this morning."

"Ah yeah, she showed up about half-hour ago." He opened the gate and came out of the booth.

"You guys stay working all kinds of hours, huh. Mr. Khoury and that other doctor showed up not too long ago, too. Go ahead and park, I'll open the door so the lovely lady doesn't have to come all the way down."

Jack wasn't sure if he'd get in trouble for doing so, but he wanted to kiss him right now.

Jack took a moment to remember the way to Ashlei's lab and came to the bottom of the spiral staircase they climbed early this morning. He retreated back into the shadows when he saw Ashlei being aggressively escorted by a dark-skinned man, trailing a slightly smaller thin man. Her head was bleeding.

Once out of sight, Jack climbed the stairs and saw the door just closing as he reached the landing. He tried to listen at the door, but couldn't make out the muffled sounds.

"What am I doing?" he said to himself, leaning against the door.

On the other side of the door Mike attempted to tie Ashlei's arms in back of her.

She moaned loudly; her arm had swelled significantly and the pain was now fighting fear for her attention. Mike winced and relaxed his grip on her right arm.

He pulled her hands and tied them together with hemp rope, tugging only lightly on both arms. She clenched her jaw.

"Sorry," he said, "I need you secure."

Her shirt was wet and sticking to her now. Her shoulder to her elbow and head were all throbbing intensely. She didn't know how long she could tolerate this position but had a feeling that this was the least of her concerns.

He's wrong, I know exactly what's going on, but I can't let him have the advantage of knowing that.

"Mike, why are you doing this?"

"Did you think I wouldn't notice that you were roaming through my virtual computer the other day? What were you looking for?" he asked.

"I didn't realize it was your VCC," she lied. "I thought it was Claude's." She took a breath between shots of pain. "I was looking for a program we had been working on together."

Persaud was leaning back in a chair across the room, elbow on the desk, watching the interrogation. She felt like his part in all this was minor.

"My VCC was locked with a hand scan and pass code, there was no way you could get on it without manipulation!"

"It was already accessed, and once I realized it, I closed it immediately. I didn't want to get fired. Is that what this is all about, Mike?"

"You're lying! You are too smart for me to believe you didn't realize this was my VCC. And did you think I didn't notice that a box in the back room had been opened with a vial missing? What were you looking for?"

Claude. Defeated, she tried to reason with him. "I'm finding it difficult to believe that you are involved in something so awful. You owe it to everyone who believes in what you've done and are doing to do the right thing," she pleaded. "You are one of the reasons I was excited to work here at Exylon—I've followed your work since I first realized I wanted to work with human genetics. No one is as passionate as you about the work they're doing and to jeopardize it all by—"

There was a knock on the door.

Persaud sat up. He took large strides across the room and used the same handkerchief Ashlei used to stop the bleeding on her head and shoved it in her mouth.

Another knock.

"Security," Jack said, hoping this would get the door open.

Mike called back, "We're working here and cannot be disturbed."

"I'm sorry sir, but there's a gas leak and we need to get everyone out. No exceptions!"

With no alternative, Mike looked at Persaud in frustration. "We'll be out momentarily," Mike called back.

"No exceptions sir," he repeated and tried the knob, but the door was locked.

Persaud whispered to Mike. "Perfect, actually. We'll deal with her when all is clear and we get back in. They'll find her tomorrow thinking she was gassed. Our hands are clean. No questions," he said, pleased with his idea.

Mike pursed his lips, his brows coming together as one. "I suppose our options are limited here."

He waited for Persaud to pull Ashlei's chair out of direct sight of the door and then opened it.

Jack didn't hesitate as the door crept open; he pushed it all the way and punched the first person in the doorway. Mike fell to the floor immediately. Jack figured he had no time to let the other guy know what was happening, he had to attack him. Mike grabbed his ankle as he stepped over him, causing him to go down hard, hitting his face on the floor. Persaud stepped in and hit Jack on the back of the head with the butt of his gun. Pulling him up, partially dragging him, he dropped him not far from Ashlei. Semi-conscious, Jack could taste the blood pooling inside of his mouth, his tongue going straight for the gash where his tooth went through his lip.

With blurred sight he looked over at Ashlei, her mouth blocked by a bloody handkerchief, her eyes wide, looking desperately at him. He sighed, relieved she was still alive.

"Who are you?" Mike asked getting up from the floor.

"Thack," he painfully said through a swollen lip.

"Why are you here?" Persaud cut in.

"Tat is why I hare," he said, pointing up at Ashlei, then spitting a mouthful of blood on the floor—causing Ashlei to gasp.

Mike answered a call. "Well, we have a situation. Yeah, her friend showed up. Not exactly sure. Is that necessary? Alright. Yeah, bye." He disconnected.

"John's on his way here from Boston," he reported to Persaud.

Mike removed the handkerchief from Ashlei's mouth—she took in a deep breath.

"Jack, are you alright?" The throbbing in her arm took over again.

"I'm okay, you?"

"Not my best day ever," she responded.

Persaud was pacing back and forth like a predator ready to pounce on its prey.

"We should take care of them before John gets here."

"No! He wants us to meet—said he wanted to handle it himself."

"He thinks we screwed up! Doesn't want us to screw up again, I'm sure!" Persaud surmised.

"Perhaps," Mike said, unconcerned. Persaud sneered at Ashlei and Jack.

Internally, Ashlei was smiling at the satisfaction of causing the bruise on his throat.

"It's unfortunate that I didn't actually paralyze your larynx."

He shoved the handkerchief back in her mouth.

"I opted to inject your fetus with the nanobytes sooner rather than later!"

Ashlei eyes widened—he disregarded her muffled shriek.

- 56 -

ELISA WAS GRIPPING THE SEAT so tight with both hands that her knuckles were white.

"Ya know if we go down, gripping that seat is probably not going to save you," Claude said.

"Shut up, it makes me feel better. It seems like you're going a little fast to be so low to the ground."

"Ground-hugging is going to keep us off radar detection." He looked over at her. "Don't worry, I'm trained to fly these things and I wasn't half bad. The night vision gives us a pretty good view in the distance." He pointed to the green tinted windshield. "See all those red blips?"

"Yeah."

"They indicate obstacles like trees, buildings, mountains. The terrain from Boston to Albany along this route is pretty straight forward. We're not going to run into any buildings. Our blips are just trees here and there, this is the safest route. I've made this trip many times by many modes of transportation, so fortunately I'm familiar with the layout. What we *do* need to concern ourselves with are pylons."

"Pylons?"

"Power poles. They will let me know where the power lines are. Our day will have gotten a whole lot worse if we run into one of those."

Elisa noticed lights in the distance behind them. "Claude, is that another chopper behind us?"

"Yeah, I see him. We're way under signal detection, whoever they are, they are looking for us. Must've been sent by John, hold on!"

Elisa quickly gripped the grab handle tight as her body leaned sharply to the right.

"What are you doing?!"

"Trying to lose them."

"Are you crazy! You said this was the safest route! You're gonna veer off ?!"

"They're right on us, damn!"

Claude pulled back on the lever to elevate their altitude, careful to remain undetected by air traffic control.

There was cracking behind them as bullets whizzed past them.

"What… they're shooting machine guns at us, Claude!"

Claude steered a sharp left; Elisa held herself up from falling into him. She pointed to the red dots in the tinted windshield. "Big blip, big blip!"

He pulled back on the lever again, just barely missing a wind turbine, then picked up speed and avoided a straight, predictable path when they were hit on the side.

"Get down low as you can!" he yelled. She slipped down into her seat.

Elisa heard pings on her side of the chopper where they took another hit. "Claude!"

He kept straight now, to gain speed. Claude felt a shift in his steering, when they took another hit to the back rotor.

Elisa gripped the seat tighter. "Why are we moving like that?"

"They hit our rotor. It's not that bad or we wouldn't still be here," he yelled.

Far enough ahead, he took a sharp right and disappeared from sight.

Claude carefully navigated into a cove, barely large enough for them to fit. They waited, hovering as low to the ground as they could without actually landing. The whopping of their blades intensified from the whirling of the other chopper. It was circling around overhead.

"I can't hold us here like this for long," he said, struggling to keep them elevated and from moving in any direction. Too far to the left or right, they would touch the sides of the cove and destroy the blades and probably themselves.

"So, we just wait them out? They're going to eventually see us when we get back in the air."

"Yup, but we'll be behind them." Claude tried to get a good look through the mirror at the damage from the bullets that struck them. The graze left a long gaping hole on the side of the chopper. The sounds above died down.

"I think they've moved on." He carefully pulled out from the cove and stayed as low as he could to the ground, then pulled the lever to elevate the chopper.

Elisa continued to grip as though her life depended on it—because it did.

Their pursuers were just up ahead; Claude picked up speed.

"Why are you going faster?!" Elisa screamed.

As soon as he was within range, just as they saw him and turned, Claude fired, hitting the tail rotor and sending them into a spin. The next shot struck the pilot. Elisa got a glimpse of Guardzilla in the co-pilot seat as the chopper leaned to the side and fell twirling to the ground. As they passed over the wreckage, it went up in flames.

Her body rigid, Elisa realized that she had been holding her breath and let out a big breath of air.

"Got anyone else you think you can trust that we can call?" Elisa asked sarcastically.

"As a matter of fact, yes."

$$-57-$$

John rushed off of the Night Hawk, hoping to settle the problem at Exylon quickly.

Entering the lab, he was immediately faced with Persaud's bruised throat.

"Krish." He patted his back. "They got the best of you, my friend." "Yes, well, I returned the favor," he responded.

John looked over at Ashlei, whose face was streaked with both tears and blood.

"Miss Quinn." He took the handkerchief from her mouth. "I just left your sister and your beau, but it seems they stole my chopper and are, I would assume, heading this way."

"Good!" Ashlei spat.

"You won't be seeing them though. I have friends in all kinds of places, my dear. I've arranged for them to be pursued and shot down. After all, they did steal a government aircraft. The report will read that they were non-compliant when ordered to land."

Ashlei gasped. "No!"

"My, but you do bear a good resemblance to your sister." She pulled her head back from his hand, cupping her chin.

"I've heard good things about you Ashlei, it's a shame we've had to go this route. Yours is the kind of ingenuity we need to saturate the population. Claude shared your paper on expiration dates as a mutation of our DNA. I enjoyed your fresh perspective."

He shook his head and said to himself, "Pity, the offspring of two intelligent minds would also be an asset."

"You're sick! You really think that you are something special! You and your Restituere are insane! And what you will be saturating the earth with *is* just that. *Your* disease!"

"Hmmm, sisters think alike too."

"You're probably going to need some ice for that," he said to Mike, who was holding his head on the side of his black and blue eye.

"And who have we here?" John looked back at Mike, referring to Jack. "A new player?"

"Jack's a friend of Ashlei's. We were not expecting him."

He raised an eyebrow. "So I gathered from your call."

He put his arm around Mike's shoulder, softly stating, "No worries my friend. I could tell that you were not up for this task. We all have our abilities and inabilities. There's no shame in being inadequate in certain areas. Your genius is what we need, you are no aggressor!" John raised his hand in declaration. "But some of us *are* up for the job." He looked to Persaud.

- 58 -

Claude gently landed on the Exylon insignia next to the smaller chopper with the same company logo on the side. He pointed at Night Hawk, the larger government helicopter, on the other side.

"John!"

He had reset their course for Exylon, once Jack had informed them Ashlei was there and he didn't get a chance to warn her. They slid out of the chopper, grateful for the time they had had to rest from their injuries.

They were met by Diego and another security officer at the door to the building.

"Hello, Mr. Monark. Everything alright?" the guard asked, taking them in. They were dirty and smelled of smoke. Elisa pulled her sweater closed to hide the blood stain on her shirt from the gash in her side, while Claude pulled his shirt over the gun in his waistline.

"Yup, working tonight. We're meeting Mr. Vanburen and Mr. Khoury here."

"Yes of course, busy night; they came in earlier. They didn't look… as weathered though."

"Ha-ha, yeah, rough night," Claude said and moved passed them.

"Well, goodnight."

"Can I help you with anything?" the guard asked, noticing Claude's limp.

"Nope." Claude patted his leg. "Like I said, a rough night. Work doesn't wait though, so… here we are." He swiped in and they entered the building.

"Goodnight," he and Diego said in unison.

"Is that normal?" Diego asked his superior, pointed back as they headed toward the booth at the front gate.

"All these scientists are freakshows, especially that Khoury guy," he responded, shaking his head.

Making their way up to the second level, they heard muffled voices from outside the door. Claude pointed to another door ten feet down, and crouching low, he motioned Elisa to do the same. Slowly opening the door, they both slipped in. Claude raised his head to the barrel of a gun pointing at his forehead. Holding the gun was a man Claude had never seen before. Persaud grabbed the gun that Claude had shoved in his waist, and motioned them to join the others on the other side of the room.

"You're not exactly stealthy," Persaud stated, following behind them.

John stared in bewilderment seeing Claude and Elisa escorted toward him. Persaud quickly looked to John as they dashed off toward Ashlei.

"No worries Krish, they're not going anywhere."

As Claude untied Ashlei's hands, her face scrunched in anguish from the released movement of her arm. Immediately her arms begin to tingle from the blood flow returning to her appendages. Claude visually searched her body for signs of trauma.

"Just the gash in my head and I think my arm may be broken," she offered.

"I'm so sorry about this," he said, kissing her.

Continuing on her way to Jack, five feet away on the floor, Elisa scowled at Mike, sitting in a chair rubbing his swollen face. *Good, Ash or Jack got one in on him.*

She kneeled down beside Jack. "Thank you for trying to save Ash. I'm sorry I dragged you into this."

Still groggy, he attempted a smile. "My life needed a little color anyway, right."

"Mmm, you look awful," she said, gently touching the cut on his lip and cringing at the lump on the back of his neck.

"Right back at ya," he replied, realizing his speech had returned to normal despite the painful hole in his lip.

"Let's get you up," she said, pulling a chair over to him and lifting under his arm as he struggled to assist her.

Jack was just beginning to see a little clearer—the fog beginning to lift from his head. *So much for being a hero and saving the girl.*

"I'm truly impressed to see you here." John grinned widely. "I can't wait to replay my security footage later to see exactly how the two of you managed to get away from my security guards. I fear I am overpaying them."

He stood face to face with Claude. "I shouldn't be surprised, Claude. I do like you. One of your reigning qualities is your resourcefulness. My mistake though, I should have been in tune to the desperate nature of your need to save your love and your unborn child. That is a strong drive for anyone."

"Go to hell," was all Claude could muster for his old mentor, undeterred by the pistol pointing his way.

Mike and Persaud were taking in the interaction.

"Well, how wonderful that you will all be together when you go. Your love, your love's sister, and…" He tilted his head. "I'm not quite sure where you fit into all of this, Jack, right?"

Jack glared at him.

Ashlei pleaded, "If Restituere is truly looking to save the human race," she looked to Mike, "VM9 is an opportunity and only the beginning. We're so close to accomplishing your goal, Mike. If you're worried, like you said, about going backwards, returning to your research is another way to avoid another famine—to go a much more productive way! That's a start! There's no need to kill anyone!"

Mike shifted in his seat, looking at the floor.

Claude glared at John. "Ash, they are planning on taking this way beyond what we comprehended. They're going to administer a sort of germ warfare using nanobytes, with thousands of already planted drones around the world infused with them, that will be set free when they release them. Those nanobytes are going to kill within minutes!"

Ashlei gasped.

"They're going to kill millions!" Elisa added.

"What are you talking about?" Mike asked, looking from Persaud to John.

Claude was surprised by the puzzled expressions on Mike's and Persaud's faces. He looked to John. "Holding back from your cohorts, are you?"

"John?" Mike asked again.

John kept his cold stare locked on Claude.

"We have developed a solution that the other members of Restituere will, I'm sure, be excited about as well."

Mike didn't even know, Elisa thought. Persaud grinned.

Mike cocked his head to the side. "You have been planning this?"

"Have succeeded!" John exclaimed. "Well, shortly—tonight I will have completed the final stages."

John never understood Mr. P's reluctance to share their plan with the other Restituere members. He expressed his concern over the acceptance of such an extreme objective, but John was sure they would all be pleased with the results.

"Mike! Why so glum? This is a time to rejoice! We have exceeded beyond expectation!"

Mike felt a sharp pain in his chest, shaking his head. *The expectation was never so extreme.*

"So, the nanobytes will kill everyone in their path? How does that help your cause?" Ashlei asked.

Elisa answered for John. "Targeting with infrared. I'm sure some of which were part of that list you found, making sure they're striking the right demographic. Their own bodies unknowingly serving as a beacon."

"John, this wasn't talked about among the members." Mike's tone was defiant.

"And I will say to you what was taught to me, you cannot simply expect a plant to grow, it needs water and sunlight. Plants need to be nurtured. Great things don't just happen, they're reared. You of all people should understand that, Mike."

Mike's thoughts were in disarray; he said nothing.

Jack nudged Elisa, tilted his head toward her and parted his hair.

Alarmed, she anticipated another wound. She narrowed her view and leaned in. "What are you…" His fingers cleared the way revealing a seven-digit number.

"Your conspiracy theory was right all along, huh. I hold no obligation to a number they decided for me," he said.

She was stunned by his revelation and by what his tone reflected. She searched his eyes for a meaning.

John threw his hands in the air and re-addressed the four liabilities in the room. "Back to our dilemma!"

Claude stepped forward. "You shoot us and anyone in the building will hear the shots."

John smirked. "True. But here is how this is going work. I'm going to inject you with the nanobytes," he pointed to Claude with the gun. "You move, trigger happy Persaud shoots her," he said, redirecting the gun at Ashlei—Persaud smirked. "I inject you," he said pointing at Jack, "you move, Mike shoots her," he said, referring to Elisa. "And so forth. You have already laid out your plan to use the nanobytes for your own agenda, remember, it's encrypted on your computer. When they find you all here, your story will be that you decided just to take your friends and your life instead. Or, if you decide to get aggressive, your shootings were in self-defense of us trying to stop your family plan. I assure you, this is much more civil for you all. Please don't get me wrong, this is a predicament I'm not at all happy to be faced with. You aren't exactly my target group, but I will not let the four of you hinder the growth of the future of our planet."

Persaud pulled out the syringes he had been itching to use since they got there.

Elisa stood, desperate to reason with him. "Where do you think this planet would be without the people you don't think are intelligent enough to lead it, the very people who take care of the things that you are unwilling to do?!" The force of her words ignited the sharp pain from the gash in her side. "These are the people who till the fields that are harvested, and mine the coal that you burn, and raise the animals that you eat, and build the homes that you live in. You *need* these people! What you're planning just doesn't make sense!"

Claude had to approach this carefully. "This is what you call civil, John?! You're a phony! A swindler! You have no devotion to this planet or the people on it! You hide behind that face, but what your arrogance strives for is control of life and death. You are pretending to play the role of God! This is about power for you, not concern!"

John's face turned red.

"Have you ever heard of biologist Max Klieber or even Geoffrey West?" John asked through clenched teeth. "No response, anyone?"

They were not about to give him the satisfaction of engaging in an agreeable conversation.

"Well then, let me enlighten you all. West picked up the theory where Klieber left off. Their premise was that larger animals live longer than smaller animals based on a mathematical formula. The elephant and gnat's hearts beat the same amount of times, but because the elephant is so much larger and requires more time to grow and thrive, the cells of an elephant work much harder and its heart beats at a slower rate than that of a gnat. The elephant's life will continue on longer because of this."

"Your point?" Claude interceded, tired of his cocky monologue.

"My point… is that, though they only studied this theory in animals and plants, this same idea can be applied to humans. I am referring to the mind, however. The larger, stronger, healthier mind is meant to endure. Whereas the weaker, feeble-minded—the insignificant gnat, if you will, is destined to live only but a small portion in time in comparison."

"The difference is, they are *not* being genetically selected, *you* are taking them out unnaturally!" Claude said.

"We are not the bad guys. We are simply an organization who has taken into our hands the responsibility of saving mankind from itself. And if action isn't taken by Restituere, the type of human beings we are extinguishing are going to continue to populate and 'pollute' the planet and steal its resources until they are once again depleted and the world is right back in the crisis it was in after the Transitional War. It's simple logic," he said, raising his hands in the air.

Persaud handed the nanobyte-filled syringes to John.

He turned to Jack. "It's only fair, unfortunate friend, I've heard from everyone else. And you… what have you got for me?"

Jack simply said, "You're an asshole." John laughed hysterically.

"I think that's the best speech yet! Touché! I guess you would see it that way."

Jack stood. "Actually, the way I see it is that you had taken an oath, just like me, to apply your skills to benefit society. You swore to practice the scientific process based on logic, intellect, integrity, and uncompromising respect for the truth. And you sir, have broken all of these promises made."

Jack lunged at John, taking him off guard. He stumbled back, while they struggled for the gun. Mike grabbed at Jack, attempting to pull him off John—the gun fired.

Unable to take his eyes off Claude and Ashlei, Persaud inched his way closer to see what was going on. He turned momentarily to try and get a glimpse, still holding the gun on the others. Claude stepped forward to help Jack. Persaud shook his head in warning, turning the gun on Ashlei.

"What's going on?!" Persaud called. "Mike… John, what's going on?!" He shifted a bit more to try and get a better view. The commotion settled quickly and Jack rolled to the floor next to John. There was blood covering them both.

John struggled to reach up, feeling the warm liquid pulsing from his throat. Dark red drops fell to his face when he raised his hands to confirm what he already knew. "Mike." He gurgled. "Mi…"

John lay there, gun in hand, eyes fixed at the ceiling. Lifeless. Elisa could see the blood pulsating from his neck. *Jack went for his carotid artery.* In Jack's hand lay the little jack knife that she teased him about. The lump in her throat grew. She whispered, "Jack."

"Oh my god, oh my god, John." Mike shook him and the gun dropped to the floor.

"Is he dead?" Persaud asked. "Mike, is he dead?"

"I think so. Yes," Mike affirmed. The words fell out of his mouth. Feeling the weight of their actions, he sat on the floor next to John with his hands on his head staring at the blood pouring from his throat.

None of this was supposed to happen!

Claude decided not to wait for the assailants to refocus. Stepping in front of Ashlei, he pushed her away, lunging at Persaud. His gun went off instinctively, brushing Claude's side. Elisa felt the momentum and rushed toward Mike.

Ashlei raced in to help her sister.

Mike desperately scrambled for John's gun when he saw Elisa rushing toward him.

She stepped on his hand just as he reached it, kicking him back with her other foot. They both heard the break in his arm from the force.

Mike cried out in pain.

Ashlei stomped her foot on Mike's face to force him all the way down to the floor.

Elisa picked up John's gun, shoving it into Mike's cheek, nicking the skin. She pushed her knee into the chest of his small frame, using all her weight, pain and anger to inflict as much injury as she could. She turned, looking toward Jack's still body. She couldn't see where his gunshot wound was. *There is so much blood!*

"Ash, check his pulse."

Ashlei put her fingers to Jack's neck, looked at Elisa and shook her head somberly. Elisa found herself now standing above Mike, kicking him over and over. He curled in a ball, crying out in pain each time.

Claude and Persaud struggled for the gun. Claude was injured, but his youth and skills should give him the advantage. Persaud managed to flip him around and get his thick arm around Claude's neck. The gun went off again as he struggled to maintain control. Grasping for air, Claude began to lose his strength. He quickly pulled on Persaud's wrist and grabbed his groin with the other hand, yanking hard. Persaud's grip loosened and Claude flipped back around, and now had him in a front hold; pushing his head down, he kneed him hard in the face. He fell to the floor. Before he attempted to get up, Claude put his foot to Persaud's throat, while Ashlei quickly retrieved the gun and held it on him.

Both doors burst open and five security guards rushed in. "Hands up everyone!"

Elisa and Ashlei both laid their guns on the floor, and did their best to raise their hands, despite their injuries.

Diego was rapidly aiming his gun from Claude to Elisa to Persaud. His eyes fell on the pool of blood around Jack. Elisa began to move toward Jack. When Elisa began to move toward her lifeless friend, Diego allowed her to go—his shaky gun hand following her.

She held him in her lap crying over his death—over the revelations of the events of the day.

Ashlei knelt by her sister and put her arm around her. "I'm sorry E."

"I didn't know his expiration date was two years from now, but that's two years he could have had. He gave that up for us."

Moments later, Albany police officers arrived and swarmed in around the room pushing security out, making them spectators. After assessing the scene, the first officer to enter called out, "We have two deceased males; one male and two females, beaten but lucid; and another male with an unidentified wound bleeding from his right side, also lucid."

Another officer, touching his earpiece, requested paramedics.

Moments later, Mike, was hoisted onto a hover stretcher and pushed out of the room.

The officers parted the way as their chief senior officer marched into the lab. He viewed the carnage around the room and looked for someone who could give him the best answers.

Persaud was slumped in a chair, blood trickling from his mouth—his throat black and blue.

The officer strode across the room approaching Claude, glancing down at the blood seeping through his shirt.

"Medic!"

An emergency medical technician rushed over. The decorated man pointed to Claude's side. "Take a look."

Claude lifted his arms, while the medic gently pulled his shirt up. He looked up at Claude.

"Looks like just a graze. It's just a flesh wound."

"Bullet," Claude informed him.

"Uh, yeah. I can just bandage it for now," he said and stepped away to get his medical kit.

Elisa's heart was breaking. She covered her mouth as she watched the paramedics pull a tarp over Jack and push him out of the room on a stretcher.

The officer hadn't taken his eyes off Claude. "What's your name?"

"Claude Monark."

"Mr. Monark, what's *your* version of what went on here?"

"Don't answer that, Claude." A strong deep voice came from behind the officer.

The officer swung around to face the man who was impeding his investigation.

"Agent James Stone, DPCS investigations."

"So? And I'm Detective Walters, Chief of Police! On what authority do you have…"

From the disk in Stone's hand, a presidential seal was produced, lighting up the space just above his palm. The Orbis sphere spun around, bouncing a green flash of light every two seconds off the stunned chief's face. A new swarm filtered into the room: all government agents dressed in black from head to toe, taking their positions.

"We will be taking over this investigation. Thank you for your assistance," he said and flashed him a solid smile.

The chief pursed his lips, his face changing to a dark red.

Government always wants all the glory!

He twirled his finger in the air. "Wrap it up," he called to his men and stormed out of the room the same way he entered.

As the last of the Albany Police Officers left, Stone followed behind, glancing at one of his agents on the way out. "I want two agents on Mike Khoury."

With John and Jack's bodies removed and Mike on the way to the hospital, only the four remained. Claude watched Persaud closely, unsure what a desperate man might do in his position. Though these agents were serious—he'd be no match.

The agents carefully assisted Ashlei and Elisa, escorting them to the third-floor administrative offices, along with Claude.

They watched as Persaud was separated and brought into another room—leaving them wondering about their own fate.

- 59 -

THE THIRD FLOOR AT EXYLON was much plusher than the rest of the building. Crystal chandeliers hung from the ceiling in the hallways and the navy-blue carpet ran in and out of each of the nine rooms. Ashlei welcomed the soft impact, since each step she took felt like a sledge-hammer to her shoulder.

"Seems like an eternity since I interviewed in there," Claude said of the dark deserted office they passed by.

The suite they entered housed a gray sofa, a couple of wingback chairs and a coffee table. The agent escorting them motioned for them to sit, again scanning the dried blood trailing down their heads; dirty, bloody, ripped clothing; and smelling the stench of smoke. He retreated to the door they entered, turned just on the inside, and stood in military formation—staring dutifully ahead.

When James Stone entered a room, authority emanated from him. After ending his long military career as a Colonel in the Orbis Air Force, he had taken on the task of heading security at the Bureau of Population Control and Statistics. At six-feet-four and with a stern demeanor, his presence normally made one immediately stand to attention, but his captive audience could barely stand at all. Claude had only officially met Colonel Stone once, but had seen him many times in passing at the Nutriment Facility. He held a high regard for him as a decorated officer in the military, which was why he was the one who Claude called from the helicopter.

Colonel Stone dragged a chair over to the couch where the three were sitting like it was filled with feathers. His brown, rugged skin bore a scar across his left cheek and a few visible on his hands. He appeared to be a man you didn't mess with. Pulling out his identification, he introduced himself and began to speak.

"I am aware you are all in need of medical attention, so I will try to keep this brief for the moment. There's a great deal that has happened I will need you to fill me in on. I want to say upfront that whatever transpired is confidential and must remain classified. Claude, I don't need to fill you in on the ramifications of classified information being exposed."

Claude nodded.

"As soon as we are done here, I have a car waiting to take you all to the Medical Center to get treated." He looked each one in the eye. "You are to speak to no one but me, understood?" They all nodded in agreement, too exhausted to argue.

"I will also provide you with a briefing as to the information you will relay regarding your injuries."

They told James Stone everything: about Restituere, the mass deaths, and how there was a secret lab on level K at the nutriment plant. They informed him about John's plan and explained in detail how he was going to carry it out using "nanobyte warfare."

Claude said, "There are employees of the bureau who are part of this. Some of whom tried their best to kill us. You may still find some of them on John's property and the others, well, I'm sure you've already come across the wreckage about twenty miles east of here. You may also want to check John's estate for whatever device he was going to use to set the drones in motion."

"And, we lost a friend tonight," Elisa said flatly, exhausted and all cried out. "Dr. Jack Derrin. He gave his life for us and honestly, John's plan might still have been executed if it weren't for Jack."

James Stone lowered his head. "I'm very sorry for your loss. Then he is a hero. And obviously, a very good friend."

"I'm going to make a couple of calls and arrange for your hospital stay. Once you're healed up, we'll meet again."

He stepped into the next room and the three slumped back into the couch. There was a much-needed calm silence they soaked in. Ashlei closed her eyes and laid her head on Claude's chest, while he rested his head on the back of the couch.

Elisa's shoulder and side were throbbing in full force, now that her adrenaline had faded away. She zoned out, looking at an old photo on the wall of the celebration of the opening of Exylon. The group, who she assumed were the founders or maybe CEOs of the company, were getting ready to cut the ribbon to begin many years of discoveries and innovation that created and built much of the technology used every day. Something was nagging her about the photo. Her eyes began to close as she faded, when she identified the familiar face of the gentleman to the right in the photo, shaking the hand of another. Suddenly she sat up straight, wincing from the jerking motion of her injured arm.

"Claude, we have to go!" she said quietly, shaking his arm.

Startled, he quickly sat up pushing Ashlei up with him. "What's going on?"

"Okay folks." James Stone returned. "You're all set. I'm sorry you got caught up in this, but from the looks of those guys in the lab, I'd have to say I'm glad you're on our side. Still, until we investigate this thing in its entirety, my agents will stay with you—for your safety." He handed them each a card with his contact information on it. "I'll touch base with you in a few days."

He nodded to the waiting agents who suddenly came to life and led the three out of the building and into a waiting government car.

- 60 -

IN THE BACK OF THE black government hover car, there was plenty of room for the three to spread out and recline while they were transported to the hospital. Ashlei took in the same view that stood before her the night she had gone to dinner with Claude for the first time. Riddled with pain, she welcomed the sensation of warm memories flowing through her.

That seemed like forever ago.

Now that they were alone in the back of the car, Elisa painfully twisted to face Claude and Ashlei, speaking low so the agents wouldn't overhear her.

"We have to go to Lake George."

"What?!" they said in unison.

"I couldn't figure out why the picture in the office was nagging at me!"

"What picture?" Ashlei interrupted.

"The one on the wall of Exylon's founders… whatever, it doesn't matter. Robert Frederick was on the board of Exylon!"

"Okay… of course, the Frederick family helped to build the company, producing a lot of its inventions actually," Claude said.

"Well, it was bugging me because it reminded me of another photo I'd seen a couple of days ago—a bunch of guys on the golf course posing for a friendly photo."

The two stared at her, bewildered.

She rolled her eyes, jetting her hands out. "Robert Frederick is Reed's grandfather!"

"And?" Claude questioned.

She continued. "I didn't know who John was at the time, and when I met him, I couldn't figure out why he seemed familiar."

She took a deep breath, holding her side fruitlessly, hoping it would suppress the pain.

"He was in that photo I saw of him and his buddies playing golf." She struggled to say his name a second time aloud. "Standing with Reed Frederick."

The lump in her throat grew, she didn't want to be so sure.

"Not unusual for Reed to be friendly with the head of a federal agency. They pretty much own the government!" Claude stated.

Ashlei asked, "So, they were in a picture together, what does that mean?"

"That means this isn't over! Think about it, how was John able to fund this plan to activate these incendiary nano bombs all over the world? The Fredericks own half of this region and beyond!"

Claude crossed his arms. "Well, John makes a pretty good living."

Elisa scrunched her eyebrows. "Umm, not that kind of money! Did he distribute them himself ?! Reed has been traveling a lot according to Jack. He was teasing him saying, 'I guess the rich get to show only when they need to make an entrance.'"

"Who knows how big Restituere actually is, maybe others helped with distribution," Ashlei pointed out.

Elisa's eyes no longer felt heavy. She had definitely gotten her second wind of the night—running on full adrenaline.

Ashlei wrinkled her nose. "I'm not sure Reed fits in. Why would he risk everything he has?"

She looked at the federal agents in the front seat, leaned in closer to Ashlei and Claude and lowered her voice again. "I don't know. Maybe because he *does* have everything or maybe everything is not enough. Anyway, I overheard him talking to another doctor not too long ago about a woman, who I assumed just lost her baby to a short expiration date. Reed's response was, 'She should appreciate the fact that with her low income she doesn't have to have the burden of a child who will also provide no real contribution to society.' He smoothed it over with instructions to help her family to transition with the loss. I was more concerned about the vial I had just taken to really give that conversation any thought about what it meant or maybe I just didn't want to see. But I'm thinking clearer now, and that ideology falls right in line with the rest of Restituere's mantra. And he *is* an administrator of nutriment injections."

She pointed at her sister. "And Ash, didn't you say once, 'guilty by association!'" She reminded her of the comment she made about Claude working with Mike.

Ashlei sneered at her sister. "Maybe you're right, John's plan seems too big for it to be just him. Mike and Persaud seemed oblivious. He would have needed someone else. So why do you want to go to Lake George?"

"Because that's where the Fredericks' family estate is and if he had something this big in the making, he'd need the privacy and room to spread out," Claude responded, convinced maybe Elisa was right.

"Jack mentioned the other day that he had plans with him, but Reed canceled because he was going home—meaning his family home!"

Elisa lowered her eyes and sighed. "Look, I'm not saying I want it to be him. I'd love to be wrong, I really like Reed. But I can't shake this, he's definitely involved, which means there's a chance those nanobytes could still be launched."

They pulled into a dark, isolated side entrance of the hospital.

"Claude, we can't have gone through all this for nothing. Jack can't have died for nothing. If there's a chance that I'm right about this, we have to go there and prevent him from sending that signal to launch those things."

Claude sat and thought for a moment. "Getting away from these guys is gonna to be a problem. They were given an order, they're going to make sure we make it to our destination and stay there."

"You can't be serious about going ourselves, why don't we let that Stone guy handle this?" Ashlei said.

"No way is he going after a Frederick! They're the government's bread and butter. By the time they investigate, *if* they investigate, it'll be too late," Claude stated. "And if we tell them of our suspicions, they'll stop us."

The agents open the doors on either side, reaching in to help Elisa and Ashlei out of the car.

A woman in a plain gray suit, along with a slightly younger, shorter woman in dark blue scrubs greeted them at the door.

"Hello, I'm Leslie, hospital administrator," the gray suit said, "and this is Ginny." Ginny smiled and waved awkwardly. "We're going to see you to your rooms."

Leslie flashed an unfriendly smile and scanned the agents top to bottom, then addressed the three disheveled people with them.

"I hear you've had quite an ordeal," she continued as they fell into place behind her, the two agents trailing.

"Yes," Ashlei spoke up, reciting the fabricated tale they were all briefed on.

"We can accommodate you on the fourth floor. You'll be in the older part of the building, but at least it's discreet."

"We may have caught a break," Elisa quietly informed Claude. "Those old rooms have balconies, believe it or not. I'm sure they're locked, but maybe we can break the lock."

"And what, climb out and scale the building from the fourth floor?"

"No. The rooms are side by side. We can climb over to the next one and—"

He held his hand up. "Let's just see if we can come up with a sane plan."

"It is a good plan—the only plan," she mumbled.

Exiting the elevator on the fourth floor, Elisa's eyes lit up when she saw Paul, wearing his familiar baseball cap, blond-streaked black hair peeking out.

Paul stepped back, sizing up her company. "Hey Elisa, you look like hell." He locked eyes with her. "You alright?"

"Yeah, acquired a few bumps. You get called in for a procedure?

"Yup, leaving now." He paused for a moment, hesitant to leave.

"Have a good night, sir," an agent said, moving them along.

She mouthed to him to listen for her call. He nodded inconspicuously.

Should she tell him about Jack? What would she say? It was not something you tell someone in passing. He deserved for people to know he was a hero, that took time to explain.

Though the hospital unit was old, it had been renovated. Elisa and Ashlei had a shared room and Claude's was a private room right next door. As predicted, there were balconies outside each.

Ginny stood to the side of Leslie, ready to explode inside. Being a part of a secret assignment was the most exciting thing that had ever happened to her.

"Ginny will be taking care of you this evening," Leslie began. "She will do an assessment and then send you down to x-ray for some testing. I will check in with you tomorrow morning, try to get some rest." She turned on her heel and militantly walked out the door, motioning to Claude to follow.

"I will see you to your room, Mr. Monark."

"I'll be right outside the room," one agent informed Elisa and Ashlei, while the other followed Leslie to Claude's room.

"There are gowns on the beds, you can wash up if you'd like and I will be back in just a minute to get some information," Ginny said.

Elisa immediately called Paul when their nurse left the room.

"Paul, I don't have a lot of time, but I need you to trust me and not ask any questions right now."

"Are you in trouble? Who's the muscle with you?"

"Those are questions, Paul. I'm sorry, I just don't have time to answer anything right now. I need your car."

"I'm on call, covering you remember, kinda need it."

"Please, please trust me. I need your help."

"Okay, I'll figure something out."

"Thank you. Can you meet me in the back of the hospital at the dock where the central supplies are unloaded?"

"I'll head there now," he said.

"I'll be a few minutes."

She dialed Claude's phone. "We need to be at the dock in the back of the hospital, now. I have a car waiting there."

"Okay, if we can get one agent to stay with Ash, then we'll only need to worry about one."

Claude entered their room still on the phone, his agent rearranged outside their door with the other.

He wrapped his arms around Ashlei, holding her gently. "How are you doing?"

"As well as can be expected. You?"

"We have to go. I think it goes without saying that you need to stay here. I will not risk losing either of you again."

"I'm not going to fight you. I realize I'm not just looking out for myself anymore."

"There you are, Mr. Monark! You haven't changed." Ginny scolded, entering the room. "Transportation is here to take you down to x-ray."

"Sorry, it's a bit breezy in those gowns, can I change after?"

"Uh, sure." She frowned.

"Perfect!" he whispered to Elisa, "I'll meet you at the dock."

"Okay, you'll already be on the ground floor. Take a left in the hallway and follow the supply dock signs."

He sat in the waiting wheelchair in the hall, his assigned agent following close behind.

Ashlei grabbed Elisa's hands. "For what it's worth, I'm sorry. I hope you're wrong about Reed. And please be careful, this kid is gonna need his or her aunt. And I need my sister."

"Thanks, and I will." She carefully gave her little sister a hug. "Now change into your gown, I'm going to get you some extra blankets," she said, winking at her.

"My sister is pregnant and not feeling well," Elisa said to the agent. "I'm going to get her a cool cloth for her head and a blanket."

He smiled and nodded.

When she was out of his view, she headed for the EXIT sign above the stairs door and made her way to the basement to meet Claude.

~

Paul sat in his running car outside the docks hoping, no one was around to question his conspicuous position. Since seeing Elisa, he'd been trying to make sense of her situation. Two big, obvious, government stiffs, a guy with a limp, and what looked to be Elisa's sister, all escorted by the medical center's icy head honcho. His concern deepened. They looked pretty banged up and she sounded desperate. He heard the door to the dock open and got out of the car.

~

An x-ray technician met Claude in the room as he was wheeled in. "Can I use the bathroom before we get started?"

"Sure. Go out this door," he pointed, "and take a left, down the hallway and it's on the right."

"Be right back," he said to the agent, getting out of the chair and turning the corner.

He looked back to catch the agent looking down the hall after him. Claude slowed at the bathroom, slightly opened the door and gave another quick glance back to find the agent had returned to his post in front of the x-ray room. Claude quickly headed to the end of the corridor and made a left through the double doors to the main hallway, nearly knocking Elisa down in his rush when she exited the stairwell.

"Nice timing," he said.

"We don't have a lot of time; they are going to notice when I don't come back with blankets."

A big black and white sign ahead read **Supply Warehouse/Dock**, with an arrow underneath pointing right.

They turned into the supply warehouse, threading their way through the heavy traffic of boxes filled with medical equipment and supplies and exiting through the door leading to the dock outside. Elisa giggled, "I feel like a little kid sneaking away from our parents."

"Except our 'parents' carry guns and won't gently scold us if we get caught!"

The rain seemed to be slowing down. Elisa welcomed the light sprinkles on her face. *I can't wait for a nice warm shower.*

Too hurt to hop off the dock, they both sat and eased their way down. Paul saw them approaching and got out of the car.

"Paul this is Claude."

"Hi."

"Hi, thanks for the use of your car."

Paul nodded.

Claude looked the car over. *It's got wheels*, he silently said to himself.

"No questions asked, but I'm expecting one hell of a story when you get back from wherever."

Elisa thought about Jack and kissed him on the cheek. "We'll talk."

"You're gonna need to drive," she said, tossing Claude the keys and eased into the passenger's seat.

Claude looked at the console. "Not a hover. Okay, I just need a second to get familiar with this old-style antique of a vehicle."

He could see Elisa staring at him in his peripheral vision and turned to see her grimace. "That I am so grateful we have! You didn't let me finish!"

He frowned and shifted a knob by his hand in the center of the console and the car jetted forth, throwing both of their heads back.

Elisa rubbed her already-sore neck. "*Can* you drive this thing?!"

"I got it, it's just been a while." A couple more shifts and the car continued on smoothly. Claude gave her an arrogant grin.

"So, he just gave you his car, no questions asked."

"The wonderful thing about working with a team of people in critical care is that we work closely together for hours and days at a time, and in dire situations where you need to trust each other. These people become your family. And yes, they'll have your back, no questions asked."

- 61 -

REED CLICKED THE DISCONNECT on his phone again. He was pacing the living room now after spending the last half hour pacing his lab. The open windows allowed the cool summer breeze, coming off the lake, to carry in the fresh earthy scent from the heavy rains that had passed through earlier.

He stopped and sat on the rugby-striped couch. This was his mother's favorite room. She loved being on the water and everything that came with it. The room was decorated with coastal themes and hues of blues, greens, and yellows contrasting with the traditional conservative spirit of the house.

He brought forth his thoughts about Elisa, knowing the nagging knot in his stomach stemmed from his loss. A loss he had tried to prevent. *Perhaps if I had been honest with her, she would have understood my goal, my vision. If only it was explained and she didn't just stumble upon our plan, maybe she could have been reasoned with. No time for regrets.*

He began to pace again.

There's a reason John's not answering. He repeatedly tapped the phone in his hand.

Something's not right, he's not this irresponsible; not tonight of all nights, this is too important to him. To all of us!

He dialed Mike again. No answer. "Dammit!"

Passing by the mantle, he reached up and collected a wood carved moose, then haphazardly fell against the back of the couch, caressing the intricate details of the museum replica. He recalled the day his mother had bought it. The day she died. They each had a penny to toss into the make-shift babbling creek the big moose stood in. They made their wishes and then she bought him this miniature copy to remember their trip. Reed hardened his jaw and put the moose back on the mantle.

I can't wait for him any longer, looks like I'm going to have to launch without him.

- 62 -

ON THEIR WAY OUT of the city, the last of the raindrops dwindled and clung to the windshield until the wipers completely erased them. Claude let his thoughts drift to Ashlei. He thought about the moment she had told him he was going to be a father. She was sitting on the table, across from him, fidgeting nervously. The midday sun illuminated her face in a way that he'd thought nothing else could possibly be so beautiful. It was in that moment that he realized how much he loved her. He grinned, allowing himself a moment of happiness. *We can't afford to fail!*

"Any ideas about what to look for when we get there?" Elisa asked, interrupting his bliss—jarring him back to reality.

"I'm not sure. We know he has these drones set up all over the world. They most likely need to be activated by a single source so they are launched simultaneously. And again, it makes sense that the source is at the Frederick estate."

Claude pulled the car onto the highway, careful to maintain proper speed in spite of the desperate need to get to the Frederick's estate quickly. Any delay could have cataclysmal results, but he knew all too well that the authorities deemed vehicle traveling a privilege and would revoke that privilege as they saw fit.

"I'm gathering you were romantically involved? With Reed."

"You could say that."

"I'm sorry. But, if you're right, we're doing the right thing." He paused. "We may be in a position where... things may not go well."

"Shoot first, ask questions later. I'm aware of that." Her gut hurt.

"So, you know what he's capable of. Reed came from a highly intelligent and adaptable family. How much do you know about their history?"

"I'm aware of the obvious, that their family is a household name and if you're using a product they probably had their hand in creating some part of it." *I am also aware that he is really funny and a great kisser, among other things, and maybe the man I potentially planned on having a future with.*

"That family had thrived long before the Transitional War, making their fortune in computer hardware and investments. Producing everything from video production equipment to virtual reality simulation and even hair products, as well as becoming the largest maker of medical equipment like computed tomography and magnetic resonance imaging."

Elisa allowed her head to rest against the window as the vast darkness passed by, listening as Claude enlightened her on the way up to Reed's home. *This feels a little like deja vu,* she thought, recalling her history lesson of the Bureau on the flight to Washington D.C. with Claude earlier this morning. *This morning... feels like a million miles away. The government was responsible for expiration dates; Mike was involved with the mass deaths; and Reed, I never would have thought Reed capable of masterminding a plan to wipe out so many of the inhabitants of the earth! He was such a good friend to Jack, a great physician, and at one point I thought maybe he and I... Guess he fooled everyone. This day has taken a turn I'd never expected!*

She closed her eyes, hoping to rid herself of the headache creeping in from all sides. This was a drive she'd taken many times since she was a child. Reed's family home was located in the heart of vacation haven, at the edge of the Adirondacks. She would rather be traveling up this way to go camping, kayaking, or hiking. She thought briefly about how Jack had already tackled forty-two of the forty-nine Adirondack high peaks, setting his sights on finishing the remainder by the following summer. *I thought it was just a time frame he'd set to motivate himself to actually accomplish his goal, I didn't realize he was trying to beat the clock.* She could hear Jack's voice encouraging her to write, *"Life is too short not to do what you love."* And the letter from his wife—*"can't go through it again." That's why she left! When I men-*

tioned having a woman in his life he said, 'Not fair to someone when I'm not around.' "Oh Jack," she barely whispered. *I'm so sorry I didn't see.* The ache in her heart was one more pain added to her body right now.

During the day, Interstate 87 was a beautiful route with its dense green tree line and mountainous backdrop, but at night it was mundane. Law enforcement monitored this stretch of road heavily during the summer months, so she was sure this was why Claude was staying within the speed limit. She tried to stay focused on him.

"During the Transitional War they concentrated on developing equipment and parts for the military, making components for aircraft and manufacturing munitions like ammo, explosives, grenades, et cetera. Graham Frederick, Reed's great-grandfather, was considered one of the great heroes, reconfiguring the strategy of germ warfare, the same technology Reed is using to unleash his nanobytes. He won several battles and some say that it was he who gave us the advantage that eventually allowed us to end the fighting. If you can call it a war won. The Fredericks dove right into the war with full support."

Claude found giving Elisa a history of the Frederick family legacy allowed him to redirect the focus from the pain in his side caused by the graze of the gun shot. He looked over at her; her head was pressed up against the window. She looked so much like Ashlei, though her hair was slightly longer. There was a fire in Elisa's eyes, which was more of a deep passion that lived in Ashlei's. They were very similar in many ways, yet so different. He'd forgotten how annoying the sound of tires were against the road, being fortunate enough to own an affordable hover car usually reserved for the more well-off.

"Of course, after the war, with worldwide communications and reserves being compromised and impossible to tap into, the government had once again turned to the Fredericks to rejuvenate their retired and obsolete products as we moved back into the dark ages, if you will. And as you know, they still hold the biggest monopoly on many businesses here in the northeast, scattered throughout the states as well as overseas. My point is, they're smart and resourceful—we need to be aware of that going in."

"It seems as though Reed has everything, except his sanity," Elisa said, a bit saddened.

$$- \text{63} -$$

Pulling up to the Frederick estate, Elisa and Claude were greeted by a sign above the archway that read "Frederick's Hollow." Claude turned the headlights off and backed up down the road they just came in on.

"What are you doing?"

"We don't want him to see us coming, I think we should walk in from here."

Scrunched down behind the hedges along the edge of the property, Claude scanned for security.

"Reed was expecting John by now, there's no telling what his plan was for activating the drones. He could have done it already," he said.

From the ground, lights shone up on the old craftsman-style house, which stood as distinguished as it did three hundred years ago when the family established itself in the area. Situated on five acres with the brick and stone house overlooking the waterfront, the backside faced the quarter-mile road coming in.

"Look, the lights are on in the neighboring cottage. Why do you think he has lights on in both places?" Elisa wondered aloud.

"Not sure. There's only one car though."

"Yeah, that's Reed's hover Volvo."

"There's a window partially opened, we can slip in there," she said.

"Uh-uh. There's laser security set around the house. As far as I can see."

She squinted to see too.

"Trust me, it's there."

He scanned the landscape, moving closer to the lake. His gaze led to the branches of the tree on the front side of the house, then followed to the roof and to the open window in the attic.

"Bet it's not fixed up there, though."

She looked up. "That's not a good plan! The thicker branches are too far from the house anyway."

He moved in closer, looking around the front of the house. "It's our best bet. He has triggers covering the ground."

"What about underground?"

"What are you talking about?"

"There's a tunnel around here somewhere that Reed used to play in till his mother found out and had it closed it up."

"How does that help us if it's closed up?"

"He said it was blocked off with a stone or something, maybe we can move it. Or, it could be collapsed, I don't know, but it's worth a try."

"Where?"

"Let's go back this way, he said he used to come out near a little creek by the neighbors. If you noticed, we passed one on the way in."

They climbed in the car allowing it to creep back another quarter mile until they came to the creek. Claude searched the car, finding a flashlight and pocket-knife.

"Don't shine the light yet, it's a beacon out here," Elisa said. "I don't see any big rocks, do you?"

"Follow the creek, it's…"

"Here, there's something here," she called out.

The obstructed opening was covered in moss and bushes all around. "That's not a rock, that's a boulder!" Claude said. "Are you sure this is it? It doesn't look like there could be a tunnel behind that."

"It must be it!"

They tried to feel around it in the dark.

"Here, let's see the light." She got on her stomach, pulling on the cut on her side. "This is it, there's an opening behind it. But it's impossible to get in there, that's got to be over a thousand pounds!"

Claude jogged back to the car and backed it up. He searched the trunk for a rope and something to get through whatever blockage they might come to at the end of the tunnel. He tied the rope around the boulder. Revving forward, the boulder moved slightly. He pulled forward again and the rope broke just after the boulder fell into a divot in the ground ten feet to the left and settled in.

Elisa peered into the tunnel with the flashlight and tightened up.

"It's only about four feet, we'll have to crawl."

"Okay, let's go," he said.

"Ya know what, I don't think I can. Let's go back, there's got to be another way!" she said, staring into the darkness. "We don't even know if there's a way in at the other end!"

"There's an entrance into the house, it's blocked off I'm sure. And if there's not, we'll come back and figure out another way, but right now, this is our only way in."

"I can't." She backed away.

"Did you get stuck in an elevator or something as a kid?"

"No, no trigger, just really don't like small spaces. I guess I didn't realize it would be so tight."

"This was your idea and it's the only logical one. He won't be expecting anyone to get in this way."

"He's probably not expecting anyone at all! Other than John, who would have been walking through the front door!"

"He will be if we trip any of those alarms." He grabbed onto her shoulders.

"We have the opportunity to save a lot of lives. We've already wasted a lot of time; you have to be bigger than this, fight it! You're not alone."

She slowly got on her knees and crawled in behind him, their knees wet from small sitting pools of water. She tried to imagine herself as small as she could.

"This was probably a drainage pipe or something at one point. At least we shouldn't really see too many bugs in here."

The tunnel suddenly went completely dark, except for the flashlight. The boulder had settled back into its original place, covering the entrance.

Elisa gasped. "Move faster!" she demanded. And he did.

They crawled at an incline for what felt like an hour to her, but was only ten minutes.

"The tunnel ends here," he finally said. He put his hand up to the surface. "Looks like they put up a wall. Sheet-rock." He raised the crowbar he had taken out of the trunk. "I'm sorry I complained about that old car, a hover car would never have needed this."

"Claude, I can't breathe," Elisa said, alarmed.

"I'll have us out of here in no time. It's humid down here, plenty of moisture in the air to weaken and crumble sheet-rock easily. If this was put up when Reed was a child, that makes it about twenty-five, thirty years old."

"Let's just hope we're down far enough that Reed doesn't hear the banging," she said.

He swung lightly then increased the pressure, the pieces of sheet rock fell in chunks.

"Move back," he said, shimmying himself back as well. He kicked the wall several times and on the fourth kick, his foot went all the way through. Stale, mildewy air hit them from the other side. He kicked enough of the wall to push their way through.

They jumped down out of the tunnel, emerging into an old stone cellar that seemed to have been closed up for years. There were some boxes pushed up against the wall and three lounge chairs stacked next to them.

"Reed played down here as a kid? I've had nightmares about places like this," Claude said.

Elisa pulled on a door handle. It didn't open. Claude tried. "Must be a lock on the inside." He felt all around the door. Then he looked all over the floor and on the dusty shelves.

"What are you looking for?"

"Nails, something, thin metal or hard."

Elisa looked on the other side of the cellar and in the boxes. "What about this?" She held a Christmas ornament of skis with a little metal ski pole attached. "Is this hard enough?"

Claude broke the pole off, pushed it up into the top pin of the hinge on the door and tapped it several times with the crowbar until it slipped up and out, falling on the floor. He did the same with the other two hinges.

The door opened up to three stone stairs, leading to a small portion of the basement. Claude passed by a set of stairs rising to the main house.

Elisa headed up the stairs. "Where do we start?"

"Maybe a den or an office." He opened the door at the bottom of the stairs. "Wait, down here!"

She climbed back down the stairs, thinking about what she'd say to Reed when she saw him. *What if this is all just a crazy idea and I'm wrong? Perhaps I let this insane day get to me and I've accused an innocent man. I mean, is this really the same guy I enjoyed conversations with; joked with; the same guy I shared my bed with? I won't really know until I see his face—till I can look in his eyes.*

This door led to the rest of the basement, which stretched the entire length of the house. Schools of fish swam vigorously all about in the lake through a large picture window.

"We're beneath water level," Claude said.

Elisa tried to ignore her increased heart rate. *It beats the tunnel,* she told herself.

"This set-up also looks like it's been here for quite some time," she observed, trying to distract herself from the feeling of being trapped in a tomb.

"Yeah, and it appears that this is where Reed has been spending his time," Claude added, pointing to a coffee mug on a table. He felt the side. "Ice cold."

"Claude." Elisa nodded to a gun Claude had missed, next to the mug. "We may need that."

"I'm still not looking to kill anyone," he responded.

"That ship has sailed."

He grimaced at her.

"Just as a scare tactic. You said the Fredericks shouldn't be underestimated, right? And if we have to confront him, that crowbar may not be enough." She felt like she had gotten punched in the chest, just thinking about hurting Reed.

"Some of these posters on the wall look like they date back over a hundred years. Are these advertising their business quests?" Elisa asked.

"Yeah, like I said, a prominent family that goes back a long time."

"Weren't newspapers, books, anything publicly written banned at that time to preserve resources?"

"You are correct. However, Orbis, anyone with money or power, even today, are exempt from such laws."

"Look at this newspaper article pinned to the wall." She read, *"Dr. Graham Frederick revives the use of the incendiary bomb and leads the fight against enemy forces defeating yet another adversary."* She looked back at Claude. "This confirms where Reed's inspiration came from."

She continued, "Huh, just under it, another article talking about how he was later scrutinized and reprimanded for his excessive and inhumane use of employing it. Can't make up their minds."

"There's a door back there, maybe what we're looking for is there," Claude pointed out.

Passing by piles of newspapers, books, awards, and what looked like unfinished inventions, Claude commented, "This place looks like a historical wasteland."

Elisa rushed to open a door, hoping to find a space she didn't feel was closing in on her, but instead found a room half the size of the first, set up as a lab.

She gasped. "There's animals in those cages!"

"Apparently, Reed is into far more than just eliminating the human race," Claude said.

He flipped through the pages of notebooks he found spread out on a six-foot lab table in the center of the room.

"You think those ocean waves are meant to keep the animals calm?" Elisa speculated about the tranquil crashing waves replaying against a far wall.

Claude barely noticed she spoke. "There's locations listed; city, states, countries—all crossed out—like a check list." He flipped through the next. "He's been busy, these things are filled with exact locations from Russia to England, to here in America."

He picked up another which read "Ameliorate Project" on the front and continued to flip through.

He glanced up at her. "Have you ever heard of the Ameliorate Project?"

She shook her head.

"They're experiments, I think," he added, pointing to the cages.

"What kind of experiments?"

"Not sure, he has notes jotted down here documenting height, weight, behavior, some other stuff. He's not really organized."

Elisa pushed around vials and syringes with her finger that were left next to a large stainless-steel machine. "More evidence this is where he's been working. I'm sure we'll find what we're looking for here," she said.

"That's a cell and chromosome harvester," Claude offered, glancing up again, noticing Elisa moving around a large machine next to an examination table. "Not what we're looking for. Haven't seen one in real life, but they had been used in the study of human genes many years ago. The Fredericks probably invented it!" he said sarcastically.

Elisa moved closed to the animals, the chimpanzee cages were labeled, "Mother-Linda," "Father-George," "subject-Matilda."

"Matilda had been following my every move." She put her hand up to the cage, hoping the chimp would feel her empathy. *Her eyes look so human.* The chimp slowly moved to the front of the cage and touched Elisa's hand with her finger.

"Hi girl," she said softly.

She glanced over to the mouse cage. "That's Pete and Fred, according to the board clipped to the cage," she announced to no one.

Elisa's body stiffened when she heard Reed's voice. Matilda silently rushed to the back of the cage.

"Maybe this will tell us what he's doing here," Claude said, switching on a recording of Reed.

He was sitting in a chair in this lab with data spread out in front of him.

"His hologram is so advanced! I can see every detail. Impressed, Claude walked around the life-like projection of Reed and swiped his hand through his head. "Scary real."

Elisa bent down, staring face to face as if he was really here in front of her. She didn't recognize the Reed she knew; his eyes were remote and dim—shrewd, void of empathy.

The hologram continued. "… using variations of genes; stop codon poly morphism in ACTN3, Cyr61, SERPINE1, SHANK3-chromosome 22, DCC-chromosome 18, ZRHX3-chromosome 16, hundreds of other genes involved in strength, intelligence, memory, lifespan, and healing, Project Ameliorate has produced varying outcomes thus far. Considering my results with the mice and chimps, the collection of genes in chromosomes that I have interlaced in hundreds of combinations have proven my data, showing this type of regeneration to be highly successful. Both Matilda and Fred have shown a high intelligence in comparison to their parents and others of their species, along with superior physical strength and agility. I will continue to monitor their progress throughout their lifespan, noting longevity. Subject 16, blacktip shark, formula will need to be reconfigured."

They both looked around for a blacktip shark, finding a covered empty tank they hadn't noticed in the corner of the room.

The recording continued: "I'm tapping into an instinctive intelligence that just needs to be boosted; a memory of things we've never learned; creating a strength that will allow for normally, unattainable capabilities; a healing process that will allow for the longevity of life that has already been assured. With further experimentation I will create an individual who will prove to be the next generation of human being. And they will thrive without the obsolete, feeble body and feeble-minded attributes of our predecessors."

He leaned forward and back again—hands folded.

"The women in this study who were injected with the gene variation faced disappointing results."

Elisa looked at Claude. "He's experimenting on humans?"

"Only one subject lived beyond birth and I'm afraid I had the error of already injecting the expiration date nanobytes prior to my own variation of genes. The child lived for only three days, which is promising. I have already repeated the same formula on my next subject."

"Synthetically structured savants," Claude said. "I have to say, Reed has taken this family of inventors to a whole new level."

Elisa flipped to the next page in the notebook Claude had discovered.

"I'm sure these are the women."

Mother	File	Occupation	Injection Date	Due Date	Status/Date
Lisa Marx	07867	Physicist	04012167	08292167	08012167
still born					
Rita Maker	07836	Mathematician	04162167	10152167	07302167
premature birth-death					
Amanda Rosenthal					
still born	05769	Lawyer	02212167	07102167	07052167
Lolita Messenger					
miscarriage	05908	Engineering	05262167	10032167	06272167
Kim Carpenter	06789	Biochemist	04242167	09162167	05292167
miscarriage					
Sarah Michaels	06805	Neurosurgeon	01092167	06222167	04302167
miscarriage					
Paulette Derringer	07689	Aerospace engineering	03252167	08112167	06042167
premature birth/death					
Shauna Burgess	06798	MD, fellowship in vascular surgery	02262167	07172167	07152167 successful full term birth.

Infant expiration date 3 days post birth.

Scratched in pen, a side note—"Do Not mix in with expiration date nanobytes!!"

"How would he get all these women to volunteer for this?"

"He wouldn't," Elisa said. "These are his patients—they don't know."

She stared, fixated on the paper.

"How do you know that?"

Her face tightened, and she quietly said, "Shauna is my cousin."

"Oh, oh Elisa I'm sorry. Ash told me. I thought it was an expiration date though?"

Her sadness turned to anger. "It looks like that asshole forgot to not use an injection with an expiration date while he was experimenting on her baby!"

"What are you doing?!" Claude called out as Elisa dashed over to the cages.

"I'm letting these animals free." She started with the mice; they scurried free from the cage and went behind a cabinet.

He grabbed her hand as she began to unlatch Matilda's cage. "You can't just let them out, they may be aggressive. We don't know what he's been doing to them."

"Exactly! We can't let him hurt anyone or anything else!" she cried.

Matilda and her parents grabbed their bars and began shaking them, grunting.

He took her by the shoulders. "There's no time to deal with them right now. We'll come back for them; I promise."

She nodded and looked past him. "Claude, look!" Wiping her tears, for the first time noticing a large metal door at the back of the room. She pushed past him and rushed toward it.

"Careful, we don't know what's on the other side!"

Composing herself, taking Claude's advice, she opened it slowly. "Great, it's another underground tunnel," she said, stepping in.

"It must be heavily sealed to protect it from the pressure and water of the lake," Claude said, feeling the surface.

"Where do you think it leads?"

"A good guess would be that cottage," Claude pointed out.

Elisa's heavy heart had turned to a burning in her stomach. Looking behind them, the tunnel felt a lot tighter. She looked ahead and it seemed like the door on the other end moved further away as they made their way closer. She picked up the pace, not sure if she was moving quickly to get through the confines of the tunnel or to find Reed.

Claude was almost at a trot trying to keep up with her, though he was not opposed to moving quickly to escape the stale air in the tomb-like tunnel. He feared she might act irrationally if they did find Reed.

He grabbed her arm. "Hey, we can't go barreling in there! Whatever's on the other side of that door, we have to proceed cautiously."

$$- 64 -$$

Staring at another large metal door, Claude carefully lifted the heavy bar handle out of its cradle and pulled it open. He drew his head back. "Do you smell smoke?"

When they slid around the door into the room Elisa tensed, the hairs on her neck rose. Immediately they could hear the crackles from the fire.

"There's a fire going in the fireplace!"

This room was very different than the last. Smaller, lived in.

Claude homed in on the half-full whiskey glass next to the couch as the melting ice shifted.

Reed took the last step on the staircase and recoiled, faltering only for a moment when he saw Claude and Elisa standing in the doorway of the connecting tunnel.

"Elisa," he said to himself. Something in him was glad to see her, but his priority, his instinct was to protect the sphere. He glanced at a single square counter in the middle of the room and back to Elisa and Claude.

It only took him a moment to regain his composure. "I have to say, I am very surprised to see you." He made his way further into the room. "You are resourceful. Weren't you two detained at John's house in Boston?" he asked, uncomfortably.

"You mean executed? Clearly not! John wasn't as bright as you thought. He's dead now," Elisa said flatly.

Reed flinched.

Any reservations she had about confronting him were gone. Seeing him now, knowing what he'd done, what he was capable of, had stirred a rage in her that she feared.

"Not sure what you think you can do here; my drones are already set in motion."

No! they both thought.

Her body shaking, she bolted forward—her words charging him with betrayal. "You looked me in the eyes, knowing you were the one that killed Jessica!"

"I was only aware when I saw you at Shauna's appointment that she was your relative. That was botched, I will admit, but I will not apologize for trying to create a better future."

Claude stepped forward; his tone defiant. "You're trying to eliminate half the planet while messing with the DNA of the remainder! What gives you the right to play God?!"

"Clearly, you found my lab in the main house. The brain is an organic instrument. The vast human cerebral cortex is full of specialized labyrinths prepared to function on command—some have innate mathematical abilities, some analytical, some musical." He reached his hand out. "You may see them as savants. As soon as it's formed, that magnificent organ," he tapped his head, "begins to convey what's already there, however in most, it lays dormant. I am merely guaranteeing that our brains and bodies are living up to their potential. I simply want to make humankind a better breed of people—mentally and physically—the way *God* intended."

Elisa noticed that Reed was careful to stay close to a large black orb stationed on a square counter in the center of the room.

That must be it! Maybe we can still stop them or maybe he's lying about launching already! I need to get closer.

She spoke up. "Once you start messing with nature, you have no idea what the outcome will be. You may be creating a race of monsters!"

She looked to Claude and back at Reed. "There's already evidence that expiration dates have accelerated our evolution. You are only furthering potential catastrophe."

Reed's jaw stiffened. "My father is over eighty years old; his expiration date is not for another ten years. He has and will live in pain and dysfunction for the remainder of that time. My mother—killed herself after years of dealing with her mental and physical conditions!"

As a kid, Elisa recalled, there were reports of the Frederick heiress dying on her expiration date. A tale to spare their humiliation, no doubt.

"Living until your expiration date does not account for dementia, malformations, or debilitating diseases that keep you lingering on in your own personal prison—along with the many other inconveniences that make life not worth living." He began to pace.

"I see kids who don't have a chance because they are genetically connected to their parents who, to put it bluntly, are idiots. I hold the opportunity to create a place where everyone left and worthy will thrive. Where everyone has something to offer. A future with unlimited possibilities! My current research and experiments with 'Ameliorate' are only touching the surface!

"That is really how you're justifying all this!"

He addressed Claude. "Is our work really much different? You're doing the same thing every day with your VM9 project—genetic engineering, correct? Taking the very best traits from different plants and making them the greatest version of what they can be. Our global government… rest assured, has the same interest in altering human kind for the 'benefit of all' in their little vault of secrets. Editing genetic mistakes—I'm taking the very best traits of ourselves to create the greatest possible version of what we can be as human beings. I'm just executing a solution to an extensive, abiding problem."

"The thing about arrogance," Claude said, "is that you think you've already won." He rushed at Reed, unaware that he was prepared for this.

Reed reached towards the orb, picked up an object beside it, and holding on with both hands, raised and discharged it, lifting and throwing Claude into the air where he landed on the other side of the room, hitting his head on an old steel stool.

"No, Claude!" Elisa shrieked.

She moved toward him, gasping at the blood pooling around his head, then paused as Reed raised the weapon toward her.

"You know, when I realized you were involved, I tried to do what I could to deter John from hurting you. I'd really hoped you would accept things the way they were once I made these changes and perhaps you and I could actually… see where we were going. He made it clear, however, that you were going to see this through till the end and eventually, make your way back to me. Clearly, he was right."

Elisa was fixated on Claude. *If I don't stop the bleeding, he'll bleed to death.*

"This was something my grandfather invented many years ago." He continued to speak while admiring his weapon. To Elisa, it looked like a deformed vintage hair dryer, though the mouth of the weapon was much wider and top heavy.

"However, our government really had no suitable use for it, so it sat around for a very long time with all the other discarded inventions of my forefathers. I've always thought it was a neat little gadget," he said, looking at it from all sides. "He called it the pressure cannon. Your friend is," he cocked his head to the side, looking at Claude, "oh, about a hundred and seventy to a hundred and eighty pounds I'd say. I have this set at three thousand pounds per square inch, which means it launched him about four feet in the air and about ten feet beyond where he was standing."

Everything seemed to have disappeared around Elisa. Heat pouring off her, she felt as though she could explode and send the shards of her hateful thoughts directly through him.

"I'm sorry Elisa, I don't even know how you got involved in this."

Blinded by hate, she already saw her hands around his neck and charged after him, making the same mistake as Claude.

The blast felt more like a powerful surge of pressure than pain. She felt herself lifting into the air and flying halfway across the room. Everything went black and then she felt the pain searing through her head. Struggling to open her eyes, she recovered only enough to see Reed moving toward her. She could now feel where her head hit the floor from the warm trickle down the side and into her ear. She hurt everywhere and had no desire to get up even if she could. Her left arm and leg felt as though they were no longer attached, though she could see that they were still there. She was pretty sure her right arm, which she was lying on, was dislocated again.

Reed crouched down next to her, hanging his head slightly, still struggling with the need to kill her, and wiped the tear from her cheek. "Why do you have to be so damn persistent!"

"Mr. P," she whispered.

He smirked at her connection.

She mustered, "Reed, how could you?"

He softened for just a moment at the vulnerability in her voice. "How? Because I can and I should. You deserve a place in the new world, it's too bad you can't see it for what it will be. But now, you are just collateral damage. You have no idea how sorry I am about that."

Unable to lift herself, her anger carried her words through her pain.

"That is not a world I want to be in!" Still desperately trying to reason, she continued, "Don't you realize that every person is a contributor in some way? One person may not contribute to science directly but can be an inspiration to spark someone who will be. One person can nurture those who will create or implant an idea that will ignite the next mode of technology to keep our world moving forward!" She struggled to speak. *Are there words actually coming out of my mouth?*

"Everyone has a purpose! Whether to destroy, leaving room for new growth or to be that new growth. And no one has a right to determine who will play that role! Neither you, nor our government. You *are* the disease you claim you are eradicating!" she pushed out of her mouth.

"You know, John killed Jack!"

Reed's face scrunched up in despair, giving Elisa the opportunity to pull the syringe she'd taken from his lab out of her pocket and lunge with it toward his arm. He grabbed her wrist mid-air, she screeched in pain from the grasp and the syringe dropped to the floor. Though distraught, he admired her resilience and smiled. *Yeah, it is really too bad.* He winced when he felt the sting from a needle plunge into his leg. Elisa released the second syringe she had in her right hand when she was sure it had emptied fully into him.

He stood and backed away in a panic. "Nanobytes?"

Elisa replied, "Expiration time, five minutes."

He desperately looked around trying to think of an answer that he knew didn't exist. Hands on his head, he looked back at her.

"Fuck! What have you done!"

"I've executed a solution to our abiding problem."

Furious, still clutching the pressure cannon, he raised it toward her.

Several shots were fired and Reed crumbled to the floor. Claude lowered the gun, letting it fall to his feet.

"Claude!" Elisa thought she called, but nothing came out.

He sluggishly made his way over to where she lay, easing his way down. "Huh, I guess there was one person I wanted to kill."

"You're not dead," she whispered.

"Not dead, just feels like it," he said, holding his head wound. Claude cautiously moved toward Reed and felt his pulse.

"Is he dead," Elisa barely whispered, "because I don't want him popping up in ten seconds with a second wind." She reminded him of her mistake back in the maze. "That would be pretty stupid," she let out a soft breath, "on our part."

Claude painfully chuckled. "Even when you're down, you're not. You look to be in pretty bad shape though." Illuminating the band on his wrist, he punched in the number from the card that James Stone gave them, giving him the address and telling him to send an ambulance.

"I think he was lying, he may not have launched the drones. We need to make sure no one can activate them," Elisa said. "It's got to be that large black ball looking thing with the flat top." She pointed, unable to get up. "On that counter. Did you notice that he went right to it when he came in the room and hovered around it like he was protecting it?"

Claude quickly, but gently removed Elisa's sweater from her and tied it tightly over the gash on her head, stopping the blood still trickling out. Easing his way up, he stumbled across the room, grabbing a t-shirt, which was draped over the back of the couch. *He won't be needing this.* He wiped the sweat and blood from his face then wrapped it tight around his head, creating a makeshift bandage.

"This is like nothing I've seen before," he said. "Looks old school— vintage. My guess, another Frederick design." He looked at it from all angles. *Of course, the Frederick name is carved in the side.* He ran his hands along the sides, the top and bottom.

"I don't see anything remotely indicating where this thing opens up. Open sesame! Reed Frederick!"

"Shit, I don't know!"

"Claude, you have to get it open!"

"Yeah, I get that!" he said, frustrated.

He got down on his knees, feeling and searching all around.

"These look like sensors on the side." He waved his hands over the sides again. Nothing.

"Hmm." He looked at Reed's crumpled body on the floor. Rushing over, he grabbed onto each arm and dragged him toward the orb. He pulled a chair just in front of the orb, and struggled to pull him into it. The throbbing in his head was almost unbearable. Claude held Reed's hand in each of his own, and slid them along the sides of the orb, pulling Reed's body forward, his head banging into the orb. Four doors on the top slid open from the center out.

"Okay, something's happening," he said, pushing Reed back in the chair.

"What do you see?"

Identification, the orb demanded. "What?"

Claude pulled Reed forward and placed his hand on the top. Nothing. He tried the other hand. Nothing.

"Retina," Elisa said, remembering the small balls at the nutriment plant.

"Yes!" He pulled Reed forward and pried his eye open while holding his body up with his own.

Another door slid to the side.

Password, the orb demanded.

"You've got to be kidding me! We have a problem! There's a timer. He wasn't lying, it looks like a countdown. He already set this thing to activate the drones an hour ago. Remaining time before it sends a signal is six minutes thirty-two seconds!"

"What's it showing?"

"There's a square keyboard with numbers and letters."

"A passcode!" she said. "At least it's not voice activated."

"Start thinking about what it could be!"

Claude was already typing.

"No, no, no, no!" he called, trying to stop the doors from shutting.

He desperately pulled Reed forward again, this time his body slipped from the chair and slumped to the floor. Claude struggled again to pick him up. He slid his hands around the sides and pried his eye wide to re-open it.

"Try Restituere," Elisa offered.

"Just did that." He typed in "restore."

The doors slid shut again.

"Don't have time for this!" He pressed his throbbing head wound, cringing. "Could use Ash on this one." He repeated his dance with Reed's limp body.

Wish I could think clearer. Elisa felt herself lulling into a sedate state. "You knew him, any thoughts?"

"Well, I missed the whole 'mutate the worthy population' part of his split personality."

Claude tried again. The doors slid shut. "Dammit!"

"Try Ameliorate!" she blurted out.

Claude typed the letters. The orb doors closed.

"This thing may have a limit on attempts, we need to get this right!"

Her head was swirling. Pieces of the last twenty-four hours were all melting together. Ashlei's face, the fiery bushes in the maze, Restituere. Helicopters and pressure cannons were hovering in a vast array of colors in her head. *My hands and feet are floating…* Split personality… Split personality! Mr. P!—email!

"Transcendent em illume," Elisa said quietly. "Transcendent em illume!" she called out louder.

"What does that mean? Are you sure?"

"Just put it in! t.r.a.n.s.c.e.n.d.e.n.t. e.m. i.l.l.u.m.e."

Claude typed in the letters just as Elisa called them out. The doors remain opened—the countdown stopped. The timer read 37 seconds.

He looked all around to make sure it was disabled and nothing else needed to be done. Reed's body slumped to the floor again. Wiping the sweat from his face, he gently slid down, pulling Elisa against him.

She stared blankly just beyond them to the body on the floor. "It means to go beyond or surpass. Mr. P's plan for the world. Reed's plan for humankind. To become a super-human race." With her adrenaline now fading, she struggled to talk, feeling herself slip in and out of consciousness.

Claude could faintly hear the whooping sounds of helicopter blades in the distance. The medivac and government officials arrived within minutes, with James Stone following close behind.

An agent examining Reed rolled him from side to side. "No blood, no holes," he announced, surprised, looking up at Claude.

"You may have shot in his direction, but you missed each time."

The second agent called over, "We have a bullet hole lodged in the canister over here." He continued to look around in that area. "Another here in the floor." He counted two more bullets lodged in the wall just beyond where Reed stood.

Claude's gaze fell to the empty syringe on the floor close to where Elisa had laid moments before. "Good girl." He smiled.

Elisa was being pushed out on a hover gurney, having totally lost consciousness.

"Is she going to be alright?" Claude asked the medic who was adjusting her IV fluids.

"She's in bad shape, but nothing she won't recover from," she said.

"I gave her pain meds and a sedative. Looks like you can use some pain meds yourself," she pointed out as another medic came to examine Claude's head. Another stretcher was pushed in.

"Yeah, I could," he agreed, grateful to be able to lay down.

Claude opened his eyes to James Stone's stern features staring down at him. "It's a good thing you two can't stay out of trouble, we'd *all* be in trouble if you followed orders."

Claude closed his eyes again and grinned as he was loaded into the helicopter.

- 65 -

Two weeks later Elisa, Claude, and Ashlei had the rare honor of being a part of an Orbis meeting, held in Washington DC, reserved only for delegates of the House of Representatives. The three sat in the balcony above the room full of members of each region from every corner of the globe.

Around the circular room, delegates from the past clung to the walls, each distinguished portrait overseeing the current meeting. Nine other forums around the world displayed delegates from their own region, paying homage to the ambassadors that came before them.

"Considering the events that exposed and brought to light the ill effects and dangers of the long-standing expiration dates falling into the wrong hands, there will be a cease and desist of all nutriment injections around the globe. We have the concurrence and cooperation of every member of the Orbis council, who have each discussed the matter with their home Parliaments." The representative from France, hair pulled back tightly in a bun displaying her plain features, pursed her lips and shifted in her chair as she paused.

"This will not go well when the entire world learns of the origin of expiration dates and how they've been manipulated over the last century, though with good intentions." She looked around with conviction.

"In 2011 there were 6.2 billion people on the planet; in 2060 there were five times that many people—30 *billion* people on a planet with limited resources. The natural order of the earth had been disrupted—there was evidence that the planet was dying. Natural resources were being depleted at an exponential rate, and what wasn't being consumed was being contaminated. Coal, oil, and other minerals had been overmined, scavenged, and sold illegally, becoming almost nonexistent. Polluted air, oceans, and fresh water resulted in disturbed and dying dependent eco-systems. Saturated with people, there was little land on which to grow and produce vegetation. It was clear that there would come a time when limited resources on our planet would no longer be enough to provide for the billions of people who were in need of them. Their situation was dire. We hope that with time, the world will understand that this was a desperate measure our forefathers felt was best for everyone and that we are now trying to rectify a situation that we were grandfathered into."

The light in front of France's member went off and switched on before England's representative. He began to speak.

"We recognize that expiration dates are no longer a viable option for population control. And in fact, population numbers have been adequate and population control itself, as it had been maintained, may no longer be entirely necessary. Our animals had gotten healthier—stronger. Vegetation has begun to rejuvenate on its own, air quality has improved nearly fifty percent! These are only a few of the vital elements making progression and moving us forward. As you know, there have been many discussions with our young biologist, Claude Monark," he motioned in Claude's direction and all eyes turned to him, "about several different advantageous ideas he'd been working on, delving deeper into possibilities already ventured and tapping into territories we've not yet explored." Tipping his head, he looked over the rim of his glasses at the listeners around the room. "Including utilizing our boundless space above, in the skies—perhaps floating cities!" Looking back up at Claude and smiling, he raised his hands as if offering him up as a gift. "We are encouraged with the prospects that Mr. Monark brings with him. In addition, this cease and desist is not only prudent, but necessary. Mr. Monark, in his research, had discovered that expiration dates have accelerated our evolution and, in some cases, have threatened to eradicate whole families."

There was a low buzz among the delegates. Questions about this new information were spinning around the room. England's delegate waved his hands down to quiet the room.

"We have taken steps to make sure that Mr. Monark has everything he needs at his disposal to continue investigating this phenomenon. We have a long road ahead to change what has been done, creating a new trust with the people and building an abundant future. There will be provisions and committees put in place to guarantee that we will never be put in this situation again."

The light before England's member went off and the light in front of America's representative illuminated. President West began to speak.

"Perhaps Restituere had been a blessing in disguise." Several members' lips curled and eyebrows were raised. "I strongly believe everything happens for a reason. This radical group was the catalyst for the beginning of the end of the only way of life we've known, though this was certainly not their intent. Nevertheless, without their cowardly acts, our attention would not had been brought to the greater threat. Of course, John Vanburen and Dr. Frederick's plan to eliminate a great portion of the population, if carried out, would have been devastating and would had altered a great many things, though they are not the threat I'm speaking of." He paused and lowered his voice slightly. "I believe there are a great many of us who embraced expiration dates because it was instilled in us from birth, and when we acquired the knowledge of where they were sourced from, it was instilled in us that it was for the good of the planet and the only way for mankind to survive. But did we ever really think it was okay? Once we were laden with this privileged information, did we really think it was acceptable? I can tell you all now, that every night when my head hits the pillow, a fresh face enters my mind. Not always one I recognize, but someone's child, someone's mother, someone's friend," he looked up at Elisa and Ashlei, "someone's cousin."

He returned to the delegates. "And I know it's not right. But I buried my head, as all of you have." Some heads were lowered, some nodding. "Because it was the only way—we thought. But did we ever think to look for another way? The greatest threat to our people is our complacency. Never again! Vow with me now to never allow our complacency, our blind eye, or ignorance, whatever you want to call it, to get in the way of doing the right thing." The air in the room livened with energy. His six-foot-two frame stood and faced Ashlei, Elisa and Claude observing from the balcony.

"We owe a great deal to Elisa Quinn, Claude Monark, Ashlei Quinn, and Dr. Jack Derrin—who gave his life. If not for the heroics and initiative of these four, we would be here in this room discussing a very different future."

One by one the representatives stood with all eyes on Claude, Elisa, and Ashlei and began to applaud.

They looked to each other and slowly rose from their seats, made uncomfortable by the acknowledgment, and for the first time truly accepting their own important part in this.

"I can't believe they're clapping for us," Ashlei said from the side of her mouth.

"We did something good," Elisa replied, smiling out at the group of people staring up at them. "We changed the world. Not bad for a bunch of quintessential geeks."

- 66 -

THE THREE EXITED THE ROOM with the meeting still in session. Elisa and Claude were released from the hospital only a week prior, and were displaying the residue of battle with bandaged heads, bruises, and Elisa's arm still hanging in a sling.

"How does it feel to be the new director of Population Control and Statistics?" Elisa asked Claude, nudging his arm with her good one.

"I'll let you know when this all feels real. And when we can change the name to something more appropriate."

"We're fortunate that Reed input the coordinates of the drones into the orb, making it easy to trace and collect them, otherwise any one of them could have had a disastrous outcome," Ashlei stated.

Elisa let out a breath. "How does one go about retrieving thousands of drones? Not a task I'd like to take on. At least with the contact list you found on Mike's VCC and the other names they found, we won't have to worry about Restituere after they've all been rounded up."

"Other than the ones that receded into the shadows," Ashlei added.

"Fortunately, they weren't the brains of the operation and will most likely not cause any trouble," Claude pointed out.

"Seems like the only brain left is Mike and he will be away for a long time," Ashlei said.

Claude debated whether to tell them of his visit to Mike at the prison the day before.

~

Face to face with Mike, Claude couldn't remember why he came.

The invisible partition between them flickered in and out, exhibiting the neglect of the prison; the upkeep had been in decline for many years. Still, it would mean electric shock if either inmate or visitor made a serious error in judgment and attempted to make contact during the few seconds between the fluxes. The walk in was bittersweet for Claude. The satisfaction of knowing that the man who was an accomplice to destroying so many was rightfully where he belonged. He looked around. And yet it seemed like such a waste of a great scientist to have him end up festering in this place. The brick walls dripped condensation and smelled of mold. The lights were dimmed, Claude assumed to conserve energy. There was no point in wasting precious resources on the forlorn.

Mike's eyes lit up when he first saw Claude. He clasped his hands together and sat down in front of the partition.

Mike's bruised face still wore the stitches required after the beating he took from Elisa. In just a couple weeks, he looked much older than the Mike who held a vision for making a better future—a fallen man. Scars he would bear for life.

"Thanks for coming to see me, this is a surprise. There are some things I thought I'd never get to say to you."

"Such as?" Claude asked.

"Such as, I am so very sorry this all happened."

"Said the fly to the spider."

"I understand your skepticism and I take responsibility for the accelerated dated injections. Though, I do still feel very strongly about a radical solution, I had no idea about Mr. P's—Reed's, and John's plan. Ashlei wasn't dead by the time you got to her because I was trying to stall long enough to come up with a plan to release her. I never wanted either of you to get hurt," he said ruefully.

Claude's eyes narrowed. "Why would I buy that you had an agenda? And you don't even like me!"

"I respect you! I respect your work ethic and your intellect. Still, I was angry that John removed me from my project and put you in charge."

He leaned in closer to the partition, careful not to touch it.

"A little secret. I'm not exactly a people person." He grinned at his own admission. "You are many things I am not: outgoing, funny, good looking. You have friends who care very much for you. I thought, 'you have it easy.'"

He sat back. "Like you, no! You have too much sarcasm for me." They both chuckled.

"Actually, it's easier not to like you than to stare in the face at all of my shortcomings," Mike admitted.

"Well, you had that cool helicopter thing going for you." Claude swirled his finger in the air. "We were all pretty jealous of that." He chuckled and added, "And you are very respected in the scientific community."

"Perhaps I was," he reflected briefly. "Why are you here?" Mike finally asked.

"Because something told me you weren't a complete asshole.

Claude decided against telling Ashlei and Elisa about his visit.

~

Ashlei wrapped her arm through Claude's as they strolled toward the exit. "Can I peek in on your thoughts? You look awfully engaged."

He grinned, placing his hand on hers. "I was thinking about how very excited I am for you, accomplishing your childhood dream and changing the course of expiration dates, while getting started on your next goal, now that we've been given unlimited resources to continue our work."

"Getting out into the field and actually getting hands on is more than I expected this soon in my career. I feel like I can conquer the world right now!" she said, grateful for the new opportunities she'd been given.

Elisa opened a memory on her phone of her and Shauna at the age of twelve, arms around each other giving the peace sign to the camera. They danced and laughed about her wrist—what she wouldn't do to hear that laugh again. Claude and Ashlei looked back as she fell behind.

"You okay E?"

She smiled. "I will be."

$$- 67 -$$

ELISA WAS STILL RELISHING the fresh springtime air she had taken in on her way into the hospital. It had been a long, drawn out winter, and she was happy to feel the warm breeze on her face again. The whirlwind of events, not quite a year ago, almost seemed like a distant dream, yet so much had changed. She carried her newly published book, *After the Date,* in her bag. Inscribed on the inside cover: *"To mom—I decided to trust my heart."* Although anxious to show it to Ash and Claude, she decided to wait—today was their day.

Stepping onto the maternity ward floor she hesitated a moment, somberly remembering the last time she'd been here in this unit, and the devastating news they'd all received. She felt reassured that, at the very least, nothing like that would happen to any family ever again, though it would still take many years for expiration dates to run their course.

Elisa hugged her parents, who were just exiting the room. "Just in time!" her mom said, as her dad's face exploded with excitement.

Claude looked to Elisa as she entered the room. "I think she's ready."

"Arrgghh…!" Ashlei belted out with her next contraction.

Elisa dropped her things in the chair and assumed her position at her sister's head. Ashlei forced a smile in between contractions.

"I'm glad you made it!" she panted. "Sorry we couldn't join you for the last high peak adventure. Jack would have been so proud of you finishing them for him."

"*We* finished them for him!" She squeezed Claude and Ashlei's hands. "You just couldn't make the last one for a very good reason."

"Arrgghh… !" Ashlei cried out again, squeezing Elisa's hand back.

Ashlei's doctor entered the room, slid his hands into sterile gloves and positioned himself at the foot of the bed. "Alright, on the next contraction, push."

Elisa joined Claude in encouraging Ashlei, while she gave birth to the loveliest baby she'd ever seen.

"She's so beautiful." Claude beamed, getting a quick glance before the nurse wrapped up their newborn baby girl and whisked her away.

"Did you see?" Ashlei asked him.

"She took her away too quickly." Claude continued to watch after her.

Elisa was applying a cool cloth to her sister's head; she could hear her delivery nurse in the next room.

"Huh." She called the doctor in.

Everyone tensed up. "Is everything alright?" Claude practically yelled. The nurse bypassed Claude's question.

"The baby is healthy, doctor, it's just…"

Elisa nervously approached, heart racing. She felt a tinge of a recalled fear from the last time she'd been in the birthing room.

"What's wrong?" Elisa bluntly asked.

The doctor said, "Well, we've done a thorough search and there's no date anywhere on baby Rose."

Ashlei slipped back in the bed, blissfully gazing at Claude, grappling for his fingers. She held his hand in hers. He moved in closer, embracing her carefully. She spoke softly. "Rose and all the newcomers from this day forth will have a freedom of not knowing that we never had."

Claude, Ashlei, and Rose Monark were inducted into the history books as the family of the first documented child to be born in a hundred years without an expiration date.

THE END

Book Club Questions

1. Was the ending a surprise to you? Why or why not?

2. What plot element surprised you the most?

3. Who was your favorite character? Why?

4. Who was your least favorite character? Why?

5. What was your favorite moment in the book? Your least favorite?

6. If you got the chance to ask the author one question, what would it be?

Acknowledgments

I would like to express my sincere thanks to my publisher, Kat Biggie Press, Alexa Bigwarfe and her incredibly skilled team; Nancy Cavillones, Raewyn Sangari, Michelle Fairbanks, Mandi Hawke, Sarah O'Dell, and the rest of this amazing team. Thank you for holding my hand and leading me through the publishing process. I would like to convey my deepest appreciation for your guidance and support, while you worked tirelessly and diligently to make sure this book was the best it can be. Thank you to all the expert and skilled professional women brought together for Women and Publishing, whom I can honestly say, along with Alexa, I would not be where I am.

My sincere appreciation to my editor, Scott Pack, for challenging me and for helping me to see my vision. Thank you to Dakota Nyght for your strong efforts with the last-minute copy edits. Thank you to my early readers and dear friends, Shelly and Toni Cestaro, for your invaluable feedback.

I express my gratitude to my husband, Harlan, my children, my family and my friends for your patience and tolerance while I spent long hours, days, months and years writing. Thank you to you all for believing in me and in this story.

About The Author

 MARDINE PERRINS is a writer and a Registered Cardiovascular Invasive Specialist in a Cardiac Catherization lab in upstate New York. Forever fascinated by the unknown and questioning the unexplored, you'll find her curiosities in her work.

She enjoys camping; hiking; extensive time in, on or by the water and considers herself an amateur photographer. She currently lives in the Albany, NY area with her husband, children and two cats.

You can visit her online at
www.mardineperrins.com and on facebook.